CURTSEY

ALSO BY MARNE DAVIS KELLOGG

Bad Manners

CURTSEY

MARNE DAVIS KELLOGG

WARNER BOOKS

A Time Warner Company

Warner Books Inc., 1271 Avenue of the Americas, New York, NY 10020

W A Time Warner Company

Printed in the United States of America
First printing: April 1996
10 9 8 7 6 5 4 3 2 1

Library of Congress Cataloging-in-Publication Data

Kellogg, Marne Davis.
    Curtsey / Marne Davis Kellogg.
      p. cm.
    ISBN 0-446-51837-9 (hardcover)
    1. Women detectives—Rocky Mountains Region—Fiction.
  2. Socialites—Rocky Mountains Region—Fiction.   I. Title.
  PS3561.E39253C87   1996   95-41992
  813'.54—dc20   CIP

Book design by Giorgetta Bell McRee

For my parents—the most loving, generous and fun people I know, who seem to be accepting the societal changes of the late twentieth century with a clamoring sort of grace.

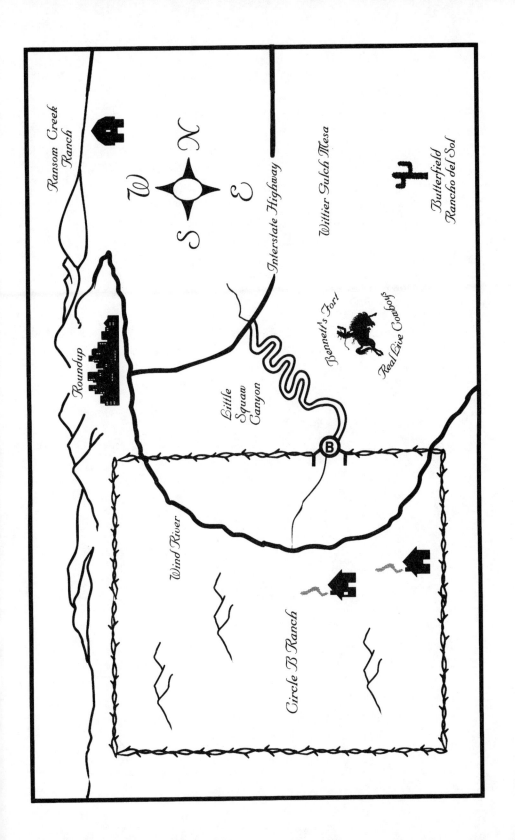

Chapter One

Friday afternoon

Well, according to my father, the unthinkable, the insupportable, the intolerable has happened: ladies may now tee off before noon on weekdays at the Roundup Country Club. It happened pretty much the way I predicted. The chairman of International Telecommunications Industries, Inc., came to town to explore the possibilities of moving the megabillion-dollar corporation's headquarters to Roundup.

Since the 1860s, which was the beginning of what we call civilization out here in Roundup, Wyoming, our economy has depended on the riches of our vast land, whether it's cattle or sheep or railroad transit rights across our ranches or the exploration and development of oil and gas. So we've boomeranged along, catapulting our economy forward with wars and retreating just as dramatically with victory. The cycle repeats itself every twenty years: big boom in even-numbered decades and big bust in odd. With the collapse at the end of the 1980s, the city and state fathers determined to begin to attract businesses that could remain stable. Telecommunications fell into their top category since, they determined, mankind will never stop talking.

I personally have mixed emotions about Roundup's new economic development plan because when big companies move west, they create lots of jobs and a lot of new people move to town and they aren't western-type people. All they care about and talk about are the great lifestyle and the beauty. They don't care about the land. They don't care about the lack of water. They don't care about how the United States Government is always trying to screw the ranchers. They're users and bleeding hearts. They don't have guts and they don't have backbone. They are not westerners.

Westerners can be anywhere or come from anywhere. It's a state of mind. Westerners are independent, hard-working individuals with a positive attitude. They are not hand-wringers, worry warts, whiners or victims. In short, they are not what the press and certain liberal members of Congress think we all should be: a weak-kneed mass of jibbering jelly.

That's what I think, anyway. I am Lilly Bennett, westerner, in case you wondered.

Anyhow, here comes International Telecommunications Industries. All their brass rolls in and all our brass rolls out. Red carpet. Whatever they want. Well, it turns out that the chairman of ITI, Inc., wants to play golf at the Roundup Country Club because the course is so famous and the only time she has available is at nine o'clock Friday morning.

That was the end of the "No Ladies on the Golf Course Before Noon" rule. "The toothpaste," as the late Bob Haldeman said in his only memorable words, "was out of the tube."

"And that," said Mother, "is why we won't be at the Children's Hospital Christmas Barn Dance tonight. Your father is in a deep funk and has gone out to the ranch to go hunting. As a matter of fact, I'm surprised he hasn't stopped by your house for a cup of coffee."

"I'll watch for him," I said.

* * *

It was less than two weeks before Christmas and the day was blindingly bright and sunny and I was snuggled on the chaise in my bedroom trying to catch a quick nap before leaving for town. I'd gotten home from Jersey, one of England's rocky, windblown Channel Islands, at midnight, having successfully tracked down and taken into custody a fellow who'd considered himself so securely beyond and above the law, that he didn't even need to pay his child support. And when he realized that my U.S. marshal's badge and shiny handcuffs and extradition papers and handsome young male deputy weren't some kind of bedtime game I'd flown all the way to England just to play with him, he was really mad. Made me smile, because I hate it when people who have all the assets and opportunity in the world try to slime out of things.

I am the former chief of detectives of the Santa Bianca, California, Police Department, and now operate my own firm, Bennett Security International, from my family's ranch, the Circle B, which lies east of the Wind River Range outside of Roundup, Wyoming. I am also, by sheer fluke, a U.S. marshal whose district is a honky-tonk, ticky-tacky, tourist-trap village—Bennett's Fort—owned by my cousin, Bucky Bennett. The Fort lies adjacent to the ranch, and, according to the four-color brochures Bucky sends out by the millions every spring—apparently to every retired motor-home owner in America, judging by the tourists who pass through—its jail has Wyatt Earp's actual desk and chair, six-shooters and saddle bags. The most recent "Wanted" poster dates back to 1913. What Bucky's brochures don't say is that the U.S. Justice Department occasionally houses high-profile prisoners there and the tourists have no idea that the fellow they see wringing his hands back in one of the two little cells is really incarcerated. But he is. Anyhow, the Department doesn't use the Bennett's Fort jail very often, and aside from infrequent prisoner escort requests, such as my quick trip to Jersey, my status as marshal requires little responsibility and provides limited jurisdiction. However, the credentials are very handy for access and clout when I need them.

"Are you listening to me, Lilly?"

"Of course I am, Mother," I said. "What did you say?"

"I said, I've just come from a Ball meeting and am absolutely tearing my hair out over these girls that are running it this year." Roundup's Debutante Ball, the symphony's major annual fundraiser, was happening in five days, and, like the Opera Ball in the fall, the symphony gala was Mother's Christmas-season linchpin. God forbid it should be her family. "They have simply no idea of how to do anything. No sense of propriety. And listen to this: two of the girls say they're going to wear *trousers*. To the Ball." I could hear her shudder.

"I don't know what to say," I said, not admitting the thought had often crossed my mind and glad someone besides me had tested the waters.

"Well," Mother huffed. "There isn't anything to say, is there? Everything's just going to hell in a hand basket." She blew out her breath. "Well," she launched off again after a moment, her recovery quick and complete, "back to this evening. Who are you sitting with?"

"Some German baron. I can't remember his name."

"Oh, my," she said, fully recovered. "It must be Baron and Baroness von Singen und Mengen. They're the only German aristocrats around here at the moment. Yes, you wouldn't know them. They moved here while you were in California. Well, you're in for an experience. Honestly, with all the *friends* who are going, I don't see why you can't sit with some of them."

"They invited Richard, and he invited me."

"Well, of course. Rita von Singen can give millions to the opera. You know she's from Dallas."

In Roundup, when you say "Dallas," you need say no more. It means a whole different way of seeing the world. Not necessarily a worse way. Just totally different. For instance, a hundred years ago, when I was promoted to chief, and it was a very, very big deal and I was on all the network news programs and I was excited and calling up all my friends and they were all calling me ... well, when I called a friend in Dallas to tell her, she said, "Oh, doesn't it just make you want to run out and buy a big emerald?" You could never think of that unless you were from Dallas. Not in a million years. So when Mother said Baroness Rita von Singen und Mengen was from Dallas, it was a tip-off, a heads-up, that we were dealing with a different breed of cattle.

Sun glinted off the windshield of my father's old dirt- and hailstone-pitted yellow Jeep Wagoneer as it crested the hill into the Circle B's main valley and rolled through the barren fields, where the wind had blown all the snow into the fences and the surrounding forests.

"Daddy just pulled up at Elias's," I said, watching him stop way down the road at the main ranch house where my older brother lived.

"Oh, good," Mother said, not bothering to hide her relief at knowing where my father was. "He'll probably have a few cups of coffee with Elias and then come home. Anyway"—she cleared her throat—"to the subject at hand: Rita von Singen was Rita Haye, as in Haye Tool and Bit." I could picture my mother perfectly, her smooth gray hair carefully coiffed, and her smooth, well-tended, light skin carefully made up. Not too much. Not too little. She was probably wearing an old luncheon suit and sitting at her dressing table, phone caught in the crook of her neck and shoulder, rearranging her jewelry. "And her mother was a Robertson," she rambled on. "Naturally, they've absolutely no background, but with all those millions, well, you get my drift. And at some point, they took her to Europe and put her on the international debutante circuit and bought her this German baron, Heinrich von Singen und Mengen. Everyone calls him Harry. And he is absolutely divine. I don't know why you don't ever come home with someone like that."

"Richard's pretty good," I said.

"Well, you're absolutely right, darling. He's even more attractive than Harry. *And*"—she paused for effect—"he's an American. If you know what I mean."

Chapter Two

Friday night

What Mother said about Richard Jerome was true: he was not only attractive and an American, but he was also tall, good-looking, successful, long-divorced, wealthy, mature and straight. And mine. For the moment, anyway.

He is a perfect example of how you don't need to come from the West to be a westerner. He'd scandalized his old New York social-register family—"It was a real bring-out-the-smelling-salts deal," a Main Line friend of Mother's told her—by making one of those complete mid-life, mid-course, just-hold-your-damn-breath-and-jump-off-the-end-of-the-high-board corrections from a staid, solid, buttoned-down, regimental-tie conservative New York City Morgan-Guaranty banker and Metropolitan Opera trustee who longed for the wide-open spaces he'd come to love spending summers on his family's ranch in Buffalo (Wyoming) to General Director of the Roundup Opera Company, one of a handful of major world-class opera companies in the country. And, on the side ("because," he explained, "if you hung around opera singers all day every day you'd go nuts") became a star of the summer rodeo circuit as a team roping champion, specializing in heels, or tails, as we call them. His London School of Economics degree helped him keep track of his winnings.

Like the von Singens, and who knows how many other people, Richard had moved to Roundup while I was away and we'd met a couple of months ago at Walter Butterfield's seventy-fifth birthday party—the one where Walter got his head blasted off by a twelve-gauge—and we'd been practically inseparable ever since.

That evening, as we whistled down the road through the beautiful Wyoming night in Richard's big Mercedes convertible, with iced champagne in a bucket on the console between us and Christmas carols playing on the radio, I clinked my glass against his. "Cheers," I said.

"Cheers," he answered. "Here's to us."

Us. I'm glad he couldn't see my smile. It was a little too big.

Billions of stars flooded the black windswept sky. There was no moon and the temperature had plunged to fifteen. We started up into the mountains, and before I knew it, had turned into the gates at the entrance to the Lorillards' ranch, Ransom Creek.

Ransom Creek may be only about forty-five minutes up the interstate from my family's ranch, but it might as well be on a different planet when it comes to appearances. The Circle B is just a plain old, get-down, low-down ranch. Ransom Creek is what people from out-of-town expect a ranch to look like, and that's probably because the Lorillards are from Manhattan. They moved to Roundup a long time ago—he came to run some company or other—and they liked the area so much they stayed, and built this incredibly beautiful ranch house and enormous barn that they donate every year for the Children's Hospital Christmas Dance. Decorators fly in from all over the country—we always say they're the world's most famous ones, but that may be an exaggeration—and team up with local celebrities and turn the Lorillards' tack rooms and thirty oversized box stalls into dining rooms of every imaginable type of Christmas fantasy.

As the tires of Richard's heavy car raced over the hard-packed snow, large spruce trees twinkling with small Christmas lights appeared here and there in the dark, quiet forest. And when we rounded the last bend into the main valley of the ranch, the sight took our breath away. The house, the barn, all the trees, everything blazed with light, magnified hundreds of times by the snow and reflected back by the moon and stars in the velvety sky. Candles flickered in all the windows and wood smoke curled from all the chimneys.

"I've never seen anything so beautiful," I said. "This is the sort of thing you see only in pictures."

"Spectacular," Richard said, as we crunched to a slow stop next to a wrangler who waited to take the car. "It gets better every year."

"How many times have you been to this?" I asked.

"I don't know." Richard shrugged. "Few. Two or three."

Well, I thought that was interesting. Of course I don't know why he wouldn't have been. He'd been living here, and I hadn't, and I suppose it was possible he had had some sort of a life before he met me.

As I stepped out of the car, my first impression was one of being embraced, transformed by the rich Christmasy fragrance of pine and fresh greens that came from the two large wreaths on the shiny red barn doors. Music and light flowed into the night with the friendly, warm welcome that the West is famous for.

"Welcome to Ransom Creek," said Mr. Lorillard, a tall, smiling, gentle-looking man in his seventies. He had on a string tie and fringed leather vest and shook Richard's hand firmly, giving me a polite once-over as he did. "This is the first decent date you've brought to this shindig."

Well, I thought, this is getting better by the second.

"You're right," Richard said.

"Merry Christmas, Lilly," said Mrs. Lorillard. "We're so pleased to meet you." She was also tall and slim, with a strong face and salt-and-pepper hair pulled back into a bun. "Please help yourselves to a drink. The bar's right through there in the tack room, past Sally and Bob." She passed me along gracefully and greeted whoever had arrived just after us.

Sally and Bob were two golden Percherons in brass-studded black leather collars with red and green bows tied into their manes and tails, their hooves as shiny as patent leather. They stood patiently at the door of the large tack room where rows and rows of perfectly conditioned saddles sat on racks on the walls, and dozens of immaculate halters and bridles, leads and harnesses swung from brass hooks, each marked with a small brass name plate.

"Do you suppose they really have this many horses?" I said to Richard while we waited in line at the bar.

"I doubt it. I think it's mostly for show."

"Oh, my God." A woman spoke behind us in that instantly identifiable, exquisitely clenched, Long Island, Piping Rock Club accent. "I absolutely *adore* tack rooms. They just *do* something to me. I mean, my God, can't you just *smell* it?" She inhaled deeply. "God, I love it in here. Just feel what it's done to my heart. Oh, my darling, just *feel* it."

I glanced up at Richard out of the side of my eyes. "Who is that?" I mouthed.

"Just keep going," he whispered. "Don't look around. Two Jamesons on the rocks, please," he said to the bartender.

"Richard, is that you?" the voice said.

Richard looked at me and I started to laugh. He turned. "Joan Chamberlain," he said. "How are you?"

"Divine," she said. "But we never see you anymore, darling. And I need you for dinner next Tuesday. My super friend, Leslie, will be in from the city and she's just *dying* to meet you."

"Thanks for thinking of me, Joan, but I'm really not available. I'd like for you to meet Lilly Bennett."

Joan was petite, and her blond, shoulder-length hair was parted on the side and hung down perfectly shiny and straight. She had hazel eyes, pink lipstick and white teeth and wore tight jeans on her perfect little body and a tucked-in cowgirl shirt and a checkered bandanna. I bought some jeans not long ago that I could tuck my shirt into and still breathe, and I threw them away. They were so huge, I looked like Mitzi Gaynor in those giant sailor pants when she sings "A Hundred and One Pounds of Fun" in *South Pacific*.

"What a great pleasure to meet you," she said without changing her expression. "I've heard a great deal about you. Do you know my husband, Dickie Chamberlain?" She pushed an overweight, sweating fellow forward.

"Yes," I said. "It's nice to see you both."

"Doesn't this tack room just send you *spinning?*" Joan panted. "It reminds me so much of Daddy's farm and all the fun. You know, I believe we're at the same table tonight. Richard, darling, meet me later under the mistletoe. We can pretend you're one of Daddy's grooms. Just teasing, Lilly." Then she laughed like a horse.

I opened my mouth to say something but Richard clutched my arm tightly in his hand and excused us and we left the tack room and went back into the main part of the barn.

"Is that one of your old girlfriends?" I said. "No wonder you were glad to meet me."

"I'll tell you about her later. Totally neurotic. Dickie Chamberlain's fourth wife."

"In from the city."

"You got it. Let's look around."

We entered the barn's magical, luscious glow of golden light and shadow. Massive black wrought-iron candelabra stood at the entrances to the box stalls, the length of the barn, creating the illusion that you were in the Great Room of some gigantic Cecil B. DeMille movie set. Overhead, long evergreen swags, trimmed with small white lights, crisscrossed the high ceiling, looping up to large wagon-wheel chandeliers with bulbs that looked like candles. At the far end of the room, a cowboy band played a lively western tune, while the singer tapped a tambourine against her thigh, and smiled and twirled, making her full calico dress and lacy petticoat and long dark hair swirl out behind. An unforgettably delightful combination of lovely perfumes, tangy barbecue sauce, horse manure, hay bales and whiskey filled our heads as we strolled along arm in arm.

"Well, well, well. Will you look who's here. Lilly Bennett."

Chapter Three

I recognized the voice instantly and thought, Oh, my God. This can't be true. But it was.

I turned, and there he stood. Dayton Wylie Babcock, Jr. My first lover.

He looked just the same. Small, wiry, argumentative and uncoordinated. Dayton had always had a lot of money—originally from oil, but that business has been more distressed than usual for years, so I'd heard that he'd diversified, semi-successfully, into entrepreneurial schemes and questionable real estate development deals which he pitched to new arrivals to Roundup. He was a creep, a jerk, a user, a bright-eyed little monkey who got his teeth into your Achilles tendon and would not let go and would not stop jibbering. He moved around a lot on his toes when he talked, like a boxer. In the late sixties and early seventies he'd been the wunderkind of the international petroleum world, an enfant terrible tolerated for his genius and willingness to accept high-risk, high-wire oil leases and deals, many of which, particularly the foreign ones, had made a few people very rich. But Dayton, now in his late fifties, wasn't an enfant anymore. Now he was just terrible. And evidently, the town just could not shake him off its pant legs.

I stood there, next to Richard—tall, trim, elegant in his navy suit and cowboy boots—and looked and looked at Dayton Babcock and could not imagine what I'd seen in him, except that I'd been seventeen and filled with powerful urges, and he'd been twenty-nine and rich, with a private jet, something not many people in Roundup, except my father, had. I think, basically, Dayton's jet, not Dayton, turned me on, and Dayton was never one to pass up a free roll. Me, neither.

Although I found it hard to believe, he seemed to be with Fancy French, whom I have always found to be incredibly glamorous, and even though she's never been what anyone would consider a genius, I thought she had more on the ball than to go out with someone like Dayton.

"Fancy," I said. "I'm so glad to see you. You look absolutely wonderful."

Fancy and I have known each other ever since we ended up in adjacent stalls sneaking cigarettes in the ladies' locker room when we were eleven. Her family had just moved to Roundup from Beaufort, South Carolina, and our parents had become great friends, so naturally my mother never missed an opportunity to remind me what a wonderful girl Fancy was, and that even though I might disagree, she was actually one of my best and closest friends, and I should never forget it. Consequently, Fancy asked me to be maid of honor when she married someone whose name we've all forgotten, and five months after that, two weeks before her divorce from that fellow was final, her daughter, Lulu, was born and she asked me to be the godmother.

That's just the way it used to work, or else you went away for a few months and had the baby and gave it up. And then, just about now, it would be showing up at your front door, thirty years old, saying, "Remember me? Any bad diseases I should know about?" Or: "Can you lend me a kidney?" Stuff like that. Sweden was always an option if you had the money and hadn't waited too long. But the Frenches were Catholic, so Sweden was out, but divorce on the grounds of desertion was in. And Lulu, who had visited me regularly in Santa Bianca when she was little, was a treasure. Fancy had definitely made the right decision.

Someone told me, my mother probably, because she had always been much closer to, and fonder of, Fancy than I, that Fancy had joined AA and gotten herself headed in a new direction. I'll say one thing, she looked fabulous—sleek and slim and trim and confident. Totally pulled together. Her hair was still blond and fluffy and her eyes as blue as her name, and her pale, white, seamless skin was made up impeccably.

I was happy to see her, but not nearly as happy as I was that I'd spent some extra time on my makeup and put on my long, Christmas-red, chamois dancing skirt and starched white western bib blouse and red-and-green bandanna and Larry Mahan dress boots. What am I saying? I spend hours on my makeup every day and, frankly, don't feel I have much to show for it. I think I've entered a major high-maintenance, damage-control period of my life. For the amount of time and money I spend, I should look spectacular. All I look is the same.

Fancy and I kissed hello.

"I'm so thrilled you've moved back," she said in the lingering Carolina low-country accent. "Everyone's missed you so, all those years. Especially Lulu."

"Saw your picture in the paper this morning," Dayton said. "Got your man."

"Always do," I answered.

"Since when did the federal government start transporting prisoners on the Concorde?"

"The government doesn't. But if I'm in a hurry, I have no problem saving the feds some money and spending my own," I said. "I paid for his ticket on the Concorde and then Christian happened to be in Washington, so we flew the rest of the way on his G-Five."

Christian Bennett is my younger brother. He runs the family newspapers and banks and commutes to work from the ranch in a

Sikorsky S-76 helicopter, and jets around the world, attending to his business, in his fancy new Gulfstream V.

Dayton snorted air derisively through his nose and gave me a nonplussed look. "Do you know the von Singens?" he said. Richard just stood there quietly.

"No."

"Harry and I are in a couple of deals together," Dayton told me importantly. "I set this whole thing up tonight. He's the biggest social climber I've ever known. Come on, Fancy. There're the Antonuccis."

"I'd think the only person a baron would have to be a social climber around would be a king," I said to their backs.

"That guy is one of the biggest assholes I've ever known in my life," Richard said.

"You're right about that," I agreed wholeheartedly.

We joined the stream of guests wandering in and out of the box stalls, which had signs posted at the doors identifying who had decorated them and who had sponsored them for dinner.

Ever since I met Richard, I've felt special. And especially tonight, being at this party with him and seeing the way all the other women looked at him and then at me, and his telling Joan Chamberlain that he wasn't available anymore, and then that horrendous blast-from-the-past: Dayton. Well, it was fabulous. I squeezed his arm. He squeezed back.

"It's weird," I said. "Roundup used to be so little, I knew absolutely everyone. But now, it's like all the old people were picked up by creatures from outer space and replaced with all new people from a different planet. And not especially for the better. Sort of like the Stepford Wives. Like everyone has a new thirty-year-old wife and the only things she has in her closet are skin-tight jump suits and lots and lots of jewelry. I mean, look at these girls. It's practically blinding."

"I am," Richard said. "I like it."

"Of course you do. It looks like a Playboy bunny convention while old Betty's been left out there in the barn with the kids."

"Yup. Speaking of sex pots, here comes our hostess." A woman who was as vast as the barn itself hove up before us. "Lilly," Richard said, "please meet Baroness von Singen und Mengen."

"Oh, Richard." The big bowl of jelly giggled and quivered. "Give me a kiss." She raised a bloated cheek.

What can I say? She looked like a sumo wrestler wearing Kabuki makeup. I don't mean to be mean, but facts are facts. She was dressed in a way, way too-tight black satin cowgirl dress trimmed with gold braid and gold snap buttons in the shape of cow skulls. Unfortunately, some of these snaps had come undone, so you could see the swollen white rolls of her bosom and belly. I don't want to harp on the subject, but I'd truly never seen anything quite like it. I've seen a lot of fat people, we all have, and she wasn't as fat as some, but for some reason I could not take my eyes off that gap in her dress and the flab that pushed through it like rising dough. There's a very famous porno movie called *Through the Green Door* that starred some girl who had made Ivory Snow commercials, so the movie caused a lot of hysteria when she showed up in it. But the point is that there was this very fat, naked woman in that movie who personified dissipation and sensual, sexual decadence. That's whom Rita von Singen reminded me of.

She was accessorized in gold: gold cowboy boots, a gold cowboy hat that hung down her back with braided golden stampede straps, gold necklaces, gold bracelets, gold rings and a gold rope belt. Her face, maybe once a little bit pretty, was now blotched and lumpy from booze. Her hair was a curly red Afro. Not Lucille Ball orange-red, but darker, like a hennaed candy apple.

"I'm Rita Haye, Lilly." She took my hand and squeezed it. In her other hand, which had little tiny fingernails polished red, she held a large cut-crystal tumbler of straight vodka with a few lonely-looking ice cubes floating on top and four stuffed olives bumping into each other on the bottom. Her voice was clear and direct, with no trace of an accent. Her teeth were perfectly flat, as though they'd been leveled with a heavy file, and her dark-blue eyes sat back in her head and looked out defensively. "I'm so glad you could join our tables tonight. We're going to have some real fun, aren't we, Richard?"

How odd—after going to all the trouble and expense of buying yourself a title, not to use it. I would.

Rita kept squeezing my hand as though we'd known each other for years. A sort of secret, best-friends, how-are-you-really-doing? kind of grip. But I could tell that she wasn't really pleased to see me, or anyone else, for that matter. There was a franticness to her demeanor, the feeling that she was afraid everything was going to fall apart any second. What Richard had told me in the car on the way up was right: Rita Haye had lost her way. She was in some other world.

"I need to steal Richard away for a minute, but I know you know everyone here anyway." She blew me off with completely phony friendliness. "They're all just gobs of fun."

"Oh, absolutely," I said. Everyone always wanted to steal Richard away for a minute, and when there was money for the opera at stake, he didn't mind a bit. Neither did I, for that matter. Well, that's not really true, is it? Actually, I just wanted to hog him all to myself all the time, but let's get real. Rich women are the lifeblood of the arts, and from what everyone had said, Rita Haye von Singen was just about as rich as a girl could get.

She and Richard were instantly surrounded by guests eager for news of progress on the opera that was opening next week: *Ada*, Roundup's version of *Aida*, western-style. So I walked over to one of a number of small side bars, this one a prickly assemblage of elk horns—something which out-of-town decorators are typically and particularly fond of—and ordered another drink.

Chapter Four

*D*aniel French, Fancy's older brother, joined me. Their parents, Mr. and Mrs. French, had lived a sort of fey, vague existence, never really too aware of who or what their children were—for instance, that their daughter was a drunk and their son gay—and when they died, leaving an enormous estate, Daniel could finally stop living his secret life. He reveled in his freedom. He was finally one of the girls and even though he wasn't exactly wearing makeup or a tutu or tossing blossoms from a basket he was clearly, gushingly, deliriously happy, and obviously spending large chunks of the French fortune on bonbons and foie gras: all his clothes—his brown suede vest with its long fringe, his patterned western shirt, yellow bandanna and painfully tight brown suede pants—were stretched to the breaking point. I don't think the pants were tight to show off his fabulous physique the way some gay men do; I think they'd just gotten too little.

I'd always liked Daniel. He had a great sense of humor and good manners and was fun to be around. I'd heard he was so in demand as a dinner partner, he'd hired a social secretary, had hair implants, which he then streaked the same blond as Fancy's, and had had his face and eyes lifted. He looked like a round-faced, pink-skinned baby that smoked cigarettes and had a fifty-year-old, overweight body.

"Hi, Daniel," I said. "How've you been?"

"Oh, fine, fine." He took two dramatic puffs of his cigarette. "Glorious, actually."

"You look marvelous," I said.

"Do you really think so? You know, I had a little work done," he whispered. "Can you tell?"

"No. Really? You just look terrific. This is quite a spot, isn't it?" I said. "Have you been up here before?"

Daniel rolled his eyes. There might have been a hint of mascara there. "Can you believe it? Isn't it divine? Honestly, Madge Lorillard is such a treasure. And I'm so glad we have some out-of-town decorators. Madge's is Uli Magnano—do you know him?"

I shook my head.

"You will adore him. He is, without a doubt, the most talented, charming, sophisticated man I have ever met in my life, so sensitive, and with the most *sublime* taste, not one of these provincial stumblebums from around here who are always offering bargains, as if the only reason you want to decorate your house is to save money. Oh please. Save me from budgets. Do you know anyone here? You've been gone so long." Daniel took another big puff. "Speaking of divine, here comes Harry. I've been trying to get my hands on him for years. Do you know him?"

"No," I said, getting a charge out of Daniel's what-the-hell high spirits.

"Let me introduce you. Baron Harry von Singen: Lilly Bennett."

Baron Heinrich von Singen und Mengen was extremely handsome in that tightly sprung, Nazi-youth kind of way. He had short gray-blond hair parted on one side and slicked back, bright sky-blue eyes, lightly tanned skin and white teeth. Instead of cowboy boots, he wore soft Italian loafers, and instead of a bolo tie, a red paisley ascot was tucked into the collar of his tan cashmere polo sweater. His houndstooth cashmere sport coat was in soft shades of brown. His faded Levi's looked old and comfortable. Harry von Singen was as clipped, precise and elegant in his demeanor as his wife was slovenly in hers. Plus, he wasn't exactly slapping a leather riding crop against his leg but it didn't take a genius to get the picture on what the baron liked. The giving and receiving of pain. He was dangerously appealing.

He kissed my hand in a proper and charming way, not a big bowing smack like in the movies. "Miss Bennett," he said gravely, "I am honored to meet you. You are even lovelier than your photographs. Not at all what one expects to meet in a police officer."

"Well, thank you, Baron," I said. "I'm not exactly a police officer anymore but I appreciate the compliment. You may buy me a drink."

He laughed loudly for no apparent reason, a couple of sharp barks—HA! und HA!—and stuck our glasses across the bar for refills. "How delightfully amusing," he said grandly. The King is pleased. "It seems you've been abandoned. Would you care to join me on a tour of the stalls? They're quite amusing."

"I'd love to, thanks."

I took his arm and he led me down along one side of the barn and we looked in at the decorations. He knew even fewer people than I did, although a number of them nodded at him and he nodded back, perfectly at ease. It was like strolling in the Tuileries, and Daniel French trailed along like a little terrier that stopped at every bush— except that he stopped at every guest and hooted and cooed and then raced to catch up with us. Chuck wagons, placed here and there, were stocked with spectacular arrays of hors d'oeuvre. Harry and I stopped at one heaped with oysters. Real ones, not what we call oysters out west.

"Please." Harry indicated that I help myself.

"No, thanks."

"What? No oysters? They are perfect." Harry slid one down his throat and I swallowed. Yuk.

"I'm sorry," I said. "But growing up here in Wyoming, the only kind of fish we got was trout, which I don't even like, so the attraction of things like oysters, clams, mussels, scallops, squid . . . well, I just don't get it."

Harry raised his brows slightly. "Pity," he said. "Although I will tell you, Miss Bennett, I admire your honesty. Most people try to fake their way through such things. Especially, regrettably, with me, as though their sophistication will impress me, and I will knight them. Ha."

It seemed that everything that everyone had said about him was right. He was disarming, charming, and had a refreshing, self-deprecating way that made him very pleasant to be around. "Believe me," I said. "It would be virtually impossible for me to fake my way through an oyster." I swallowed again.

"I'm sure we'll come across something you'd like." Harry took my arm. "We'll make a search. I'd hate to see you starve."

Now, wasn't that a nice thing to say? Here's a guy who looks at me and thinks I could be on the verge of starving because he's used to looking at his five-hundred-pound wife.

"Lilly!" Daniel materialized with a woman of medium height with shoulder-length shiny dark hair that she pushed indolently out of her face and tucked behind an ear. Her light-blue eyes were made up à la Cleopatra, and she had what my father calls "a rush of teeth to the mouth." "Do you know Cordelia Hamilton?"

"No." I took her hand. It was like holding on to a cold, dead mackerel. "But I'm glad to meet you."

"Yes." She smiled a little too much, showing a little too much gum. "I'm happy to meet you, too." She laid a long, manicured hand on Harry's chest in a familiar, possessive sort of way, I thought. "I see Harry's taking you around."

"Would you join us?" Harry said.

"I've already seen those; I'm going the opposite direction. Most of them are absolutely ghastly, don't you agree? But it's certainly for a good cause. We'll see you at dinner." She took Daniel's arm and off they went.

I thought most of the stalls were wonderful. But what do I know?

In a stall called "Cowboy Christmas," where a small electric campfire glowed in the center of a circle of logs, and hand-carved ornaments hung from large blue-spruce branches that appeared to grow from the wall, we bumped into Richard and the baroness, who, basically, was being attended by Dayton and Fancy, who brightened up considerably when she saw Harry.

"This party is incredible," I said to Rita. "Thank you for including us."

"Oh, you're so welcome," she said listlessly. Some sort of oil problem with her skin was causing all the Kabuki makeup, including her mascara and lipstick, to slide and furrow. With her red hair and wrecked face, she looked exactly like Glenda Jackson as Elizabeth the First when she was really falling apart. "I'm not really too sure why we're doing this, I think it was Dayton's idea, but I just go along with whatever he and Harry want. I've learned that I am a completely right-brain person. Very, very creative and completely impractical. So I have to surround myself with left-brain people like Harry and Dayton to keep me organized. I don't do any left-brain activity at all anymore. It doesn't suit me."

"Oh?" I said. "Aren't you lucky you can afford to use just half your brain. So many people have to make do with the whole thing."

"Yes," Rita said. "I am. I'm very lucky."

She and Harry drifted blithely off. In opposite directions—she and Dayton to the right. Harry and Fancy to the left.

I didn't trust myself to speak, it was so clear that only half her brain, at the most, remained anyway. Tom and Sparky Kendall wandered up and the four of us just stood and stared at each other for a minute, afraid to open our mouths.

"Where in the hell did all these people come from?" I said.

"Welcome to the new Roundup." Sparky, a lifelong friend, answered, but her words were practically drowned out because just then one of the Lorillards' cooks, a big, burly guy with a scratchy-looking beard and a plaid shirt and a white apron tied neatly around his middle, stood in the center of the barn and clanged deafeningly on an iron triangle.

"Chow's on," he yelled.

Chapter Five

Our stall was called "The Three Kings," and believe me, they would have been impressed. It was a double-sized, solid-gold vault. The walls and two round dinner tables were draped with gold lamé, and the centers of the tables were heaped with gold casks of large jewels and strings of pearls and ornate gold candlesticks; even the wine-glasses were golden goblets. The gilt chairs had necklaces, and crowns and tiaras hung over their backs as though they'd been tossed there carelessly by a king too rich and busy to be bothered. Large old leather trunks, heaped with gold coins, sat along the walls.

"Wow," I said to Richard. "Very Rita."

"Very Roundup Opera Scene and Prop Shop."

"You're kidding?"

"No. Rita called at the last minute and asked us to do it—said she wanted it gold—and there it is."

"She must be a really big contributor," I said.

"Let's dance." Richard took my hand and spun me around the dance floor. "You're a good sport to come here with me tonight," he whispered into my ear and pulled me close.

"I wouldn't have missed it for anything," I told him.

After a while, we traded partners with two of Harry and Rita's other guests, Sam and Georgia Campbell.

"Tell me, Sam," I said, "I've forgotten which oil company you head." I didn't really know if he was in the oil business, but he had a large ring depicting an oil derrick in diamonds on his meaty pinkie finger.

"Spin Drift Exploration."

"Right. That's out of Fort Worth, isn't it?"

"Sure is."

Sam Campbell was heavy-set and balding, and I could tell that he was tough and hard and didn't take any crap from anybody.

"How do you know Rita and Harry?" I asked.

"I've been friends of Rita's and her family for years, known her all her life. We went all through school together. Was sweethearts."

"Why didn't you get married?"

Sam looked at me as if I were crazy. "Me and Rita? Hell, I'm just an oil-patch kid. Her daddy had his sights on somethin' bigger than me. But that's okay, she can have that sawed-off little German fag-got in her bedroom. I get to see her where it really counts. In the boardroom. We're in a few deals together." He said the words like a hurt little boy. He and Rita were clearly much more suited to each other than Rita and Harry and he knew it. "Hell. That was years ago. If I'd married Rita, I never woulda met Georgia. She's a hell of a gal."

Georgia, at least twenty-five years younger, had a nice face, spec-tacular body, capped teeth and huge shiny hair that cascaded to below her shoulders from a straight-up, four-inch, solid wall of hair at her forehead. Texas-sized jewelry glittered all over her low-cut red spandex jumpsuit, which was covered with sparkles and fringe and matched her pointed red cowgirl boots and glossy lipstick. She was nothing but a kid and stared up at Richard with a vacant, gaga smile. I could tell she'd rather be at home watching *Melrose Place* instead of at a grown-up party, a subtlety Richard appeared to be missing altogether, since he was smiling a gaga smile back.

"So you're just up here visiting?" I said to Sam.

"You could say that. Keepin' an eye on the investment here."

"Poker Creek Country Club?" I said. "I understand it's a pretty spot and a huge success."

Sam looked at me like I had rocks in my head.

"It's not to my taste," he finally said. "Plus, it's gone about five hundred percent over budget and is nothing but a big dry hole, far as I'm concerned. Literally and figuratively. I quit puttin' my dough in about six months ago. I don't know where Rita'll get the money to finish it 'cause her daddy's froze all her big cash accounts as far as I can tell, and Harry don't have a pfennig. It'll be outta the red in about fifty years. But what the hell, she's havin' a good time."

I glanced over at Rita, who was bouncing around the dance floor like a big black rubber ball, and she didn't particularly look to me like she was havin' a good time. Of course she was dancing with Dayton, who, in my recollection, did the Hop, no matter what. On the other hand, I thought if Sam gouged me or stepped on my foot one more time, I'd have to shoot him.

"Her daddy wants her to sell it," Sam was saying. "But that little pip-squeak, Dayton Babcock, thinks he can pull together some new investors. Course, he's sunk a boatload of change in hisself. If I was him, I'd find a way to burn it. Collect the insurance."

"We don't tend to encourage forest fires as financial solutions here in Wyoming, Sam," I said.

"Yeah, you're right," he grinned. "Might be a little extreme."

I could not keep going. "Let's rest."

He stopped us dead in our track. "Thank God." He breathed a huge sigh of relief. Sweat coursed down his cheeks. "I hate dancing. Let's get us a damn drink before we have to drink any of Harry's fancy-pants wine. He gives me a royal pain in the butt."

Fancy-pants wine was a good name for it, too, and I love fancy-pants wine. Nineteen sixty-one Lafite Rothschild. Yes. With roast beef and butter-and-garlic-roasted potatoes and asparagus. Oh my.

I sat between Harry and a man named Anthony "Call-me-Tony" Antonucci, who looked like a ferret, and wore his wide silk tie looped over instead of knotted, like a Montana country boy gone to town.

"I'm a lawyer, specializing in personal injury," he told me. "Let me give you my card in case you ever have any problems."

"Thank you," I said. On the back was printed: "My attorney is Anthony "Tony" Antonucci and I cannot be held responsible for any of my words or actions until he is present. Please call him for me immediately. Tony Antonucci accepts all collect calls." I looked at it and then I looked back at him and then I looked at the card again, and then I put it in my pocket, and wondered what in the hell he was doing with this group of people.

He stuck a large, practically bloody piece of beef, with all the fat on it, into his mouth and chewed with his mouth open. It was so bad, I couldn't take my eyes off it. "Are you good friends of the von Singens?"

"Nah." He looked over to the other table, to his wife's perfectly round grapefruit breasts that strained against the low-cut bright blue suede, and smacked his lips. She was sitting between Richard and Tom Kendall and they didn't look so bored. Now that's a big difference between men and women, isn't it? Men couldn't care less what they're talking about if they can look down a girl's dress. They just sit there and say, "Uh-huh, Uh-huh, Uh-huh," and fantasize about what they'd do if she didn't have that dress on. But a woman can hardly sit next to a boring man and stare into his pants the whole evening. I mean, who would want to? If you can't stand to look at his face and he's boring to talk to, who cares what's in his pants?

"How do you know them?" I don't know why I didn't just shut up, but I was fascinated at what his connection could be.

He tore his eyes away from his wife and gave my bosom a fleeting glance. "Business." He swallowed the semi-chewed mess and chased it with big gulping quaffs of the Bordeaux and then reached across the table for the decanter and refilled his glass to the top.

"You're one of the partners in Poker Creek?"

"You could say that." He inhaled deeply and then wiped his napkin all over his face the way you see a monkey do with its hands at a zoo. Like he was washing his face.

Sparky Kendall was on Tony's other side, and when the next course was served, I could hear her trying out the same questions and getting the same monosyllabic answers.

"Your friend Mr. Antonucci is interesting," I said to Harry.

He laughed easily. "Tony is a real diamond in the rough."

"Well, I'd say that you're at least half right." I hoped Harry or Rita or Dayton, or whoever actually owned that doomed country-club project, didn't owe him too much money. "Tell me about some of your other guests," I said. "Who is the woman next to Daniel? I met her but I've forgotten her name."

"Oh, ja. Cordelia Hamilton." Harry appraised her. "She's a widow. From one of your industrial capitals, Cincinnati, Akron, Pittsburgh. One of those places."

"What does she do?"

"Do?" said Harry, perplexed. "Well, I don't suppose she does anything."

Cordelia was sitting between Daniel French and John Stewart, a society plastic surgeon whom I'd met a few times before at cocktail parties and benefits. He was very masculine and handsome, tan and tough-looking with crinkly blue eyes and black curly hair, and gave off an aura of pure, unadulterated animalistic sex. Just look into his eyes and jump right into the sack. No wonder women flocked from everywhere to spend a few days in his private clinic.

Cordelia was listening intently to a conversation between him and Richard. She had leaned slightly forward toward Richard, her fore-arms resting on the table, her graceful hands laid carefully on top of each other. Her eyes flashed and her expression was intelligent and lively and calculating, and I realized I had probably underestimated her, and wondered what, if anything, had gone on between her and Richard before I appeared on the scene.

"How long has she been widowed?" I asked Harry.

"Perhaps a couple of years, I imagine. We only just renewed our acquaintance with her when she moved to Roundup. Used to see them in the south of France. She and my wife have become quite friendly. She's quite charming and amusing," Harry said in that vague, international mumbo jumbo that fills up the air at dinner parties when the guests don't know each other well. He seemed very relaxed for a German. Sort of as though he were passing the time until the next event. Or waiting for something. "I hope you have a chance to talk with her more; I think you'd like her quite a lot."

HA! und HA! I thought. Not too likely.

She watched each man's lips as he talked, which, as every girl knows, is sexy, inviting and not very subtle. John Stewart asked her to dance.

Tom Kendall asked me, and then Dayton cut in and then Richard and then, all of a sudden, it seemed the party just cut loose.

Serena Antonucci, Tony's wife, who had more hair than Georgia Campbell, had painted onto her body a bright blue suede minidress that left virtually nothing to the imagination. Nothing. I don't think she even had on underpants. She wore very high-heeled shoes. It was a novel costume for a square dance and a good thing for her that ladies curtseyed and didn't have to bow. This was a gun moll. A woman with a past. An alley cat. I was quite sure that they did things Tony's way or he smacked her around a little, and she scratched him if he smacked her a little too much.

"I've been trying to get her to limbo," Dayton whispered to me behind his hand.

"Shut up, Dayton," I said.

At one point I went back to our table and found Sam Campbell, Dayton Babcock, Joan Chamberlain and, unfortunately, Fancy French, who had been sober for four years, screaming with laughter and tossing down shots of Cuervo Gold.

Fancy leaned in to Harry. "Aren't they just the most precious addition to our town?" she said to me.

Harry laughed and gave her hand a brisk pat. And suddenly her blue eyes glittered as though she was about to cry. Maybe Fancy and Harry were having a thing, I thought, and hoped for their sakes they were. I mean, Rita and Dayton on a daily basis would be tough to take.

"Come. Let's two-step." Harry took Fancy's hand and led her away.

It seemed everyone wanted to be with someone else. Sam wanted to be with Rita, who, I think had drunk at least a whole bottle of vodka and, not surprisingly, hadn't been seen for a while. It was clear that Fancy and Cordelia and Daniel all wanted to be with Harry, but Harry didn't seem to care much whom he was with. Dayton, who wanted to be with either Serena or Georgia, both of whom wanted to be with any of the stars of *Beverly Hills 90210*, had to settle instead for guiding a staggering, maudlin Fancy out the door to his car. Joan wanted to be with Richard, who wanted to be with me. Thank God.

During a break, he came over and sat down next to me. "I'm getting old," he said.

"Why?"

"I'm sitting next to that sex bomb Serena Antonucci, the one in the low-cut blue suede."

"I know which one she is."

"I've been trying to look unobtrusively down her front to see if she's wearing a bra, but just as I start to zero in, my eyes shift to the next lens in my trifocals so I never can focus unless I get right down next to them." He shrugged. "I guess I'll never know."

"Well, number one," I said, "she isn't. And number two, they're fake. They're implants."

"Get out," Richard said.

Men.

The floor was jammed, the band was fabulous. For what seemed like hours, we were all out there, trading partners, doing do-si-dos and promenades, squares and reels, lines and waltzes.

At midnight, the band played "Happy Trails," and that was it. People began to drift toward home. Richard and I were working our way to the front door when the Lorillards' butler materialized beside us. He had my coat over his arm.

"Miss Bennett?" he said quietly.

"Yes."

"Would you and Mr. Jerome accompany me to the main house? It's quite urgent. There's been an accident."

We followed him out a side door and down a snowy path to the silent house, where the candles still glowed in all the windows, and into the large living room. Mrs. Lorillard was sitting in a chair gripping a glass of brandy while Mr. Lorillard stood in front of the fire. They both looked pale and shaken and stared at a motionless cowgirl in the armchair before them.

It was Baroness Rita Haye von Singen und Mengen, a bullet right between her eyes. Stone-cold dead in the market.

Chapter Six

*P*oor Rita. There she sprawled, all two hundred and fifty pounds of her, her left and right brains severed forever. She was frozen back as though in a dentist's chair—"Doctor will be beginning the root canal any second now, just relax." Her hands gripped the armrests, her head was back, her eyes were wide open and her mouth gaped. Her chubby legs stuck straight out in front, the boots bringing them to little golden points.

The hole in her forehead was precise, almost like she had been killed by a high-speed drill, but it was clearly a close-range gunshot wound. Clear to me, because I'd seen a few of them before, and recognized the hardball-sized black-and-red jagged circle where the gas had been forced under her skin and blown it up into a gruesome star-shaped ornament. A nine-millimeter shell casing lay in the folds of her dress. Evidently a full metal jacket, since the back of her head appeared to be in place.

Full metal jackets make crime scenes a little tidier for everyone, since they usually pass straight through, leaving small exit wounds, unlike hollow-points, which just take the back of the victim's head right off, like a fist smashing through drywall. If police officers had their way, they'd carry hollow-points, but all crimes would be committed with FMJs. The difference between going to the morgue with a parent or husband or wife and asking them to identify a corpse that's been shot with a full metal jacket versus a hollow-tip is big. In one instance it's awful, in the other, devastating. I imagined we would find Rita's fatal round lodged in the wooden chair frame. The chair's blue wool upholstery had already turned black with absorbed blood.

I looked at my watch. Twelve fifty-five. "When did you find her?" I said to Mr. and Mrs. Lorillard.

"We didn't," Mr. Lorillard said. "Robert did."

"I came in to stoke the fire and there she was," Robert the butler volunteered. He was English and white as a sheet. But very calm and collected. They all were.

"Has someone been in the house all evening?" I asked. In a gesture that came to me automatically, I took Rita's wrist between my fingers to check for a pulse, knowing even before I touched her that she had been gone for some time and there would be no bringing her back.

"Robert and the cook have been out helping at the party the whole time," Mrs. Lorillard answered. "But the house has been open. I know guests have been in and out to use the extra bathrooms and Robert has been back and forth."

"She's been sitting here for quite a while, madame," Robert said miserably. "Two hours at least. I thought she was resting, so I didn't think to disturb her. It was just when I came close, that I saw."

"Go get Harry," I said to Richard, who raced back out the door to the barn while I returned my attention to the blanched group. "Mr. Lorillard, I'm sure you have a library or study we could move to?"

"By all means," he answered, relieved, and took his wife's arm. She was starting to look a little shaky. "It's right in here." He led us through a wide, timbered doorway into a well-used, comfortable room. Shoshone and Arapaho artifacts adorned the walls.

"Excuse me," Robert said. "I'll just get something to cover the baroness."

"I'm sorry," I told him. "You can't touch her."

"It's unseemly to leave her like that."

"Do as the marshal says, Robert," Mr. Lorillard said.

"Yes, sir. I'll just bring a tray of coffee, then." Clearly, it would take more than murder to convince Robert to give up his vow to return the world to imperial civilization.

"Has anyone called nine-one-one?" I asked.

"No." Mr. Lorillard seemed surprised at the question. "We sent for you. I mean, Mrs. von Singen was obviously very dead and I saw no reason to broadcast trouble."

I understood his feelings completely, even though he'd done the wrong thing, technically. He should have called right away, but there wasn't really any need for 911. Rita was as dead as she was going to get by the time they'd found her, and since most of the guests had gone, there wasn't any reason to detain the others. I returned to the living room and took my cellular phone out of my purse and dialed the communications center at police head-quarters.

"Roundup Police Department, Sergeant Bryant speaking."

"Homicide, please," I said.

"Homicide. Chief Lewis speaking."

I would be lying if I said that everything between Jack and me was hunky-dory and that I wasn't still a little jealous and resentful of his position and power. He had all the toys—the manpower, the technical backup, and, most important of all, the jurisdiction—and I had only his professional courtesy to keep me in the mix. He still gave me some minor crap from time to time about being a U.S. marshal, about how it was a cushy job and I could still be home in time for a five-course dinner prepared for me by my illegal-alien cook. But our antagonism was diminishing since we'd worked together on a couple of big cases, which I'd solved, and for which he'd received all the credit. I still hated like hell to call him on Rita von Singen's murder because this was the sort of homicide that's right up my alley, the kind I like best—a specific victim for a specific purpose other than drugs or illegal handguns—not some gang shooting over a pair of high-top sneakers.

"Jack, it's Lilly Bennett. I'm up at Ransom Creek Ranch, the Children's Hospital Christmas Party was held here this evening, and we have a homicide. Rita Haye von Singen. Killed at close range, gunshot wound to the head, execution-style."

"Rita Haye von Singen," Jack said. "That that fat rich princess?"

"Baroness."

"Excuse me. Baroness. When did it happen?"

"Well, it's hard to tell," I explained. "The butler said she'd been here for a couple of hours, but she's a big girl, so she's still pretty warm." I moved one of her fingers from its death clutch on the armrest and it was still flexible.

I heard voices coming from outside. "I think her husband's just been located."

"Did you say 'a couple of hours'?"

"I'll explain when you get here."

"We're on our way," Jack said. "Keep it all in place."

"One of these days, Jack, something big is going to happen in Bennett's Fort or on the reservation and it'll be federal property and you're going to be calling me up."

"Right," he said. "Tell me another." And we rang off.

The door flew open and Richard burst back into the room, bringing a big blast of cold mountain air. "Harry's gone," he said.

"He's gone?"

Richard started to say something more, but Daniel and Cordelia entered behind him.

"What in the world is going on?" Daniel said. He was a little bombed. "Has Rita passed out? Come on, Cordie, let's try to get her on her feet."

"She's dead," I said. "She's been shot."

Their reactions surprised me, once they got beyond giggling disbelief and sobered up, which took about five seconds. When people who haven't seen many, or, for that matter, any, unexpectedly dead bodies, do see one, one of two things happens: they scream and cry and go to pieces, maybe even throw up; or they are wowed into stunned silence.

I remember the first time I saw a corpse. It was a security guard who hadn't checked in at his assigned time, so the police were called. One regular officer, one rookie. Me. We found him right away on the floor at his post and I thought he was asleep. It looked to me as though he had passed out or fainted or nodded off, and tumbled off his stool and maybe broken his nose or cracked his head, which would have explained the pool of blood. He was warm when I touched his shoulder and when I felt his neck for a pulse, I could have sworn there was one. Now I know it was the pounding of my own heart. So, I sort of missed my first corpse, but over the years there have been plenty more. Many, like Rita, unmistakably dead. A bullet between the eyes is pretty definitive.

Daniel was silent. He didn't turn green or get queasy, he just stared at her as though he were waiting for her to wake up or speak. "Gosh," he finally said, looking up at me. There were puddles in his big blue eyes. "She's really dead, isn't she?"

"Yes."

"Gosh."

Cordelia, who I thought would have been as cool as a cucumber, since that's the way she looked and acted, had the reaction I'd expected from Daniel. She didn't scream, but her hands flew up to cover her mouth, and her face turned sheet-white so quickly that, for a second, I thought she was going to faint. "Oh, God," she moaned through her fingers. "Oh, God. Oh, Rita." She gulped out a breathy sob and then reached out to her dead friend.

"Why don't you come in here and sit down?" I put my hand on her arm and steered her toward the study.

"Oh, God. I can't believe it. Poor Rita." Cordelia sank into the sofa and wept into a large linen handkerchief thoughtfully provided by Mr. Lorillard. Richard took her a glass of water and she accepted it, looked up at him gratefully with her now limpid baby-blues. I think she was even wearing waterproof mascara. What a phony. As far as I was concerned, she was overreacting like one of those thirties movie stars, weeping and swooning because her rich ninety-year-old husband had just been found dead in a chair at his club, like that would be a big surprise, and it kind of irked me. I wanted to kick Richard.

Daniel, who had not uttered a peep since the "Gosh," circled around in one place, endlessly, like a dog on a sofa, and finally scooched his large behind into a straight-backed armchair and smiled stupidly at the butler, who handed him a snifter of brandy.

"Where's Harry?" I said.

"He left a long time ago," Daniel answered. "Couple of hours, maybe."

"Didn't he and Rita come together?"

Daniel shook his head. "No. I mean, yes, but we were going to take her home. She usually rode with us. Or sometimes . . . " He hesitated.

" 'Sometimes' what?" I said.

"Sometimes she'd leave with Sam Campbell when he was in town."

"Like tonight?"

"Yes, I mean, no. His wife was with him so she was riding with Cordie and me. Harry doesn't like to stay out as late as the rest of us."

"I just can't believe it," Cordelia said, pulling herself together a little. "Who would shoot Rita? She was harmless."

Jack Lewis's helicopter, which had been thrumming in the distance, grew closer and noisier, and the frigid alpine world outside was illuminated brighter than day by the chopper's strong search and landing lights. Moments later, Roundup's bald, wiry, dapper chief of detectives strode into the house and took charge.

Chapter Seven

Saturday morning

The drive back was quick. The big Mercedes hugged the road like a locomotive as we raced down the mountains on the dry highway toward the rising sun, which greeted us from far across the vast snow-covered plains, giving the illusion that we were driving into a blindingly white sea. Unknown Iron Curtain singers, probably dead by now, the recording was so old, serenaded us with *Rusalka*, a melodious, obscure fairy-tale opera by Antonín Dvořák. It was next in the season, opening just two weeks after *Ada* closed.

After a few minutes of being quiet and trying to read the little tiny print of the foldout from the disc, I gave up. "What is this about?" I asked Richard.

"Rusalka is a water sprite who wants to become a human so she can marry the prince, an intention of which the prince is unaware. So, when the witch turns her into a person and she presents herself to the prince and he rejects her in favor of the princess, she kills him and goes back to the water where she's sentenced to spend the rest of eternity as a will-o'-the-wisp on the lake edge. There's more to it than that, but that's basically it."

"Thanks."

The music looped prettily through the car, waltzing around us, and as Rusalka sang of her passion, I thought about all the women who seemed to want Harry, albeit a baron instead of a prince, but nevertheless, I imagined there were scores of women, all over the world, he'd probably rejected because of Rita. Their marriage appeared on the surface to be as unikely and incomprehensible as that of Henry the Eighth to Anne of Cleves. That they were actually happy was unthinkable, untenable even, to some people. I thought about the passion of murder and the currencies that drive it. They're always the same: money, power, influence or position. Somebody wanted and expected to receive all or any of those things from the death of Rita Haye von Singen. Somebody who was well-organized and very objective and dispassionate about his or her methods. Close-range. Between the eyes. Silencer. Someone cold-blooded, maybe even professional. Someone German, maybe. But, whatever the reason, I didn't think that it was because the killer was mad at Rita personally. I could not imagine that Rita herself, who was so innocuous and grasping and desperate, could inspire a murderous passion in anyone beyond just getting her out of the way.

We wailed through Crazy Squaw Canyon toward Bennett's Fort, past all of cousin Buck's freshly painted, snow-topped signs: REAL LIVE COWBOYS said one. REAL LIVE INDIANS said another. Others promised AUTHENTIC RATTLESNAKE CAVE—OVER 100,000 LIVE RATTLESNAKES. VISIT THE JAIL IN BENNETT'S FORT—SEE WYATT EARP'S SIX-SHOOTERS. VISIT THE GOLDEN NUGGET SALOON. REAL SASPARILLY. FREE PARKING AND CLEAN REST ROOMS IN BENNETT'S FORT. WALK ON THE REAL OREGON TRAIL. COME MEET SANTA.

"I think this music's a little wimpy, don't you?" I said to Richard as we turned onto the Circle B. He had driven so fast we had gotten through only one act.

"You're so erudite in your critiques," he said. "Like when you told the director of *Traviata* that you thought, and I quote, 'the guy playing Alfredo was a geek.'"

"Well, he was."

"You're right about *Rusalka*. The music gets a little bigger here and there in the next two acts, not much, but the staging is breathtaking. It'll all come together. You'll see."

I lifted his hand off the gear shift and kissed his palm and held it against my cheek for a moment. My feelings for Richard were so strong, they scared me to death. Murder is nothing compared to love, especially the middle-aged variety. Not only do you have an ongoing tug-of-war with your heart and soul and the consideration of changes in the singular lifestyle you've worked so hard to put together and come to terms with and like so much, you also worry constantly that if your lover gets a really good look at your body, uncamouflaged by bubbles or negligees, he will be gone faster than you can say "Don't look!"

Plus, I think it's excellent to come to an understanding with your body that it is not and never again will be what it was, but I don't think we should force our self-acceptance on others. I figured this bit of wisdom out the last time I sat beside a swimming pool. I realized that at a certain point you shouldn't go wandering around in a bathing suit anymore. If you need to go to the pop stand or the ladies' room, for heaven's sake pull a sarong around you or a caftan. Don't make everyone look at that fifty-plus-year-old flesh—it just doesn't look nice.

"What are you thinking about?" Richard said. "You're awfully quiet."

"Nothing much," I said. "Going on a diet."

"Don't worry about it. You look terrific."

Right.

The main valley of the ranch was quiet; no birds, no leaves to rustle on the black-speckled aspen that blended into the terrain. I love the silence and intimacy of the hill country's winter landscape. Everything is under the snow, under the ground, sound asleep. Not showing off, not interfering with our brains and distracting us from our thoughts. It's just there in the background. Only a few blades of dry water-grass stuck through the snow which drifted in the shade of the river's banks. The water was so low, as it slid over the rocks and pebbles it made them look as if they were covered with aspic.

The valleys, which teem with Black Angus from April to October, were empty, as were the big lodgepole cattle pens. Only Elias's breeding stock remained, and they had gathered down by the river, many of them circling around the salt lick just staring at it, maybe hoping it would turn into something. Who knew what? A few bored woolly horses, whose furry winter coats made them look like stocky little Siberian ponies, wandered aimlessly in the corral outside the horse barn, sniffing the clods of frozen mud and pawing nonexistent tufts of grass. When our car rumbled across the cattle guard, they lifted their heads in unison and turned their bright black eyes eagerly toward us, hoping we were bringing them something good to eat. Some new kind of special, sweet oat from town. Just like people.

We caught Elias puffing his burly self across the ranch-house yard, his two Australian shepherds, Gal and Pal, and my little wire-haired fox terrier, Baby, who had been their houseguest, scampering around him seeing who could outjump the other. Steam shot from their smiling mouths as they leaped several feet straight up into the icy morning air, flipping and twisting and turning and tripping each other and just generally having a ball.

Elias had been a Green Beret captain, well, actually a Central Intelligence Agency officer in Vietnam—well, actually in Cambodia—where he got his legs shot up, not off, thank goodness. After that unfortunate incident, which he followed by two years of whooping it up in Aspen as a Demoral addict, he cleaned up his act and came back to Roundup to run the ranch. It's hard to say if Elias became a Green Beret because he was a misfit or if being a Green Beret made him one. Either way, he never found peace until he moved into the main ranch house and reconciled himself with the fact that he would never be the head of the CIA, or the CEO of one of the Bennett family corporations, or any other corporation, for that matter. He reconciled himself with the fact that he liked to be on the ranch, working with his championship Angus cattle and cutting horses. Elias was just as sweet as pie except when he went to town, where he tended to drink too much and talk too loud.

"Hey!" he beamed, once Richard stopped the car. "Come on in and have some breakfast."

Elias gets into Christmas in a major way and had decorated the big old rough house like Macy's windows. An evergreen wreath with a wide red ribbon and sleigh bells hung invitingly on the front door, and at every window box, upstairs and down, where hot-red geraniums blaze all summer, he had laid pine boughs strung with little lights. Electric candles burned behind the windowpanes. Santa in his sleigh and his eight tiny reindeer scampered across the roof, and in the front yard the Holy Family gathered around the Babe in a life-sized, hand-carved, hand-painted crèche he had bought in Bavaria when our grandmother took us to Europe when he was fifteen and I was thirteen. Talk about a trip. I could write a book about that one. Inside the front door a tall, fat, sparkling, fragrant Christmas tree filled the large central foyer completely while the Mormon Tabernacle Choir filled the air.

"I'm glad you're back," he said as he stamped snow from his boots on the mat outside before entering. "I was starting to get worried. I wish you'd been here for my tree-decorating party last night."

"Me, too," Richard said. "It's starting to get dangerous going to parties with your sister. Sort of like dating Jessica Fletcher: someone always gets murdered. Pretty soon, people will stop inviting her."

"Very funny," I said.

"What do you mean?" Elias asked.

"Give me a cup of coffee and I'll tell you," Richard said and we followed my brother into the house.

Elias hung his heavy sheepskin coat and hat on an old-fashioned bentwood rack just inside the door. He had on a plaid flannel shirt, a knit tie and a gray cashmere V-neck sweater. "I'll tell Marialita to add a couple of places," he said and passed through the swinging kitchen door. Then he poked his head back out. "How about some hot buttered rum?"

"Why not," Richard and I answered in unison.

Everything about Elias's home is oversized because it's required to accommodate so many ranch hands. In the winter there are just a few, maybe eight or ten, but beginning with the early-spring roundup and building in numbers over the summer to the big roundup in late September, there are sometimes as many as sixty wranglers. The main house is where all the meals get served, and where the cowboys pass their time off, shooting pool or gambling, when they're not out on the range or sleeping in their bunkhouses. It's a man's house with pine-paneled, soot-darkened walls which bear the burned-in initials, brands and artworks of more than a century of cowboys taking a few hours off between roundups or ropings or brandings or just plain herd tending. Antique Navajo Indian rugs cover the polished cedar floors except in front of the living room fireplace, where an enormous grizzly bear, his jaws open in a ferocious growl, lies flattened into a furry rug. Indestructible tartan wool cushions and pillows and bolsters soften the heavy pine furniture, and a number of Frederic Remington oils, depicting a life that is so unchanging they could have been painted yesterday, hang on the walls.

This morning, four cowboys—tan faces, scorched, peeling noses, white foreheads—were in the poolroom, which opens to the side of the living room. That's pool the game, not the hole in the ground filled with water. They played cards while a video of a PRCA Bull Riding Championship, sound off, was on the big-screen television, and two or three dozen stuffed, mounted heads of sundry wildlife, some from Wyoming, some from my great-grandfather's long-ago African safaris, kept score from the walls. Coffee mugs and ashtrays ringed the scarred table.

I stuck my head in the door. "Morning, fellas," I said and they all stood up, not because I was a Bennett, but because I was a lady and because they were gentlemen. Cowboys always are.

"Morning, ma'am," they said.

The coffeepot is on twenty-four hours a day in the poolroom and Elias provides all the beer the cowboys want when they're off duty, but it's only 3.2 percent alcohol. Hard liquor is not allowed. In addition to the pool table and TV, there are four poker tables and three slot machines. We don't have a problem attracting good hands to work on the Circle B.

Just to the left of the front door, in the dining room, I could see our places set for breakfast on the long, time-worn table. A fire blazed in the granite fireplace. Everything smelled good—the fires, the cedar floors, the wet leather of our boots and the old leather of my father's collection of antique saddles, the Christmas tree.

In spite of what Jack Lewis likes to say, our household and ranch staff, mostly members of the Vargas family, is not made up of illegal aliens. The Vargases have been on our ranch for three generations, but they stick strongly to Mexican ways, and anyone meeting them for the first time would think they had just walked right out of the Rio Grande. Well, they haven't. And we pay their Social Security, their FUTA taxes and all their health insurance, et cetera, et cetera, et cetera, in case anyone wants to know. We've also put most of them through college.

In my house, I have Celestina fix more Mexican-style food because I think it's healthier since it's based on beans and fresh vegetables instead of beef, butter and eggs. Not Elias. After a couple of hot buttered rums, we sat down and Marialita swung through the door with big platters of sausage and bacon and little grilled fillets, buckwheat cakes. ("How'd this buckwheat get in here, Elias?" I said. "This is actually healthy.") There were pitchers of melted butter and warm syrup, a bowl of scrambled eggs, a covered basket of hot biscuits and a boat of spicy sausage gravy. And about a hundred gallons of coffee. We told Elias about the murder.

"Who do you think did it?" he said and started to carve his pancakes, sausages and eggs into hash.

"I don't know," I answered. "I've been thinking about it all the way back in the car." I took my notebook and glasses out of my purse. "There are some outstanding suspects. Harry, the husband, for one. But, based simply on my intuition, I don't think it was him. Clearly, he and Rita weren't close, but I didn't get the impression he was so miserable he couldn't stand it anymore. Actually, I thought they seemed sort of kind to each other, affectionate. Didn't you, Richard?"

Richard, who had just taken a large bite of scrambled eggs and biscuits and gravy, nodded his head.

"Apparently Rita was having a long-term affair with a man from Texas, Sam Campbell," I continued. "So his wife, Georgia, is a possible. Also, from a passion angle, women are extremely attracted to Harry, which, for starters, makes Fancy French and Cordelia Hamilton and Joan Chamberlain all possibles that I know of right off."

"All debutante mothers," Elias pointed out. "All three of them have daughters who are being presented at the Ball next week: Lulu French, Mary Patricia Hamilton, and Dorothy Jefferson—Joan Chamberlain's daughter from her second or third marriage. She's from New York," he said, as though being from New York explained the number of marriages, because that's the way everybody lived back there.

"Interesting," I said, putting notations by their names. "You're absolutely right. I don't see a connection right off the bat, but who knows. Then we have the fact that this big country-club development the von Singens are involved in—Poker Creek—is hemorrhaging red ink, opening the whole world of business associates and investors as suspected, starting with Dayton Babcock." I put some buttery hotcakes in my mouth. They were so good I thought I'd fall off my chair with happiness.

"What"—Elias laughed—"Short-Arms was there?"

"Who?" said Richard.

"Never mind," I told him and took a big gulp of coffee. "Sam Campbell, Rita's friend, from the aspect of a business partner who's losing money. Some greaseball lawyer, Anthony Antonucci."

"You mean, 'Call-me-Tony'?" Eli said. "The personal-injury guy? 'You get injured, call one-eight-hundred-ANTHONY collect. I will help you. You have my name on it.'"

"You know him?"

"Nah. That's what his TV ads say." Elias helped himself to a fillet, his second.

"Daniel French."

"Daniel French?" Elias was incredulous. "He wouldn't hurt a fly."

"You never know," I said. "Don't rule him out. He was very calm around Rita's corpse and had told me earlier that he thought Harry von Singen was the most divine man he'd ever met. I don't think Daniel's quite the cream puff he wants everyone to think he is. No one who can't handle a lot of pain—physical and mental—chooses that life."

Richard and Elias both grimaced. "No shit," they said at the same time and laughed and shivered their shoulders as though chilled.

"So what are you going to do?" Elias said.

"Nothing," I answered, taking another large bite of everything we know better than to eat. "Not my case."

Chapter Eight

*T*hat afternoon, after lunch, Richard left for town to check on the *Ada* rehearsal and I took a quick shower. I was afraid to get into my big bathtub, which beckoned to me like Bali Ha'i, because I knew if I did I'd fall asleep, and I needed to go to the office for a couple of hours to catch up. Not only did I need to wrap up the report from the trip to England, I had three Bennett Security cases in various stages of development that needed attention, and my new secretary, Linda Long, whom I'd stolen from my brother Christian, had left a message that there was a bunch of stuff on my desk I needed to look at before Monday. So I pulled on a pair of old jeans and a soft shirt and sweater and worn-out boots and a long fur coat and headed into the Christmas chaos of Bennett's Fort.

Since the Marshal's Office was such a tourist attraction—VISIT THE JAIL IN BENNETT'S FORT—SEE WYATT EARP'S SIX-SHOOTERS. PEEK THROUGH THE DOOR AND SEE MARSHAL EARP'S AUTHENTIC DESK AND CHAIR—and since I needed an actual office, Buck had thoughtfully provided me with one atop the Golden Nugget Saloon. I slid to a stop in the slush behind the building, stuck Baby under my arm, and went up the steep, rickety back stairs to the second floor. Buck had this thing about authenticity, unusual in a tourist trap. Everything was authentic except the rest rooms. "That's what keeps 'em coming back," he claims. "Clean, modern rest rooms. You can get saltwater taffy anywhere." So upstairs in my office, the wind blew right through the old windows, covering everything with dirt, but I didn't mind because they provided me with a wonderful view of all the Christmas festivities on Main Street, which was decorated to beat the band.

Bundled-up families ebbed and flowed in and out of the shops, and an octet of costumed carolers stood in front of the taffy-and-rock-candy store, which was now filled with racks of candied apples, some dipped in caramel and rolled in chopped nuts, others shining in crackling red cinnamon candy coats. The sounds of "God Rest Ye, Merry Gentlemen" rose to my window. Baby and I stood looking out, she was up on her back feet, her paws on the sill, eyes bright and alert.

It was a wonderful scene and made me feel the same thrill of anticipation I feel every year around Christmas—that something fabulous (besides Jesus, of course) was going to happen. Usually, it didn't, but I never give up. Besides, this year was my first year living back in Roundup, not just visiting, so, in many ways, that in itself was a fabulous gift.

After a moment, I sat down at my desk and went to work and tried to put Rita von Singen out of my mind. But it was hard. I prayed for Jack Lewis to call and ask for my help. He did call, but only to have me recap what we'd been over the night before. It was routine. They were contacting everyone who'd been there. Rub it in.

At about four o'clock it started to snow, and then the wind picked up. Within half an hour, all the tourists were gone. I locked up and went back down the stairs, around to the front of the weather-beaten old storefront building, down the wooden sidewalk and through the swinging front doors of the saloon, where I knew Buck would be sitting at his table in the side booth perpetrating phone rape on some Hollywood producer for the right to use the Bennett's Fort facades in some TV-movie deal. I was right. He hung up just as we reached him.

"Candy from a baby." He smiled up at me, his Santa suit open at the neck. Buck was big and friendly and looked like Burl Ives. "You want a coffee and a shot?"

"Sure, thanks," I said.

"Two Jamesons and two cappuccinos, and not too much damn milk," he yelled at the dreary-looking, middle-aged bartender who slumped in front of a small TV set behind the long "Authentic Western Bar" across the room. She slid off her stool and shuffled to the impressive old-fashioned chrome espresso machine with its huge shiny tanks of boiling water.

Buck shook his head with disgust. "That girl," he began, "is a perfect example of only one of a million things people don't seem to realize about the West. They think it's so damn glamorous, but most of the people out here in the boondocks, which we all know the western states mostly are, are nothing but a bunch of goddamn burnouts. A bunch of goddamn ex-hippies whose brains are like Swiss cheese from LSD and pot and amphetamines and who-knows-what-all, who came here to hide in the mountains and get high without interference or interruption from their parents or the fuzz. Hell, they're friendly and nice and mostly harmless enough, but they'll never amount to a goddamn thing and they contribute zilch to the tax base. Just look at this mess."

The bartender, wearing a soiled, faded western-style gingham granny dress, not quite long enough to conceal her backward-tilting earth sandals, drifted over with a tray and placed the coffees and whiskeys on the table. Her gaunt, hatchetlike face was expressionless. Large ears poked through her black stringy hair that hung straight down from an ancient red flannel Santa hat trimmed with dirty gray fleece.

"Thanks, honey," Buck said kindly.

She gave him a vacant, friendly smile that pulled her chapped lips back over her bad teeth. "Sure."

I agreed with Buck. Back in the Appalachians and places like that, they have generations of impoverished families. We never had anything like that out here. Everyone was here because they wanted to be. But now the same is happening here that happened there, and we've just started our third generation of poverty. We now have the hippies' grandchildren: the children of the children of the flower children of the sixties and seventies. They live in poverty and squalor and wouldn't believe it if you told them they can lay their whole sorry situation at the doorstep of Peace, Love and Timothy Leary. They just know they're poor and cold and hungry and sick because all they eat are Cheeze-Its and potatoes.

He tossed off his shot. "Couple more," he yelled. "Hold the coffee."

A few shots later, I followed him out into the storm, and ten minutes after that pulled through the main gate at the Circle B. It was dark and the snow was really coming down, cutting the visibility to almost nothing. I drove slowly, my headlights scarcely helping as I followed the dirt road across the river, past Elias's, and up the small rise above the river to my place. Celestina had left the lights on and they shone with welcome through the French doors and made my cozy little cabin look like an ad for an expensive liqueur.

I knew even before the phone rang that Richard wouldn't be able to make it back out because of the weather, that he and Christian would have to spend the night in town. But I really didn't mind, I was so beat. I went to bed and slept like a bear.

Chapter Nine

Sunday morning

During the night, the storm worked itself into a full-blown blizzard. The snow might have been drifting down romantically, postcard style, up in the mountains somewhere, but out here in the hill country, where we don't have that many trees, or even very many hills, for that matter, it seemed as if someone were standing on the North Pole shooting snow out of a high-pressure fire hose right straight across Wyoming. And as it got light, the temperature dropped and the wind picked up even greater intensity. It was what some people would call downright miserable.

I literally dragged Baby outside and walked her once around the house, and then, without giving myself time to come up with the *excuse du jour*, leaped immediately onto the treadmill in my dressing room and started my two miles as fast as I could.

The local news was on, and obviously, Rita von Singen's murder was still the lead story.

Most of it was a rehash of the stories that had been on the night before. By mid-afternoon Saturday they had contacted a lot of the dinner-party guests for comments and observations, and reported that no murder weapon had been found and no suspects taken into custody. Therefore, since five o'clock Saturday evening, there'd been no *new* news. A challenging situation for any television reporter who has hours of air time to fill. But, this morning, the newscaster was Marsha Maloney, the co-anchor of the weeknight *Evening News*. A big shot. Something must be up.

"Sometime late Friday night, during a gala fund-raising dinner at the Lorillards' Ransom Creek Ranch, with some of Roundup's leading socialites," Marsha Maloney said, "Baroness Rita Haye von Singin' an' Mingin'—"

"It's Singen *und* Mengen. Not Singin' an' Mingin'," I said to Marsha. "It's a name. Not a Lawrence Welk dance."

"—was found shot to death in the lavish living room of the Lorillards' deluxe mansion."

"She obviously hasn't been there." I upped the speed to four and a half miles an hour and started to run. "It's nice, but hardly what I'd call lavish."

"Police have interviewed the guests at the exclusive party, and although no arrests have been made, KRUN has learned that Baron von Singin' an' Mingin' is going to be taken to town for questioning. Let's go now to Tom O'Neil, who's standing by up at the baron's ranch. Tom," she said, "what can you tell us about the situation as it now stands?"

Poor Tom O'Neil, Marsha's *Evening News* co-anchor, stood in the blizzard waiting his turn on the air and getting his lungs more frozen with each breath and trying to look macho about the whole deal. I'm sure he had thought his working-outside days were over. The von Singens' ranch house was almost invisible behind him through the snow, but it looked absolutely enormous.

"Thanks, Marsha," he said. "I'm here at Baron von Singen's exclusive ranch estate—"

"*Ranch estate?*" I blabbed along. "That's a new one. You either have a ranch, or you have an estate. Where are you from, Tom? Milwaukee? This is like watching *Lifestyles of the Rich and Famous*."

"—scene of the brutal, cold-blooded, execution-style murder Friday night of Baroness Rita Haye von Singen und Mengen following a charity dinner with some of Roundup's leading socialites. According to a highly placed source in the Roundup Police Department, KRUN has learned that the baroness's husband, Baron Heinrich von Singen und Mengen—boy, that's a mouthful, isn't it, Marsha?—a German national, is going to be taken in for questioning. Chief Investigator Jack Lewis arrived here a few minutes ago and we are expecting him and the baron to depart momentarily. Back to you, Marsha."

"Interesting," I said, puffing up a four-percent hill. "I wonder what the evidence is."

"You get back in the truck and stay warm," Marsha told him. "And we'll cut back to you instantly when they come out. Don't catch a cold."

"Give me a break," I said. "Grow up."

"Thanks," said Tom.

"I've just received word"—Marsha turned up her volume of urgency—"that KRUN *News Six* has an unconfirmed report that the police have recovered the gun believed to be the murder weapon. We'll bring you more on this story as it develops."

I stepped off the treadmill and lay down on the floor, stretched for about five seconds because everyone says we should, and did fifty sit-ups, why, I have no idea. They do absolutely nothing but make me mad. They have no effect at all on my stomach. But nevertheless, I groan through them a few times a week, along with forty leg-lifts and forty push-ups. I just made that up. I don't really do all this a few times a week, I just say I do because I think everyone does, except me. I try to work out a couple times a week, but at least I don't smoke anymore, and I walk Baby five times a day. Look, I'm doing the best I can.

Finally I stopped. I took a quick shower, pulled on a warm flannel robe, went to the kitchen, made a pot of coffee, put a mixture of All-Bran and Raisin Bran cereals in a bowl, fed the dog, put pretty crisp linens and silver and china on a tray and filled up the delicately flowered porcelain coffeepot that was part of my grandmother's Limoges breakfast set, and hauled the whole business upstairs and got back into bed. The fire blazed and the storm raged and I switched on the television with no sound so I could keep an eye on Harry von Singen's departure and snuggled down into one of Susan Howatch's long, complicated gothic novels. To my way of thinking, it is not possible to have a more perfect Sunday morning. The only way such a luxurious affair could be improved upon would be with the addition of great sex. Or even marginal sex. I had a friend once who said, "Want to know what the worst sex I ever had was like?" "Sure," I said. "FANTASTIC!!!" he yelled. I wished Richard were there but he wasn't.

My phone rang.

"Miss Bennett?" The voice had a slight accent.

"Yes."

"This is Harry von Singen and I need your help."

"Tell me what I can do," I said, looking skyward and saying, "Thank you, God" in my head. "I've been keeping track on the news."

"I have only a real estate attorney in Roundup, Sparky Kendall, and in any event I have not been able to reach her on the phone; they must be away for the weekend. I know you are a detective, Miss Bennett, not an attorney, but I know you would know who I should call. They say they may have evidence against me, but I did not kill Rita."

My adrenaline leaped. This was excellent. Better than great sex. "I'll put in a call right now to Paul Decker," I said. "He's the attorney you need and he'll come down and meet you. Don't answer any questions until he arrives and then I'll see you guys out here at the ranch for lunch."

"Thank you, Miss Bennett."

"Don't worry. You'll be in good hands. And, Harry, please call me Lilly." I hung up. Jack Lewis would crap. I was so happy.

Paul Decker, Roundup's superb, and unbelievably expensive, criminal defense showboat lawyer, could not have been more delighted to interrupt his Sunday morning to come to the aid and comfort of Baron von Singen und Mengen.

I caught a glimpse of Harry as he rushed through the thick snow and into the squad car. Naturally there were about fifty microphones shoved into his face but he didn't stop to make any remarks.

"We will have an official comment at some point later today," Chief Lewis said before the squad disappeared into the storm, leaving the announcers to reiterate for the hundred millionth time the story no one could get enough of.

Chapter Ten

By noon, the lights of Decker's custom-made, ten-wheel, silver Suburban limousine shone through the snow on the road to my house and came to a precision stop at the front gate. Decker's bodyguard, a burly Turk, darted out and slid open the side door—so big it was like watching a Federal Express ground crew open the main hold of a cargo liner—revealing a large dark interior. According to Paul's publicity, his Suburban had been outfitted with not only the expected furnishings of soft black leather seats and burled walnut, crystal decanters and high-intensity reading lights, but also a small private sleeping compartment and an ultra-sophisticated communications system.

In Wyoming, we don't think for a second of making a four- or five-hour drive to visit a client or do business, because that's how far away the next town is. And we are always prepared for disaster, because the weather comes fast and hard. Every month during winter there is a story or two about out-of-towners who thought they'd make it and either froze to death after they'd pulled over in a whiteout, but didn't have any emergency supplies to sustain them for a two- or three-day period; or else didn't pull over and drove off a butte. We never think we can beat the elements or the odds, including distance and fatigue. They're just too damn big. That's why Paul

Decker traveled with a bodyguard and a driver. The bodyguard was really there to spell the driver, not so much vice versa. All just part of the image, the Legend of Paul.

The Man himself descended, settling his black cowboy hat firmly on his head. His full-length ranch mink coat whipped around his legs in the fifty-mile-an-hour wind. Harry followed, pulling his navy cashmere overcoat and paisley scarf close around his neck. They both slipped and slid their way up the front walk in slick-bottomed alligator cowboy boots and soft Italian leather loafers, and across my cedar floors into Celestina's arms, where she traded them Bloody Marys for their overcoats.

Baby jumped all over Harry.

"Oh," he said. "What an amusing little dog."

I flipped through the notes I'd made Friday night and Saturday morning as we settled in the study, where Celestina had arranged a large tray of turkey sandwiches, pitchers of Bloody Marys and ice water, and a pot of coffee on the table in front of the fire. Usually the Wind River is right out there, right outside the windows, flowing with peaceful grace over to Nebraska or somewhere, but today everything was white; not a single shadow to demark the world.

"Tell me about the gun," I said, once they were comfortably seated—Harry on the sofa, Paul in a wing chair.

"It's terrible," Harry said. "I have always kept my father's sidearm from World War Two in my desk. It's just an old souvenir."

"What is it?" I said, knowing full well that it was some sort of Mauser, probably a 9-mm Luger, which had been standard issue for high-level Nazi officers. I just hoped it wasn't the Gestapo model.

"A Luger, of course," Harry said archly.

"A Luger with a silencer and SS runes," Paul added.

"Oh, dear," I said.

"Lilly," Harry said. Two rosy patches bloomed on his pale cheeks. "Let me assure you, I am not a Nazi and my father was not a member of the Gestapo. He was presented with the gun with the special Gestapo SS medallion as a kind of passport for his own safety."

I didn't say anything, but is it just me, or has anyone else noticed it's impossible to find any World War II vintage German who had any knowledge of, or association with the Nazis? Or even who knew any Nazis? Or to find any American who admits going to Canada during the Vietnam War? The ones with student deferments or 4Fs are just now peeking out from behind the trees.

"That may or may not be true, Harry," I said. "The only reason it's troublesome is that Nazis have a reputation as cold-blooded killers. You know what I mean? Have they confirmed it was the murder weapon?"

Paul shook his head. "They just picked it up this morning."

"Where did you keep the gun?"

"In my desk in the study at our ranch." Harry refilled his drink, sprinkling a little extra salt and pepper on the top. He sat back in the corner of the sofa and crossed his legs and stretched his arms along the cushion tops, completely at ease. Elegant and relaxed.

"When was the last time you used it?"

He shrugged. "I can't recall."

"Who else knew it was there?"

"Only Rita and Carlo, my valet."

"Okay." I made a note. "I'll call Jack Lewis a little later. It sounds like a routine check to me. They'll have preliminary test results in another hour or two. Where was Carlo on Friday night?"

"Believe me, he did not shoot the baroness."

"How do you know?"

"It's simply not the sort of thing he would do."

"Baron," Paul spoke up. "As we proceed, we're going to have to get a little more specific than 'it's not the sort of thing he would do.' When you look at the guest list, you would hope that this is not the sort of thing any of them would do."

"Well, you're quite right, of course," Sovereign Harry conceded with grace.

"For instance," I asked, "why wouldn't you do it?"

"Kill Rita?" Harry looked surprised. "Never. She was my friend."

I believed him.

"Did you have a habit of attending parties separately?"

"Yes. Frequently." Harry paused to think. "Let me explain. Rita and I had very different interests—she loved the opera and American Indians, and she surrounded herself with what she considered to be like-minded, interesting people." He smiled charmingly. "This may astound you, but I am not generally considered to be especially fascinating."

He was trying to get me to be friendly, but I wasn't. Harry had plenty of friends—and enemies. He needed someone objective on his team. "Where was Rita when you left?" I asked.

"I have no idea. I left the party right after I danced with Fancy, at about ten o'clock."

"Did you go home?"

"Yes."

"Alone?"

"Yes." Harry lit a cigarette. His face had colored again.

"Are you sure?"

Paul Decker cradled his coffee cup in his hand and frowned at me, his thick salt-and-pepper eyebrows making the large signature "V" that inevitably makes his clients feel secure, and juries righteously indignant on his clients' behalf. I knew what was coming. "I'm a little disturbed by your questions and your attitude, Lilly. You are treating my client as a suspect." Paul knew exactly what I was doing, but the remark was designed to make Harry feel better.

"I don't especially think he is," I said. "But I can assure you that as far as the police are concerned, Harry is the prime suspect. And you know as well as I do, Paul, we need to see if there are gaps in his activities or questions about his behavior that will help them make their case and cause them to stop the search for the actual killer. So if I'm insulting you by my questions, Harry, well, that's just the way it goes. Now . . ." I cleared my throat. "According to what Paul told me over the phone, you stand to inherit the bulk of Rita's estate. What does that do to the status of the country club development?"

"I need to decide soon whether to hold it or sell it," Harry said. "We have investors, and they and our bankers have been very patient, and have accepted numerous delays, but if we don't get the income moving, they will close the operation down—probably in thirty days. Maybe sooner."

"'We' being you and Dayton Babcock?"

"Correct," Harry said. "Principally Dayton. He has attracted most of the investors. Made most of the deals. He and Rita had the biggest shares. Now, of course, I do."

"Tell me about the insurance. Was there key-man coverage?"

"Naturally. Ten million each on Rita, Dayton and me."

"So theoretically," I said, "if you were to kill Rita, not only would you be able to stabilize the project's operating cash flow for a while, it would also be under your majority control. You would also collect any assets she provided to you in her will. In short, you would be well fixed."

Harry looked put out and did not answer for a moment. "That is all true," he finally granted. "But I didn't kill Rita. As I have already said, she was my friend. I miss her."

Harry was difficult for me to read. He was so open and forthcoming. So innocent and helpful. That sort of conduct always makes me suspicious.

"The same is true to a large extent for Dayton," I said. "But he would be in even better shape if both of you were dead."

"Very true," Harry agreed, visibly relieved that the subject had moved from him. "Rita used to drive him wild with all her left-brain/right-brain silliness. But I don't think it was Dayton."

"Why?"

The baron frowned slightly and then tilted his head back just a little, the stereotypical Aryan general peering at his minions across his ormolu desk. "You know how these little men can be," he said. "They get terribly excited and angry and then squirt off right away. Then they start again. They never really accomplish much."

Tell me about it, I thought.

"In any event," Harry concluded, "if Dayton had done it, he never could keep his mouth shut about it for this long. He'd have to brag to somebody."

"Lilly," Paul spoke up. "What do you think about Tony Antonucci's being there? Word on the street is that he's directly linked to the Mob."

"Who got Antonucci involved?" I asked Harry.

"Dayton."

"I think they'd probably go after Dayton first," I said to Paul. "But Antonucci's a strong contender. Harry, tell me about Sam Campbell. He told me he had a lot of money in the project."

"Sam would like it if I were dead," Harry said. "But not Rita. He worshipped her."

"His wife, Georgia?"

Harry shrugged. "I don't think she'd be smart enough to plan something so cool without a lot of help."

I glanced at my notes. "Fancy French?"

Harry paused, as though he were about to speak, but then changed his mind and shook his head.

"Are you having an affair with her?"

"No."

"Why are you hesitating?"

"I'm terribly fond of Fancy," Harry said. "She can be delightful company. But I think she would be quite incapable of murder. Don't you?"

"Not especially," I said. "Unfortunately, I think that today just about everyone is capable of murder. People lack discipline and self-control. Plus, the media provides you with celebrity and cash if you kill someone. So not only do you get rid of a problem with a murder, you also get to be a star."

Paul and Harry both looked at me politely.

"Well," I said. "I know I'm getting a little off the track. What about the plastic surgeon, John Stewart? Does he have a motive?"

"Not that I know of."

I skipped past my old friends, Tom and Sparky Kendall, to Joan and Dickie Chamberlain—Richard's old girlfriend. But Harry hadn't met either one of them before. They had been Dayton's idea.

"Cordelia Hamilton?"

"She and Rita were close, longtime friends. Cordelia would have nothing to gain by Rita's death."

"She might think she would gain you," I suggested, recalling the way Cordelia had looked at him, placed her hand on his chest.

Harry smiled. "She knows better. We covered that territory long ago. No, Cordelia would not trouble herself with a losing proposition. If she can't be the queen bee, she moves on quickly."

"Was there anyone else at the party that you can think of who would have any reason at all to kill Rita?" I asked, even though I had a feeling the murderer, or murderess, had been included in the list of possibilities we'd just reviewed.

"No. I haven't the smallest idea who did this," Harry said impatiently. "That's why I'm hiring you."

"Fair enough." I took off my glasses and rubbed my eyes. "I think that'll do it for today, unless there's something you think we've left out?"

Both men shook their heads.

We all stood up and stretched our backs. I went to the closet and got their coats and then they disappeared down the dark walk into the storm. None of us had to say out loud what a total cash-flow and publicity bonanza Rita's murder would be for Poker Creek Country Club's flagging building site and membership sales.

I returned to the library and added a log to the fire and then faxed a list of suspects to the office with some instructions for Linda to get started on in the morning.

Then I called Jack Lewis. As I suspected, Harry's relic was not the murder weapon.

"This should be in a museum," Jack said. "I've never seen a Luger in such superior condition."

"Just make sure it gets back to him," I warned. "Don't let it somehow get misplaced or misappropriated between the station and his place. Know what I mean?"

"We don't lose evidence in Roundup. This isn't Santa Bianca. Keep me posted."

"You, too." We rang off.

"Lee-lee." Celestina stuck her head around the door. "Do you want something? Fresh coffee or hot tea?"

"Tea would be great, thanks."

"Mr. Jerome called and he will be here in an hour. I put the cassoulet in the oven."

"Great, thanks," I answered absently and went to work. I was still completely absorbed in my notes when Richard arrived.

"Hey," he said in a perfunctory kind of way as he walked in and set his briefcase on one of the card-table chairs and hung his jacket on its back. I could tell he was as preoccupied as I. Completely somewhere else. Totally distracted.

He went straight to the small officer's campaign table bar between the windows and dropped a handful of ice cubes into a large old-fashioned glass. The room was so quiet, the sound of the ice hitting the fine crystal echoed like bells. He splashed in some Scotch.

I didn't know Richard that well, but I knew him well enough not to push. But it drives me berserk when men don't talk. When I'm working, I can sit someone out for days if I have to. I can die of old age waiting for someone to talk. But in my personal life? Makes me absolutely paranoid. I knew that whatever it was would come forth when he thought I ought to know it. I just hoped it wasn't me. That he wasn't giving me the old heave-ho. It's not cool to admit it, but I instantly forgot about Harry von Singen and Rita's murder completely, and went and stood beside Richard at the bar and started to make myself a drink.

"Here." He took the glass from me abruptly. "Let me do that."

I'd waited sixty seconds for him to talk. Long enough. "So what's wrong?"

"Normal opera hazards."

"Like what?" I said, thinking, How bad can it be? Someone lost his voice? Missed a note?

"Well, we had a good rehearsal and then did notes for a few minutes onstage, everybody's happy, Nikki Pantallo made a few suggestions about small changes in her role as Ada, no problem. The minute I got in the car, the phone rang. It's Nikki's agent, letting me know she would not be attending any further rehearsals until her role is expanded." He practically threw the Scotch into his mouth.

"Why?"

"She feels Eloise Scott, who's Amy, has all the good lines, the good music, all the attention."

"Didn't she know that when she signed on?" I asked.

"Of course she knew it." Richard looked at me as though I were the stupidest person in the world. "You have a lot to learn about divas."

Evidently.

"The behavior goes with the territory." He took another big swig. "It's not that big a deal, just an aggravation. Opening-week jitters."

"So what's going to happen?" I said. "Are you going to change her role? Or get a new singer?"

"Of course not," he said irritably. "You are so literal, Lilly."

"Really?" I said.

"Yes."

"Not always."

"Oh? When are you not?"

"Well, now, for instance," I shot back. "I'm smart enough to know its not really me you're mad at, even if it's me you're taking it out on. Making me pay for your stupid diva's stupid behavior."

"You're right." Richard laughed and smiled and might have relaxed a little. "We have a day off tomorrow, so I invited her and the tenor, George Monfort, out here to go riding, and for dinner. I think Nikki's homesick. Her husband's coming for the opening and to spend Christmas and New Year's with her, but he doesn't get here for a few days. I knew you wouldn't mind, and I thought maybe a little of Celestina's good food and some wine and a little personal attention from George and me would solve the problem."

"Great," I said, glad the squall had passed. "What are we having?"

Chapter Eleven

Monday morning

I got to the office at about seven-thirty. Linda had been there for at least an hour and was squinting hard at her computer screen. Paper poured from the fax as fast as was technologically possible.

"What's up?" I asked.

"There." She hit a last series of keys. "I think that's everything."

Linda Long had replaced the surly Miss Black as the librarian at the *Morning News*, which is where I met her. And I was so impressed by her thirst for knowledge, by the volume of current publications that she absorbed daily, by her ability to retain and process what she'd read, and by her advanced computer skills, that I hired her on the spot. One of the smartest moves I've ever made. My brother Christian wasn't exactly ecstatic, but I needed her more than he did.

"I don't think there's a better way to pass the time than to look through some of these society clips," she said happily. "It's just hard to believe what some people do." Her smile was eager and friendly, her eyes lively behind big glasses. Her blue suit and ruffled white blouse were as prim as the pristine condition of her desk.

Linda's from Wyoming, which is good. It means she is by nature hardworking, honest, suspicious, and keeps her mouth shut. Essential traits for my particular business. "I'm from Riverton," she'd said when I interviewed her. "We're surrounded by Indians over there. We have to watch every word we say."

The only thing I would change about her is her hair. It's long, curly and graying and should be cut. Maybe it's my particular feeling about it, which I no doubt got directly from My Mother, the Valkyrie, but frankly, I think women over thirty-five, at the absolute maximum, should not wear their hair past their shoulders. Face it, we aren't children, and by thirty-five our faces truly start to go, just a little, but gravity is definitely shouldering its way in. By forty, forget it. Cut it to your chin. Linda's about fifty. Not good.

"Did you go to the Lejeunes' wedding?" she said, sorting page after page of faxes as they flew out of the printer. "I could not get enough of it. Did you hear that she spent a million dollars on flowers alone?"

"I didn't go to it." I poured myself a cup of coffee and then went through the door into my office. Morning sun filled the room. "And I don't see how it would be possible to spend a million dollars on flowers in Roundup. But I could be wrong."

"Oh, I'm pretty sure she did." Linda kept sorting and stapling while she talked, never missed a beat. "It was mostly orchids flown in from Thailand and tulips from Holland. It cost even more than when Martin Gordon gave that big celebrity barbecue out at their country place and all those movie stars flew in from 'the Coast.'" She held up her fingers and made little quotation marks. "And when you drove down the road to the Gordons' house, he'd lined it with a bunch of buckboards and hay wagons and loaded them up with a bunch of black children—the girls with lots of little braids and bright bows and the boys in overalls and straw hats, the whole thing—and had these children wave and say hello, and then when the guests left, the children had to wave and say, 'Bye-bye, y'awl come back.'"

"You're joking," I said.

"No, it's true. It was awful." She put a stack of papers neatly on my desk. "Not only did he have to fly in the celebrities, he had to fly in the black children because we just don't have that many here. This was while you were still in California because it was a big deal. You would remember it. Lots of people were mad. Well," she said, straightening the piles, "I think that's it. I'll leave you to your reading. Let me know if I can help." She closed the door behind her.

"Thanks," I said, shaking my head at what some people do when they get their hands on a little money.

For the next two hours I scanned the columns and looked at the photos. The first time Rita appeared in the paper was two and a half years ago at the Women's Valentine Fashion Show for the Heart Association. She was gigantic next to the sleek society ladies—a full-grown prize heifer surrounded by delicate, leggy thoroughbred fillies. From then on, she and Harry were in the paper at least once a week. And unless it was strictly a ladies' thing, like the fashion show, they were together. It appeared that after about three months, she started wearing ridiculous western get-ups. Always a dress with fringe, and cowboy boots and cowboy hats—styles that would make any real cowgirl kill herself.

As I studied the photos, it was interesting to see who'd had what done in the plastic surgery department, eyes, foreheads, face-lifts, like that, and then I came to the big announcement that they were going to build the country club. "Wow," I said loudly.

"You just came to the liposuction picture?" Linda stuck her head in the door. "Can you believe it?"

Rita and Harry stood on the site of what would be the clubhouse, the Continental Divide strung along behind them like waves on the ocean, and Rita had lost what looked to be about one hundred and fifty pounds. She looked nice.

I studied the picture and looked at Linda. "No. I can't believe it."

"Dr. Stewart, of course. And his big liposuction machine. I think she had her whole body done."

"No way," I said, making a mental note to look into it. For myself.

"Really. How else could she lose so much weight in such a short period of time? Don't you wonder what they do with all that fat? Just put it in an old coffee can like bacon drippings and then put it out in the alley with the rest of the trash?" She shook her head. "That was only about eighteen months ago, and now look." Linda shoved over a new stack in which Rita got progressively heavier, until she was as big as she'd been when she was shot on Friday night, which was significantly larger than she'd been when she arrived in Roundup.

"This is pathetic," I said.

"If you say so." I could tell by Linda's tone of voice that she had absolutely no sympathy for someone with as much money and as little self-control as Rita.

There were almost as many pictures of Fancy French and Cordelia Hamilton. Joan Chamberlain had only been in town for a few months, so she had quite a lot of catching up to do. But from what I could tell about her background—which was what my mother would call "blue ribbon," only one of the many expressions she used to denote who fit and who didn't—the number of husbands she'd had, each successively richer and more prominent than the next, she would probably leave Roundup's other ladies in social dust before long, probably just before she left Roundup itself. Probably with a new husband. Like a baron, for instance.

Cordelia was extremely photogenic. I think it was because of all the teeth. She had moved to Roundup about three or four months after the von Singens and built a house near the country club, and there were a number of pictures of her at a hard-hat benefit luncheon she had thrown for Children's Hospital in her new home while it was under construction. Like Fancy and Joan, the photographer had captured her at a number of events, some with the von Singens, some with others, some with Daniel French, some with different men. The last few months, many of the pictures were of the ladies and their debutante daughters. Mary Patricia Hamilton and Dorothy Jefferson (Joan Chamberlain's daughter) were carbon copies of their mothers, while Lulu was taller and darker than Fancy. It all made me a little sorry that I didn't have a daughter. Not sorry enough that I'd go out and get one, though.

Dayton Babcock, with the help of his public relations firm, seemed to get around as much as the ladies, and the business pages announced his newest projects and then, six months later, his bankruptcies.

"I confirmed your lunch date with Fancy French at noon," Linda said, and laid the contract with Harry and my retainer invoice on my desk. I checked the documents thoroughly and then asked her to call him and give him a general, nonspecific run-down of my schedule for the day.

"What do you know about the Stewarts or the Antonuccis?" I said.

"Nothing, except that Antonucci has these sleazy television ads to call him if you have whiplash and so forth. I don't know anything about her at all. Maybe he just likes to keep her behind the scenes."

"Something like that, I'm sure," I said, opening my desk drawer. I took out a large stand-up, magnification mirror and powdered my nose and put on fresh lipstick. "Or tied to the bed."

I whistled for Baby and left for town.

Chapter Twelve

When I was little, Children's Hospital was already big, taking an entire city block close to downtown, but it had since grown into a four-block complex. Across the street from the institution, on a vacant lot, a sign had just been erected announcing that this was the new location for their Pediatric Cardiology Treatment and Research Center, to be constructed via a thirty-million-dollar capital campaign.

I parked in front of a small two-story building close to the center of the campus-like compound. CHILDREN'S HOSPITAL FOUNDATION, the sign read on the door. This was the place where the people who would raise that thirty million, along with several other million each year, worked. Unlike the rest of the hospital's facilities, which looked as if the Disney Corporation had decorated them, the Foundation offices were blue and gray, solid and conservative, designed to denote that charitable gifts were taken seriously and would not be squandered. But in spite of the serious decor, the energy was high. Phones rang, people rushed. I heard laughter.

"Elsa O'Hara, please," I said to a bright-eyed secretary-receptionist. "I'm Lilly Bennett." Her desk was invisible beneath piles of work.

"One moment." She picked up the phone, spoke into it and then said, "Go up the stairs, Miss Bennett. Her office is to your right."

Ms. O'Hara, the Vice President of Development, was waiting for me at the top of the stairs and she was exactly like her name: Prussian demeanor for the Elsa, with Irish coloring for the O'Hara. A big, busty, black-haired, blue-eyed woman, she greeted me with a firm, businesslike handshake and a friendly smile.

"Please come in and have a seat," she said in a deep, booming voice, and led me into her sunny corner office. The hospital gardens and play yards were visible through the bare tree branches, and I imagined in the summer, all she could see was green. "I'm happy to meet you. I saw you at the party Friday night and every time I came over to introduce myself, you were on the dance floor. Would you like a cup of coffee? Or a glass of water?"

"No, thanks. I don't think I'll need to take that much of your time."

"Well, I've got a copy of the guest list ready for you." Elsa reached across the desk with an alphabetical list that indicated people's table assignments, with the information in the "Amount" column tactfully deleted. "How do you want to proceed?"

"If you could just take me quickly through the names and tell me if you see even the slightest possible connection between each guest and Rita or Harry von Singen. I'm assuming you know all these people."

"Ninety percent of them, anyway. I know a great deal about them even if I don't know them directly. But this was our first contact with the von Singens." She refilled her coffee mug from a white decanter that sat on the credenza behind her desk. "They have no history with Children's Hospital, so I can't be as helpful as I could be with a lot of the other guests. I don't have to tell you that we saw them as major prospects for our current capital campaign."

"Who made the reservations?" I said.

"Dayton Babcock's office."

"How large a gift did they have to make to underwrite the room and the two tables?"

"One hundred and fifty thousand."

"Whose name was on the check?"

"It was a corporate check—Poker Creek Country Club. Mr. Babcock didn't contact us until about ten days ago, when the party was already sold out, but, as I said, the von Singens are important prospects for the hospital and Mr. Babcock was adamant that they had to have a double space. So we took what was going to be a bar-room and sold it to him."

That fit. Dayton's last-minute demands and the disjointedness of the von Singens' guest list matched what seemed to be his frantic attempts to scrape up potential new investors he could impress with Poker Creek.

We went quickly through the hundred and fifty couples on the party list, and aside from the obvious connections of the von Singens to their own guests, Ms. O'Hara shed no other new light.

I thanked her and went to meet Fancy for lunch at a little tiny spot named Tutto Bene, which, naturally, in Roundup, we call Toto Bean.

Chapter Thirteen

Monday lunch

With its eight white-linen-covered tables, Tutto Bene could not be smaller and stay in business, and it is not possible to find finer Tuscan food outside of Tuscany. Sure, go ahead and laugh, but it's the truth.

As usual, the cheerful little room was packed and convivial. Diffused sunlight glowed off the yellow-washed walls and mirrors, casting a warm glow, and the air was filled with the sounds of friend-ly voices and Christmas music and the smells of roasted tomatoes and garlic. The waiter, Peter, his salt-and-pepper mustache bristly above his white, white teeth, his starched white apron folded crisply around his waist, smiled hugely when I entered.

"Your table is ready." He indicated the small table for two in the corner by the window. "Mrs. French isn't here yet but I just opened a bottle of Pinot Noir. May I pour you a glass?"

"Absolutely. Thanks," I said.

They're extremely professional at Tutto Bene, which is very unusual in Roundup's restaurants, where the waiters and waitresses want you to know their first names and that they're really architecture students. At Tutto Bene, they never call you by your first name and they never pretend they know everything about you, even though they probably do, and they never assume that you have any personal interest in them at all. For instance, Fancy French used to be such a wild-eyed, hell-raising, meaner-than-hell, get-outta-my-way drunk, I don't think there's a soul in town that doesn't know that she's been sober for four years. (I assumed her shots of tequila the other night were a slight slip, an aberration, over which she was no doubt suffering deathly guilt.) She probably ate at this restaurant as often as I did, but Peter would serve her whatever she asked for without batting an eye.

I used to be not too sure about what to drink when I was having lunch or cocktails with a recovering alcoholic, especially someone like Fancy with whom I used to get loaded on a regular basis when we were in our early twenties. But now I've figured out we're all just getting through this the best we can, some of us drink, and some of us can't, but we can't make everyone else's troubles our own. There are more than enough to go around.

Of course, as I sipped my wine and watched Fancy park her big BMW sedan across the street, and then stand there, in a scarf and dark glasses and long fur, looking exactly like a blond Jackie Onassis waiting for the traffic to clear so she could cross, I acknowledged I'd definitely be thinner if I were to go on the wagon. What a wildly reckless measure that would be for a few lousy pounds.

Fancy crossed quickly to our table, like a brisk wind, bringing a whisk of cold air along with her from outdoors. "How are you?" she said breathlessly and bent to kiss my cheek. "I'm sorry I'm late." She sat down and arranged a soft cashmere scarf around her shoulders and ran her fingers through her high-gloss, fluffy hair.

Peter stood silently alongside until she was organized. Fancy looked up at him with her large blue eyes. "I'd like a double Tanqueray martini, straight up, please," she said. "Right away."

Whoa. Hardly anybody drinks double gin martinis anymore. Not even alcoholics.

Peter turned to go. I was aghast. I know my mouth was hanging open.

"I know you all are shocked, but I'll tell you, this Debutante Ball is driving me crazy." Fancy blew out her breath and fanned her face with her hand. "I had no idea that having your daughter make her debut could be so stressful. Lilly, you are so very, very lucky you don't have any children. I don't know what's wrong with Lulu. She's gone all the time and acts so mysterious about everything she does, won't tell me anything. And I just knew something had to give, so I just said to hell with it, I'm drinking until after the holidays and then the people from St. Mary's will come and get me. I've already called them. They're picking me up at ten o'clock the morning of the first." Peter set the martini down at her place and she picked it up and took a ladylike belt. "So you're all just going to have to put your teeth back in your mouths and get with the program."

"Have you been spending a lot of time in Beaufort lately?" I said. "Your accent is so strong."

"Well, I go back for a board meeting every quarter, but my accent's strong because I've discovered that men lak it. It jus brings 'em to their knees. Turns 'em to jelly. Of course, I spend practically all day, every day, taking care of myself, doing this thing or that. And"—she paused for effect—"I take a little Prozac every now and then. Keeps me from getting too depressed about having my parents be dead and me not drinking."

Brother. I chose not to make any of a dozen possible obvious observations, but changed the subject instead. "Fancy, what in the world are you doing with Dayton Babcock? He would force anybody to take Prozac, he's such an idiot."

"You think I don't know that?" She flipped open her menu. "He's nothing but a little no-good punk. Why am I looking at this menu? I know what I'm having. So, why am I with Dayton? Well, in case you hadn't noticed, adorable men aren't exactly falling out of the trees around here. He can be a perfectly suitable escort." She smiled blandly. "Are you helping out the police with that terrible killing?"

"Yes. And that's why I wanted to have lunch. I need to ask you a few quick questions." I wished she'd tone down the Southern Belle act a little—it was starting to get on my nerves.

"Ask away. I love stuff like this." Fancy leaned forward eagerly with her arms on the edge of the table.

"Did you know her very well?" I said.

"Who? Rita? Pretty well, I guess. I didn't care for her one bit, but since Dayton and Harry are doing some business deals together, almost every time Dayton and I go out, it's with them." Fancy sipped the martini and laughed. Her cheeks got rosier. "To tell the truth—but you can't tell a soul because I don't want people thinking I killed Rita—Harry's the only reason I go out with Dayton, just so I can be around him. He feels the same way about me. Don't you just look at him and imagine how good it must be? Well, take my word for it—it's better than your sweetest dreams. I love sleeping with both of them."

"God," I said.

"You're one to talk."

"I didn't say that because I don't think you shouldn't have two lovers—I just don't think one of them ought to be Dayton. He's such a yutz and such a bad, bad lover."

"Well, honey"—Fancy looked me in the eye—"I've given up smoking and drinking and I'm not giving up fucking, and I'll tell you another thing: Dayton's picked up a few tricks since you last slept with him a hundred years ago. He can be absolutely *electrifyin'*."

"If you say so." The gin had loosened her tongue, just the way it had in the old days. "Fuck" had always been her favorite word. I wondered how long it would be before she started getting mean again.

Once we'd ordered our lunch and another round of drinks, I asked her what time she and Dayton had left the party.

"Oh, I have no idea. All I knew was that we had to leave. As I'm sure you noticed, I'd sort of fallen off the wagon a little, drinking those incredible Gold shooters. So I asked Dayton to get me out of there before I did something untoward."

"Was Harry still there when you left?"

Fancy thought for a minute. "I don't recall. I know we danced a few times. I just don't remember."

"Did you see Rita leave?"

"No. But no one would notice her absence. She was always going off and passing out and then, if Harry'd already left, which he often did, someone would wake her up and take her home. But for the last couple of months they've been going together, like to the opening of the opera and the symphony and so forth. It just seems over Christmas, with all these parties, they're on a little different sched- ules. Of course they've had to go out lots and lots lately because they need to get new investors since her daddy cut off her money. But"— Fancy smiled over the tops of her dark glasses, just like Candy in the movie—"I've got almost as much money as Rita did and I'm going to make him so very, very happy."

Watching Fancy drink brought back floods of memories—none pleasant—of how totally she lost her judgment, all of her control, in fact, when under the influence. One time, she and some guy were spending a weekend in Santa Bianca. I hadn't seen her for a few years, and didn't even know she was in town until I got a call from the city jail at two forty-five in the morning, and the desk sergeant said she'd told him I would vouch for her.

"What did she do?" I asked him.

"Smashed out all the windows in her suite at the Four Seasons. I don't know what she's on, but she's really flying high, and mean and mad as hell. What do you want me to do, Chief?"

I didn't have to think about it for a second. "Tell her you couldn't find me and to call her lawyer when she calms down."

"Righto."

There are many, many people I'd bail out in the middle of the night, but anyone who has a history of substance abuse and is over thirty years old and still indulging in immature, rock-star behav- ior, is more than I ever would, or will, deal with. And today, years later, as Fancy smiled flirtatiously over her glasses, I could see that the same crippling weaknesses squirmed not far below the surface, waiting for the alcohol, ever ready to ambush her whole life. I'm so glad I've never been addicted to anything but cigarettes.

"Tell me about Cordelia Hamilton." I tore off a piece of bread crust and dribbled some olive oil onto it.

"Cordelia? Well, frankly, Lilly, just between us, because she is my best friend and all, I think she and Rita were lovers."

I almost choked. "Oh, please, Fancy," I sputtered. "That is too gross even to contemplate."

"Isn't it, though? But I think it's possible. Cordelia was hanging around her all the time."

I realized that she did sort of look the type. "Maybe they were just friends," I said.

"Uh-huh. If it makes you feel better to think that, go ahead. Cordelia would never make a move at me, but I think maybe she goes both ways. Like one of those dissipated Parisians in the thirties. I think she'll do just about anything with anybody. She has that ingratiating personality. You know what I mean? Kind of insinuates herself into people. Lilly, that wine of yours looks so good, do you think I could have just a tiny sip?" She reached over and lifted my glass. "Oh, my. That's just heaven. I think I'll have a little of that with my lunch. Now, let's see. Who's next?"

"Joan Chamberlain?"

"Oh, Joan. Well, let me see. I first met her about a year ago. She was dating someone here, let me think . . ." I saw a lightbulb go off in her head, but she veered away from it and said, "I can't remember who. But then she met Dickie; he and Suzanne had just gotten divorced, and so she married him. I think it's the fourth marriage for both of them. She doesn't have any friends here—looks down her nose at all of us. Very ta-ta." Fancy polished off her drink. "You can tell she doesn't give a shit about anyone or anything but herself and her stuck-up daughter."

Peter placed our plates carefully in front of us, both arranged with four perfect bruschettas—cool chopped tomatoes and garlic and basil and oil mounded on crisp toasts.

Fancy bit into one and chewed for a second.

"Do you think Joan killed Rita to get to Harry?" She gave me a cunning smile. "She's such a cold-blooded bitch, I sure wouldn't put it past her."

Thankfully, the rest of our lunch arrived. The conversation was going nowhere as far as I was concerned. Wholesale gossip bored me silly and it was clear that gossip was Fancy's life—her only stock-in-trade.

"I can't believe the Ball is day after tomorrow," she said after a minute or two. "Who are you all sitting with?"

"My parents and my brothers," I said. "How about you?"

"Well, it's kind of a mess now. Dayton and I were going to sit with Harry and Rita and some other people. But I don't really want to go to the Ball with Dayton Babcock. You know what I'm saying?"

"I know exactly what you're saying," I said.

"And I haven't talked to Harry about it but I think with him being suspected of murder and all, he might not want to attend. But he is such a superb dancer—much better than Dayton—and the people we're supposed to be sitting with might not want him at their table. What do you think? You know more about these situations than I do."

"You know perfectly well that around here a full-scale felony indictment has never stopped anyone from going to the Ball. Remember the Marquettes?"

"Oh, my Lord, who could forget?"

That particular year, the Ball had taken place just days after Mr. Marquette's wife, I can't remember her name, poor thing, had committed suicide by shooting herself three times: once in the leg, once in the purse, and then once in the head. And then she had completed the self-destruction with a remarkably defiant act: throwing the gun twenty feet up the mountainside. In a perfect example of what a soul can get away with if there is enough money to pay a team of expensive lawyers, the jury believed Mr. Marquette. Anyhow, two days after the suicide, out on his own recognizance, he'd married an awful tramp and brought her to the Ball. Things sure were buzzing that night.

"Besides, if you decide to come with Harry, I know my mother would be absolutely delighted if you joined our table. If you come to the Ball with Dayton, that would probably not work out as well."

"I understand perfectly." Fancy smiled. "That's very gracious of you. I'll call Harry the minute I get home. After all, just because his wife's dead, he can't sit around the house and mope forever."

☞ *Chapter Fourteen*

Monday afternoon

I always try to keep myself pulled together as best I can just in case someone drops by, which, granted, living out at the ranch, isn't a very realistic possibility. But that's the whole point: You never know. I have always hated it when people drop by unannounced. I think most people do. You're caught unprepared. Maybe the house is a mess; more likely, you are. Maybe you just don't feel like seeing anyone. Maybe you're hiding something. That's why dropping in without warning is a founding principle of police work, and since I was in the neighborhood, I decided to drop in on Cordelia Whitaker Hamilton. Not because I harbored any deep, dark suspicions about her, but because I was curious.

Roundup's country-club neighborhood is filled with enormous, beautiful old houses, most of them built just before or just after the First World War. The streets are actually wide parkways lined with tall old trees and with grassy medians filled with lilacs and honeysuckle and other shrubs and large flower beds that the city gardeners keep in bloom from May until the first snow, usually sometime in mid-September. The houses are set back on large, meticulously landscaped lawns. The sense is of spaciousness and grace, peace, propriety and fortitude. Not all the houses have always been beautiful, and not all of them are now. Every now and then an old house is torn down and replaced with something that is occasionally better, but generally worse, to look at.

A high, white stucco wall surrounded Cordelia's Mediterranean-style house; and straightforward cast-iron gates decorated with twin evergreen wreaths dotted with simple bouquets of pine cones, marked the front walk. Two polished-brass lion's-head knockers hung side by side on the glossy bottle-green enameled doors. Marble urns potted with dwarf spruce trees that had been decorated with tiny lights sat on either side beneath a curved portico. The roof was glazed terra-cotta tile, and all the second-floor windows, which were actually several pairs of French doors, had green shutters and cast-iron balustrades. I found the whole setup enviable and elegant.

I had pulled over for a minute across the parkway just to double-check the address and make sure I was headed to the right place, so my car was somewhat screened by the shrubs in the median. Just as I stopped, Cordelia's front doors flew open and a man, his hand covering his cheek and the side of his mouth, exited fast. It was Harry. I put my window down to listen.

"I'm sorry if I insulted you, Cordelia. Please accept my apology." He took his hand away and examined it. There was blood running down his face. "Look what you did." His voice was incredulous.

Cordelia ran out the door. She was dressed in an elaborately embroidered satin kimono-style robe and silk pajama pants. She was crying. "Oh, God, Harry, I'm so sorry. I don't know what happened to me. Please come in and let me patch it up. I know you didn't mean anything by it." She grabbed his arm.

"I have to get back to the office. I never should have come here in the first place. Again, I apologize." He pulled away and climbed into his black Range Rover. The scratch marks on his cheek were so deep, they were visible from across the street. Cordelia stood holding her shoulders and weeping in the middle of the sidewalk until he was gone.

This is a perfect example of the worst possible time to have someone drop in. A detective's dream come true.

I felt sorry for her because, God knows, I've made a fool of myself around men more times than I care to remember, but not sorry enough to give her time to recoup completely. I pulled around and parked, and as I was getting out of my car, a metallic-green Saab convertible slammed on its brakes and screeched into Cordelia's driveway on two wheels. The doors flew open and two laughing young ladies in jeans and sweatshirts jumped out—one with short dark hair: Cordelia's daughter, Mary Patricia Hamilton, and the other with a long, caramel-colored ponytail: Lulu French. They kissed each other quickly on the cheek and then Lulu ran down the driveway and threw an armload of shopping bags into the backseat of her little black BMW convertible. "Hi, Aunt Lilly," she yelled at me and waved before she climbed in and screamed off. I felt about a hundred years old. It seemed like yesterday that those girls were Sparky Kendall and Fancy French and me.

A black maid in a black uniform and crisp, snowy apron answered the door.

"Is Mrs. Hamilton in?" I said. "I'm Lilly Bennett. She's not expecting me."

"Please come in," the woman said kindly, in a soft accent. "I'll see if she's available."

The inside of the house, judging by what I could see from the entry hall, was even more elegant than the outside. The floor was polished slate. A wide staircase curved up gracefully at the far end of the foyer, in the center of which sat a large, round inlaid Biedermeier table with a blue-and-white Chinese export brazier that overflowed with white lilies, tuberoses, and hydrangeas. To the right, through an archway, was the library; and to the left, the living room, each with the finest rugs I'd ever seen. Old and well-worn, but with succinct, rich colors. And big. I wondered if my mother had been in this house. Even she would be impressed.

The maid reappeared from the hall that led past the stairs. "Mrs.

Hamilton will be down directly," she said. "Will you join her for tea?"

"Yes, thanks."

"Please make yourself comfortable in the library."

If I had not been working, I could have spent my whole afternoon, uninterrupted, in Cordelia's study, looking at the small oil paintings arranged here and there on the mahogany shelves among the leather-bound books. Several silver- and leather-framed snapshots of all different sizes sat randomly on the shelves and tables. The Christmas tree, which stood in front of double doors to a small enclosed garden, was about ten feet high and almost invisible behind masses of ornaments and lights, strings of cranberries and popcorn.

One year, I spent hours stringing that stuff, and hung it up and it looked so festive, and overnight, Baby went out and very carefully ate every single piece of popcorn, leaving only gooey threads of cranberries on the bottom third of the tree. I haven't tried that one again.

Beautifully wrapped packages, most of them from Neiman-Marcus and Bergdorf-Goodman, lay in a controlled jumble beneath the branches, glittering and shining in their gold and silver and pink foils and wired organza ribbons. A wide, flat sterling silver bowl of Christmas cards and a big arrangement of creamy roses sat on the coffee table in front of the fireplace, where the remains of a small fire sputtered along. Above the mantel hung a gauzy impressionistic portrait of Cordelia and Mary Patricia in a garden when Mary Pat was a little girl. Cordelia sat on a marble garden bench, cool and calm in a filmy dress, while her daughter stood at her knee in a short organdy frock and had a pink ribbon in her hair.

I added another log to the fire and sat down on one of the matching burgundy paisley love seats that faced each other across the table, and flipped through the cards. There were only a few of them, and all from people I'd never heard of, except for Harry and Rita, who had sent the picture of themselves on the building site when Rita was thin. After about five minutes, the maid came back in, her step firm and steady, and placed a large tea tray down in front of me. Cordelia was right on her heels.

"Lilly." She extended her hand. "Good afternoon. I'm sorry to be so casual, but I wasn't expecting company." She had pulled on some loose charcoal gabardine slacks, an ivory silk shirt and a camel cardigan sweater. Her only jewelry was a string of pearls.

I stood up. "I really apologize for dropping in on you like this. I hate it when people do it to me, but I was in the neighborhood and I have a few questions having to do with the investigation of Rita von Singen's murder. I hope you don't mind."

"Of course not," she said and sat down. She had no visible reaction to my statement and there was no visible sign she'd been sobbing hysterically a few minutes earlier. She was pale but her eyes weren't particularly puffy. Her makeup and poise were just fine. It takes my face hours to get back to normal after I've been crying. "If I can shed any new light, I'm happy to help. Milk or lemon?"

"Neither, thanks. I saw your daughter and Lulu French pull in. They're both making their debut this week, aren't they?"

"Yes. Mary Pat's home from Hollins. I gave a little luncheon for them on Saturday. I can't tell you what an effort it was." She poured the tea expertly and passed me my cup, dismissing the subject. "Help yourself to the sweets." She placed a Spode plate of iced Christmas cookies on the table close to me. I took my glasses, pen and pad out of my purse.

Cordelia looked at her hands. "Rita was my closest friend in Roundup. And I've been running that whole evening over and over in my mind." She made a small shrugging gesture and an unsure smile tightened her lips. "It was such an odd group, no one really knew each other very well at all, as a group of friends, anyway. I keep thinking what I could have done to help her. I'm sure I could have done something."

"I don't know what," I said, "short of shadowing her. Had you been friends a long time?"

"Well, we've known each other for years and years. I came here from Pittsburgh two years ago, not long after my husband died. I thought a fresh start would do me good. I was in bad shape, because, except for Mary Pat, I'd basically lost my whole family. My parents. My husband. It's a story I know you've heard often, but I felt so surrounded by my loss that it was all I could see. I was paralyzed." Tears filler her eyes. "And now, Rita. It's just not very fair, is it?"

I shook my head. "I'm sorry," I said.

Cordelia pulled a linen handkerchief from the sleeve of her sweater and shook it out with a flutter before she dabbed her eyes. "Oh, I'll be fine. I've survived a lot. I'm sorry," she said modestly. "I generally don't lose control of myself like that in front of people."

No, I thought. Only twice in the last ten minutes. First with Harry, now me.

She cleared her throat. "Anyway, Rita and I knew each other when we were girls, and then, over the years, Howard and I frequently ran into her and Harry on the Côte d'Azur, and we'd had such a wonderful, fun time with them." Cordelia grew silent for a moment and took a deep breath. "Well, anyway, they had moved here and were having this marvelous western adventure and kept telling me to get out of Pittsburgh. So I did."

"When did you meet her?"

"Rita came to Madeira, just for our junior year. We hit it off right away. We had a lot in common—hated our parents." Cordelia warmed at the memory. "Just like all sixteen-year-olds. Well, my mother was already dead by then, but Rita and I both thought our fathers were real bastards." She held up a hand. "Don't misunderstand, they didn't beat us up or rape us or anything like that. We hated them mostly because they wouldn't give us Thunderbird convertibles and all the money we wanted, and made us go to school."

I could tell Cordelia was a master of manipulation. Very skilled. She flowed from emotion to emotion, always trying to make you keep up.

"Rita's father pulled her back home after she and I got caught

hitchhiking to Fort Lauderdale for spring break. We were so bad."
She laughed. "I'm really going to miss her. Sam Campbell and I are
probably the only people in the world who will."

"Don't you think Harry will miss her, too?"

"I don't know, it's hard to say." Cordelia looked at her watch. "I'm
sorry, but I've got to race off to another Ball meeting. I'm going to
be so glad when this thing's over. Hopefully we'll wrap up the seat-
ing today. But I'll tell you, Harry didn't kill his wife. He has nothing to gain from her death but his freedom, and he likes being fet-
tered because it lets him keep playing around without getting
attached. I think Fancy killed her."

"Oh?" I realized even more acutely that this woman never worked
without an agenda designed to keep her ahead of the pack. I've
always rejected the phrase "control freak," because I contend that
anyone with any brain, success, intelligence and ambition should
want to be in charge of his or her immediate circumstances if possible. Maybe that's just the westerner in me. But this attitude of
Cordelia's was different. It was so calculated. Almost cold-blooded.
Like watching a wolf move through the woods.

"She's desperate for a new husband and she and Harry have been
carrying on what they think is a secret affair for quite a while; of
course everyone knows about it."

Cordelia stood up, anxious for me to leave, but I wasn't quite
ready.

"Have you ever had an affair with him?"

She shook her head. "I wouldn't have done that to Rita, but truth-
fully, now that she's gone, I'm not saying it hasn't entered my mind
to be—as they say—the first on his doorstep with a casserole. I'm
sorry, but I really must go."

"I understand." I gathered my stuff. "Is Harry gay?"

"Gay?" Cordelia exclaimed. "Oh, my God, no. That is one thing
I can tell you unequivocally."

"Aren't he and Daniel French good friends?"

"Not that good. Believe me, that would be a permanently unrequited love for Daniel." She was starting to get edgy, rushed, angry at my foot-dragging.

"Why did you slap Harry's face a few minutes ago?"

"Oh, Jesus," Cordelia snapped. "That's none of your business. We had a misunderstanding. What, are you spying on me?"

"No." I stood up. "He left just as I arrived. One more question and then I'll let you get back to your schedule. Are you experienced with firearms?"

"Very." Cordelia's smile was disingenuous. "As a matter of fact, I am the Country Club Women's Skeet Champion. This is my trophy." She picked up a small silver-plated nut bowl and held it toward me like a proud child.

"Congratulations," I said.

"It's silly, I know," she said, suddenly self-conscious, and placed the bowl back on the table. "But I really enjoy shooting. I also carry a thirty-eight in my car in case of trouble. You can see it if you like."

"Yes, please. If you have time."

I followed her through the house into the kitchen, which had one of those eight-burner gas stoves, four wall ovens, a double-wide Sub-Zero refrigerator and a large center island with sinks at either end. "You must really like to cook," I said.

"You would think so, with all of this, wouldn't you?" She laughed. "But actually, I only come in here occasionally. I avoid food as much as possible."

With remarks like that, I knew Cordelia and I would never be friends.

We passed through a breakfast room with an antique refectory table and ladder-back chairs with faded Pierre Deux cushions, through the utility room, which had a commercial-sized washer and dryer and four large sinks, two of them filled with more white lilies, roses and hydrangeas, into the garage. She opened the driver's side door of her British racing green Range Rover and pulled the weapon from the door pocket. A shiny, lethal, little black Glock 19. It looked brand-new. A wadded-up pair of black kid gloves came out of the pocket with the gun and fell on the floor. Cordelia stooped quickly to pick them up.

"There those are." She balled the gloves up in her hand, but not before I caught the strong, unmistakable scent of cordite. "I've been looking for these."

"How long have you had this?" I said, sniffing the barrel.

"Couple of years. I've only fired it once."

"Do you mind if I get a warrant to have it tested?"

I could tell she did.

"Well, yes, I do." Cordelia's jaw jutted a little. "It gives me a great sense of security to have it with me in the car." She laughed, embarrassed. "I'm sorry to be such a chicken."

"I understand," I said. "An officer will pick it up in an hour or two. We probably won't keep it for long, and frankly, I don't think anything will happen to you on your way to or from the Debutante Ball meeting, but I can arrange to have a patrolman accompany you if you like."

Fortunately, she had the grace to blush. What a boob. I didn't like her any more than she liked me, and I can't tell you how glad I was I hadn't eaten any of her stupid Christmas cookies.

Chapter Fifteen

I called Elias from the car. He was in his office. "I'm on my way home," I said. "Are you free for a few minutes?"

"Sure, come on by. I'll give you a cup of coffee."

"Is Richard still there?"

"They're just getting saddled up. Do you want them to wait?"

"Nah."

I pulled up in front of the main training barn and parked next to Richard's car, sorry I'd been too late to join him and the diva, Nikki Pantallo, and George Monfort for a ride through this perfect late afternoon, which was freezing cold and crystal-clear. The sky was especially far away, and a blue you'd have to see to believe. I shielded my eyes and looked across the valley and up into the hillsides as far as I could, but they were nowhere to be seen.

The life-sized bronze sculpture of Elias's champion Angus bull, Wind River Ranger, greeted me at the top of the stairs to the second-floor office. Today Ranger sported not only his permanent decoration of Elias's Hill School tie around his huge neck, but also had cowboy hats hanging from both of his horns. Not too dignified for a specimen of his background and breeding.

Elias was leaning back in a swivel chair that looked as if it were on the verge of exploding, as did his flannel shirt, which strained, against all odds, to stay buttoned over his bulging belly. He flipped the end of his Prince Charles tartan wool tie back and forth while he talked on the phone. His manure- and mud- and straw-caked boots were on the desk, in the middle of what looked like an oil lease.

I waved hello and helped myself to a cup of coffee and watched the foreman working with a three-year-old quarter horse in the riding ring below. The foreman's name was something like Bob Smith, but everyone called him Art, after Arthur Murray, the dancing instructor, because he had a way of working with these quick-witted cutting horses that let them surpass mere excellence of footwork and attitude and tenacity. He taught them to waltz with whatever partner he picked. I watched Art introduce the young sorrel gelding to the steer he wanted singled out, and then he simply held on as the horse and two dogs took over, darting back and forth, back and forth, the gelding often keeping its rear feet in one place and pivoting, worrying the steer, pushing it farther and farther from the herd, and finally isolating it, literally cowing it into submission until it stood stock-still, locked in place by the horse's eyes.

I never get tired of watching the horses work. Like a good detective on a case, a well-trained cutting horse is single-minded in its determination, once the subject is identified. The culprit can try to run and lose himself in the herd, but ultimately he can never escape because the horse and dogs won't let him. They have his scent and they'll hunt him till he drops.

Elias hung up and took his feet off the desk and held out his mug for me to fill. "Well, Chief," he said. "What's up?"

"We have some interesting things going on, Elias." I briefed him for about twenty minutes until Richard and our guests galloped up, laughing and pink-cheeked from the frosty air.

"How is it going?" I asked him when we got back to the house and had gone upstairs to change for dinner. Nikki and George were busy freshening up in the guest rooms downstairs. "Is she still going to boycott the rehearsals?"

"George has been stellar." Richard splashed water on his face and then covered it with shaving cream. "Kept reminding Nikki all afternoon about the great roles they've sung together and the *Bohème* they're doing in San Francisco in April, about how much he can relax and enjoy singing with her, so she brings out the best in him, and how he always has to be on his toes with Eloise because her voice is unpredictable, gets a little screechy every now and then. Talked about how excellent the casting was because it made him, as Rex, edgy to be around Amy, and happy to be around Ada."

I put the finishing touches on my lipstick. "Good going," I said.

"What?" Richard looked at me as he dried his hands. "You think the casting was by accident? That's the director's responsibility, to pick up on those little chemical idiosyncrasies among the artists. Maximize them."

"Oh, yeah?"

"Yeah," Richard said, and snapped me with the towel. He was much more relaxed.

It turned out to be a very special evening. Nikki Pantallo and George Monfort were delightful and she came to dinner dressed like an off-duty opera star visiting a ranch. Tight jeans with high-heeled strap sandals and red cotton socks with little sparkles, and lots of makeup and scarves and rings and necklaces.

"One forest fire snuffed out," Richard said as the helicopter lifted off, turned its nose toward town and zipped away. "Thanks."

"My pleasure."

We fell into bed and slept as though we'd been shot.

Chapter Sixteen

Tuesday morning

The morning dawned warm and beautiful enough for Richard and me to go for a ride. We drove down to the barn and went in and found Art tightening the cinch on Hot Spur, Richard's huge palomino stallion. My little quarter horse bay mare, Ariel, watched from over the door of her stall, her big brown eyes bright and shiny. With her heavy, thick winter coat and shaggy legs, she looked the way Baby does when her fur's gotten long and curly—like an F·A·O Schwarz pull toy. I kissed her warm muzzle and then picked up the stiff brushes and gave her back a few quick strokes before tossing on a thick brown wool saddle blanket that had a "Circle B" brand burned into each corner. She rubbed her head against my back.

Hot Spur and Ariel—names that always make Elias shake his head in disgust. "What a bunch of high-toned crap," he says. But it was just that sort of high-toned crap that attracted Richard and me to each other in the first place. Among other things. Many of them of a physical nature. Shakespeare among the savages. We found it quite amusing, as Harry would say, and were not in the least surprised when lower, less sophisticated, more ignorant forms of life, such as Elias, didn't appreciate it. Richard told him so regularly. "Face it, Eli," he'd tease him, "just because you went to The Hill School and Harvard, you're still nothing but a provincial putz." He and Richard were good friends. If I said such a thing to Elias, he'd whup my butt.

After a hard, fast, thirty-minute ride, the most time either one of us could spare, we turned our ponies back over to the foreman, went home for a quick breakfast, and then Richard took the helicopter into town with Christian and I called Harry.

"What were you doing at Cordelia Hamilton's yesterday that caused her to slap you?" I said without preamble as soon as he answered.

The question didn't seem to rattle him. "I assure you, Lilly, it had nothing whatsoever to do with Rita's murder, and it was nothing I started. It was nothing I would even consider starting. It was a misunderstanding."

"What exactly happened?" I asked.

"She called me yesterday morning and asked me to come by to pick up some papers of Rita's that she thought might be helpful," Harry explained. "When I got there, the maid showed me to an upstairs sitting room, and once the maid had closed the door, Cordelia came through another door that led to her bedroom. She was dressed in a thin, flimsy robe and she walked in and stood in front of a full-length mirror and began to caress herself and talk about how much Rita liked to watch her do that and how much she missed her." Harry paused and cleared his throat. "Well, Lilly, I'm sorry, but I am, after all, a man. And a man can watch a woman do such things to herself for just so long before he must take action."

"So you took action," I said, thinking it seemed the reasonable next step.

"Yes, unfortunately, I did. The wrong one. I told her I'd have to leave." Harry sounded rueful and chagrined. "And you saw the result. It was a terrible mistake and I am extremely embarrassed you have discovered it. I trust you will not mention this to anyone."

"You told her you'd have to leave?" I laughed. "She slapped you because you weren't interested?"

"Ja." Harry cleared his throat. "And I have the wounds to show for it. Now, if I may close that subject forever and ask if you have uncovered anything of interest yet?"

"Cordelia says you and Fancy are having an affair, and that Fancy murdered Rita."

"Impossible," he said.

"Impossible, why? Were you with Fancy later that night? Did she come out to your ranch?"

"No." Harry was adamant. "And let me be very clear: Fancy French and I are not having an affair."

"Harry, I'm working for you. You're paying me a fortune. How do you expect me to help you, unless you tell me the truth? Think again: are you absolutely positive Fancy didn't come out and meet you later Friday night?"

"Quite sure."

"Did anybody come to your ranch that night?"

"Not that I am aware of."

The tone of his response made a lightbulb go off. "You don't live at the ranch, do you? You don't have any idea if Fancy went there Friday night or not."

Silence.

"Look, goddamn it. I don't know what's going on, but let's stop screwing around, okay? Stop taking up my time with a bunch of evasive bullshit—I don't need the work and I don't need the money. You either tell me the truth or find someone else to help you. Where do you live and who are you protecting?"

More silence, but I could tell he was thinking. "I'll tell you after the funeral."

"What time is the service?" I finally said.

"Eleven o'clock."

"I'll be there, and be ready to cut the crap." Jesus.

Chapter Seventeen

I showered and dressed with particularly special care and attention to my clothes and makeup because I had an appointment with Dr. John Stewart to quiz him about Rita, and I knew that some of the country's most glamorous women passed through the portals of his private clinic. I didn't want to stumble in there looking like some poor wretch from Bennett's Fort with wind-wrinkled skin and rodeo-queen hair.

Put together in a pair of carefully tailored chocolate-brown trousers, a black cashmere sweater, black suede boots, most of my pearls, my new black Persian lamb coat and black kid gloves, I arrived at nine o'clock sharp at the pale-pink adobe walls that surround the hacienda-style hospital. Although it was situated close to downtown and covered an entire city block, the clinic itself was not terribly large and was settled in the midst of grounds that gave the sense of sanctuary, with tall trees and large shrubs fending off city noises and smells. The only clue as to where I was was a small pink-and-yellow-tile plaque by the front gate that read STEWART CLINIC. The parking valet, who was careful not to look at me too directly, whisked my car to a lot hidden behind a tall hedge.

I walked up the flagstone path, past rose beds and flower gardens tidied scrupulously for winter, and pushed open the heavy wooden front door and entered the pink waiting room. A plump young woman in a crisp white uniform, with dark curly hair, long pink nails, and studiously applied makeup waited at a bleached-pine reception desk.

"I'm Lilly Bennett," I said. "I have an appointment with Dr. Stewart at nine."

"Yes. Good morning." She smiled and handed me a chart. "He's running a little late, Miss Bennett. Please fill this out and he'll be with you shortly. May I offer you some coffee while you wait?"

She was an ideal choice for a receptionist in a plastic surgeon's office, because usually when people decide to go have something fixed, they're doing it because they don't feel too good about some physical aspect of themselves, or maybe even themselves altogether. The last thing they need is some goddess greeting them, someone who, no matter if the patient had one million dollars' worth of work done, she'd never look as good as. Someone, for instance, who looked as good as the only other person in the waiting room.

She was lanky, like Cordelia Hamilton, with silvery hair pulled back into a ponytail and unblemished, perfectly draped skin. I would say she was there for a follow-up visit. She sat on a couch with her sable coat draped over her shoulders and her legs crossed with the casual ease tall, thin, rich people have. She had on taupe gabardine pants, a cream-colored silk T-shirt, an Hermès scarf, white socks and polished leather loafers. And dark glasses. Nobody dresses like that in Wyoming unless they're passing through. Nobody. Believe me. She was reading a book. I cannot tell you how glad I was that I'd gotten myself put together. I don't know who she was, but I didn't want her going back to what must have been Manhattan or Palm Beach or Paris, telling all her friends, "Well, I know it's Wyoming, but Dr. Stewart is simply the best and you just have to train yourself to overlook the locals."

I sat in a comfortable armchair near the fireplace and sipped my coffee and read *Vogue*.

For ten minutes, there was complete silence. Finally, the phone rang. The receptionist picked it up without speaking, nodded, hung it up and said, "Mrs. Bruce, the doctor can see you now. I'll take you back."

The woman closed her book with a deliberateness that indicated she had the time to do everything in her life carefully and well, picked up her purse and gloves, got gracefully to her feet and glided down the hallway.

The room returned to silence, and then, after a few more long minutes, the front door opened and in swirled Daniel French with the gusto of Loretta Young.

"What a simply glorious day," he said to the receptionist, who smiled up at him and giggled.

"Good morning, Mr. French," she said.

"Good morning, my little dear." He spotted me by the fire. "Lilly. Oh, my goodness. What a marvelous surprise. I was hoping you'd find your way here. It's getting to be time for all of us, isn't it?"

"Good morning, Daniel," I answered. "What is this? Your home away from home? What could you possibly have left to have done?"

"Oh." He shrieked with laughter. "Meow. Meow."

He tossed his cape onto the couch and came over and snuggled into the chair next to mine and took my hand. "Tell me everything," he said.

"Everything about what?"

"What you're finding out about Rita. You know. Who did it."

"Well, actually," I said, "everyone's saying *you* did it."

"What?" He leaped to his feet. "Why, that's not true."

I shrugged. "Do you want to tell me about it?"

"Really, Lilly, you have to believe me. Who would say such a thing? Oh, my goodness." He sat back down and took both of my hands.

I didn't answer.

"That bitch Fancy said so, didn't she? She would. Well, I'll tell you one thing; she has much more interest in seeing Rita von Singen dead than I do, and everyone knows it. But if you want to know the truth, I think it was that gangster."

"Daniel," I said, "the Mob doesn't usually kill women. It's against their Code of Ethics."

"Do you really want to know who I think did it?"

"Of course."

"Well, everyone's just sort of skimming over that old love affair between Rita and that great big guy from Texas, Sam Campbell. But I'll tell you, it was serious. And it was still going on. He and Rita really loved each other, and I, personally, think that's why they were both so fat. They were eating away their blues and their frustrations and their loneliness. Sort of like me. I mean, I am happier than I've ever been, but I had no idea that when I came out of the closet it would be so hard. Or so lonely. People don't really think I did it, do they?" His eyes brimmed. "I would never do such a thing."

"I'm sure you wouldn't," I said.

Tears spilled down his smooth cheeks. "Oh, thank God, Lilly." He took a linen handkerchief from his pocket and blotted the tears away. "I'm trying to be so good all the time." He drew a long, shuddering breath.

"Finish what you were saying about Sam Campbell."

"That's really all, except that I don't think Sam did it. I think his wife, Georgia, did. I think she got sick of listening to him and his always going off to board meetings with Rita and talking about his deals with her father and his investment in Poker Creek. I think she hated Rita's guts and decided she wasn't going to put up with it anymore. She would never ask him for a divorce because I think we can all be sure her prenuptial would leave her with nothing, so she just keeps up a good front, to Sam and everyone, about how happy she is. But apparently she's been on a rampage for about a year. He was here in Wyoming, constantly."

"How do you know all this?"

"Cordelia told me. She and Rita were best friends."

"Are Cordelia and Fancy friends?"

"Well." Daniel rolled his eyes. "You know I adore my sister, but Fancy can be a handful, and her whole helpless-as-a-cupcake act has Cordelia completely flummoxed or whip-sawed, or whatever you girls call it. I'm always saying to Cordelia, 'Watch my lips: JUST SAY NO.' But she's too nice to her."

This didn't exactly jibe with the Cordelia Hamilton I knew. I didn't think she'd ever been flummoxed in her life. "Are there *two* Cordelia Hamiltons?" I asked.

But Daniel didn't hear me because the phone on the receptionist's desk rang. And again, she picked it up, nodded and replaced the receiver without a word. "Mr. French," she said. "The doctor can see you now."

"Whoa." I held up my hands. "Wait a minute. What time was your appointment?" I said to Daniel.

"Eight forty-five. What time was yours?"

"Nine." It was now nine forty-five. Rita's funeral was at eleven.

"You mean no one told you?"

"Told me what?"

"Dr. Stewart always runs a minimum of an hour late. Minimum. Oh, you poor thing. You'll be here till lunchtime."

"The hell I will," I said. Arrogant, self-important crap like that really gets me mad. And doctors are the worst. "Rita's funeral is at eleven and I'm going to be there."

"I don't see how."

"Watch this," I said to Daniel. I approached the desk and removed my badge from my purse and held it up so she could read it. "I need to see Dr. Stewart, now. Official business."

"YOU ARE SUCH A BITCH," Daniel screamed and fell back on the couch in hysterics. "I love this. I just love it when you girls are butch like that."

Chapter Eighteen

I had forgotten in the four days since the murder how good-looking Dr. John Stewart was, with his dark curly hair and tanned face and blue eyes. But whatever caused chemistry between us on Friday night had disappeared behind walls of professional distance. His and mine. I had made some judgments about his clinic before I'd gotten as far as his office: the whole place was as beautiful and inviting as could be, but it lacked warmth. And positive energy. It reflected him perfectly: he had no soul to back up his matinee-idol good looks.

In my opinion, the mark of an outstanding physician is an individual whose vocation is also his avocation. There are two kinds of people it's completely miserable and lonely to be married to: dedicated doctors and cops. I'm always sorry for their wives or husbands because they're always alone, always second on their spouse's list of priorities, behind patients and criminals. Now, if you're married to a doctor who isn't dedicated, that might not be too bad for you as the spouse, but it's very bad for the patients, especially when that doctor starts slicing up the skin around your eyes with an extra-sharp knife.

If you're married to a cop who isn't dedicated, you're married either to an alcoholic or a philanderer, usually both. So basically, if you're married to a cop, whether he's dedicated to his work or not, your life is going to be miserable.

Dr. Stewart stood up when I entered his private office, a masculine version of the facility's monochromatic southwestern scheme, and reached across the large, distressed-oak desk to shake my hand. He was dressed in a starched white doctor's jacket, a yellow-and-white striped shirt, and a red Hermès tie. "Lilly," he said, "it's a pleasure to see you. I take it from my receptionist's rattled remarks that this is not for a consultation after all? I didn't realize you were a marshal."

His attitude was so condescending, so la-di-da, there were about a hundred things I could have said, but they all would have sounded, and in fact, been, defensive. I didn't say any of them, but instead sat down in one of the pair of armchairs across from him. "Actually, I had been hoping to combine a little business with pleasure, but you're running so late I guess we'll just have to stick to business."

"May I offer you some coffee?"

"No, thanks."

"I hope you don't mind if I have some?"

"Of course not. Not at all."

He picked up the phone with an important flourish and pushed a button. "Hey, sugar," he said jovially into the receiver, "I'm dying for a cup of coffee in here. You're neglecting me." Then he laughed and winked at me and hung up. The phone immediately rang again. He listened and listened and listened, nodded his head several times and said, "Uh-huh, uh-huh, uh-huh," asked a couple of questions, listened some more. This went on for about ten minutes, during which time a nurse brought in a fresh mug of coffee for him and asked me by sign language, so as not to interrupt Doctor, if I was sure I wouldn't like some.

"No, thank you," I said, as loudly as I could without actually yelling.

I flipped through my notebook and made a couple of observations about what Daniel had said about Georgia Campbell, which I'd found semi-interesting, and some comments about Dr. Stewart, mostly pertaining to what an asshole I thought he was. Finally he hung up.

"I apologize. But that was a very complicated surgery this morning and I just need to be certain that things are going exactly as they should. Now"—he leaned across the desk, his countenance earnest—"back to your problems, Lilly. What can I do for you?"

"Let me be totally clear, Dr. Stewart. I'm not here to talk about my problems. I'm here as a federal marshal and I want to ask you some questions about Rita von Singen."

"All right."

"Was she a patient of yours?"

"I prefer not to answer that. I guarantee all my patients complete confidentiality." John Stewart's demeanor would get him into trouble one day. Maybe even with me. Maybe even today.

"Dr. Stewart," I explained patiently, "under the law, you can tell me whether or not she was your patient; you just don't have to say what you said or did to her. And I'm going to make this easy for you because I'm running short of time. Baroness von Singen's funeral is in forty-five minutes, and I could come back and see you later today, but I'd rather not."

"Well, I think I'm all booked up the rest of the day anyway," he countered.

"You don't understand, do you? When the police knock, it's better if you answer. Otherwise, they just have to go downtown and see the judge and get a warrant and take up a bunch of their valuable time and it gives them a bad impression and surly attitude about the person they're trying to talk to. So let's just get the facts as we know them out on the table, now."

"Are you threatening me, Lilly?"

This guy was so smarmy I wanted to punch him, but as I had a million times before, I forced my attitude down behind my training. I got extra cool. "Absolutely not, Dr. Stewart. I'm just explaining the facts of procedure to you, if you intend to continue to be hostile and obstructionist in a murder investigation."

"Are you implying I should call my attorney?"

"That would be totally up to you. I hadn't especially considered you as a suspect, but if you would be more comfortable with your lawyer here, by all means. It's up to you how formal you want our discussion to be."

He thought it over for a minute and then said, "I don't really see why I should call my lawyer. I had nothing to do with Rita's death. Ask away, Marshal," Dr. Stewart concluded heartily. "I have nothing to hide."

"Thank you, Doctor," I said. "Now, everyone knows that Mrs. von Singen was a patient of yours and that you performed an enormous liposuction procedure, or whatever you call it, on her, and that it was a roaring success for about four months and then she began to gain it all back. Is it true that you threatened to kill her if she ever told anyone who did the surgery?"

He looked at me straight on. "What do you expect me to say? That I killed Rita von Singen because she got fat again? That's ridiculous."

I just stared at him without speaking.

"Of course I didn't kill her."

"What time did you leave the party Friday night?"

"About midnight."

"Do you own a gun?"

"Of course."

"What kind?"

"I don't know. What difference does it make?"

This guy was not giving me one bit of cooperation and it was really starting to piss me off. "We'll issue a warrant to pick up your weapon and test it, Doctor," I said. "Where do you keep it?"

"In my bedside table."

"Is someone at your house?" I made some notes.

"You mean right now?" Till this moment, John Stewart had not become even slightly ruffled by my inquisition, but he began to color and unconsciously drummed a pen-top on his desk. "I suppose. Either my wife or the maid. Look," he snapped, "I haven't got the slightest idea who murdered Rita von Singen and absolutely no interest, and I don't see why you need to go around and upset my family and collect my gun."

"Routine. Process of elimination." I stuck my pad and pen back into my purse and pulled out my gloves and dark glasses. "I guess that's it for now. Thank you for your time."

"What about your consultation?" he said.

"I'll be in touch."

O Tannenbaum, O Tannenbaum!
wie treu sind deine Blaetter!

I turned the car radio down and phoned Elias on the way out to the von Singens' ranch in the foothills just west of town. "Where are you?" I said.

"Out in front of Fancy's workout club." He sounded bored.

I could picture Elias, staked out in his maroon Suburban, one of dozens in Roundup, eating doughnuts and sipping 7-Eleven coffee in the alley off Cherokee Street, in front of the little wisteria-blue-doored studio where all the chic people went to get beaten up every day.

"What's up?"

"Well, so far, nothing. She's been here since about eight-thirty. Oh, here she comes now."

"Probably on her way to the funeral," I said. "She'd better hurry. Keep an eye on her."

Then, before I lost the cell going over the hill, I called Jack Lewis's office and left a message for him about John Stewart's gun, and touched base with Linda at my office. Five million faxes as usual.

"There's sort of an interesting-sounding query from Florence from the Marchése Enrico Cortini," she said. " 'An unfortunate and unexpected discrepancy in the Marchése's Titian collection in his villa in Porto Ercole,' it reads. I guess that Bennett Security phone line you put in at your friend's villa is paying off."

"Finally." I smiled. "I hope it can wait, I could use a little Italy. Fax them back and say that I'm unavailable until after the first of the year and will recontact them at that time to see if the 'discrepancy' has been resolved."

"Okay," Linda said. "There's one more. A man named Dwight Alexander called to say he was in town and wanted to drop by and say Merry Christmas later this afternoon. I told him I wasn't sure of your schedule, so he should call first."

The mention of Dwight's name made me smile. I'd met him when he was the foreman of the Butterfields' ranch—primarily assigned to servicing Mrs. Butterfield—and he'd become so enamored of police work, in general, and me, in particular, during the events and investigation surrounding Walter Butterfield's murder, that he'd decided he wanted to enter the U.S. Marshal Service. He'd passed the civil service exam—don't ask me how—and was now enrolled in their academy in Glencoe, Georgia. Dwight was twenty-six years old, minimum brain, maximum sex appeal. Absolutely irresistible unless, of course, you happened to have a Richard Jerome to go home to.

"If he comes by," I warned Linda, "make sure your chastity belt's locked."

"I beg your pardon?" I heard her say, but I'd lost the cell.

A few minutes later, just as I was turning onto the two-lane, a navy-blue Porsche 914, with tinted windows, did a perfectly executed four-wheel drift past me and screamed onto the interstate headed toward town.

Chapter Nineteen

Going to find out
Who's naughty or nice.

I sang along as I followed a narrow road up through quiet wooded wilderness for a couple of miles, crested a hill, passed through a security gate, rounded a bend, and there was the von Singens' ranch house, lit up and looking as big as an oil refinery or an aircraft carrier plunked down on a mountaintop.

"Wow," I said out loud. "It looks like a giant Ahwahnee."

The brightly lit, three-story house was reminiscent of the grand old hotel in Yosemite Park with its peeled-pine exterior and soaring Sequoia support columns. But there the similarity to the elegant Sierra Nevada resort ended. The balance of the von Singens' complex consisted of walkways leading to barns and tennis courts and a swimming pool and a number of small guest houses. A paved circular driveway passed beneath a two-story-tall porte cochere at the front door, across from which, where a fountain of flower beds would normally be, was a magnificent monumental bronze statue of a buffalo. A small gathering of Shoshone Indians, dressed in their formal feathered garb, had beaten a path in the snow around the sculpture. One of them slapped the heel of his hand on a small drum hung with feathers as they rocked back and forth in a circle around the buffalo, chanting in unison. I thought they must be freezing to death.

There were a few cars in the small parking lot in front, mostly Range Rovers and Ford Explorers and Jeeps, one silver Bentley with a liveried chauffeur, and a couple of smashed-up pickup trucks that must have belonged to the Indians. The only car I recognized was the Mercedes wagon of my tall, handsome cousin Hank, the Very Reverend Henry Caulfield Bennett, Episcopal Bishop of the Wind River Diocese, who stood in the open front door next to Harry, the scratches on his face scarcely visible. Together, they greeted the guests for Rita's funeral.

Hank's not a charlatan, but he is definitely a showman. He places a high priority on the visual power of the church and spends a lot of his money bringing to Roundup the finest High Church trappings available in the world, which today included a black suit and crimson shirt and collar, the simplicity of which made the jewel-encrusted, glittering gold of his antique bishop's cross appear especially rich and mighty.

I think that people who enter the religious life, whether they're priests, nuns or ministers, mystify most of us. We all wonder, Is he really that happy? Does God speak to him or her in a more special way than He speaks to me? Tell him more? Well, the answer to those questions is No. These people just are better listeners. They listen and then they happily do what they're told. They don't equivocate or bargain or try to slime out of things. That's the difference. And that's why they are happier. They've got faith. I think it really is that simple.

We greeted each other warmly.

"I'm sorry I'm late," I told Harry. "Am I the last to arrive?"

"No, Daniel French called and said to expect him. There's his car now. Please come in." He seemed a little preoccupied, maybe because it was his wife's funeral. Or maybe he was a little miffed because I'd yelled at him, but there was a definite chill in the air.

I followed them up the front steps through the double front

doors, which were about fifteen feet high and six feet wide, into a massive room that was easily the length of a city block, surrounded by a second-floor balcony. The floor, instead of being traditional western oiled pine or cedar, was drab mustard-colored glazed Mexican pavers, with several Navajo rugs. The designs might have been authentic, but each rug was the size of about ten hogans. These rugs were so big, I had a mental picture of these poor little Indians building enormous looms that were so gigantic that they had teams of weavers who ran with the whop, or whatever it's called, from end to end until they were exhausted and fell to the side, only to be relieved by the next young Navajo. The rugs probably came from China. They can put together more, bigger, teams than the Navajos. A half dozen wrought-iron chandeliers, as large as the tires of Euclid trucks, but in the spoked design of wagon wheels, were suspended from the high ceiling with thick chains and cast a thin, bleak light. The furnishings were Frank Lloyd Wright's dreary, uncomfortable, overrated stuff, upholstered in what looked like faded, old brown flannel shirts. At the opposite end of this medieval Great Hall, hanging above the biggest fireplace I've ever seen in my life, was the pièce de résistance: a colossally gigantic painting. The face of an Indian warrior with his mouth wide open in, presumably, a death scream. His eyes bulged with terror. Blood gushed from his eyes and mouth. The background was slashes of purple and orange with red spatters. Presumably blood. Presumably his.

Well, since I'd been a cop for twenty years, it was far from the sickest thing I'd ever seen, but it was bad. Gratuitous crap.

"Yikes," I said.

"Lilly." Hank frowned at me.

Harry laughed. "Don't worry. I'm not insulted. It's terribly bad. Very sick. This is all part of Rita's Native American collection. Not at all my taste, but this ranch was her dream. I plan to put it on the market immediately."

"I'd hold off for a while," I told him. "I don't think it would look too good for you if you were to decamp instantly."

"Very well," he said coolly. "You're the boss."

Damn straight, I thought.

Two large arrangements of Casablanca lilies billowed from tall pedestals on either side of the fireplace, in front of which curved two rows of straight-backed peeled-pine dining room chairs with rush seats.

In the center of the front row sat Sam Campbell, possibly the deceased's only true mourner. He looked tired and sad as he pulled a large white handkerchief out of his back pocket and wiped it across his eyes and nose. Georgia, her glossy brown hair as big as a spiky sombrero, and her fingernails as long as daggers, sat next to him in the center of the front row. She wore a tight, short black leather skirt, a stretchy black bustier with rhinestones, a black leather jacket with enormous shoulder pads, and high heels with gold-chain trim and black fishnet stockings. A carhop in Versace. She sat with her legs crossed and circled and pointed her foot. Her eyes alternated between bored admiration of her shoe and gold chain ankle bracelet, and her fingernails, off which she furtively peeled strips of hot-pink polish which fell around her on the floor like little specks of confetti. The only thing missing was gum.

Whether or not she murdered Rita, as Daniel French claimed, Georgia was clearly getting sick of her husband's wailing grief. She reached over and patted his leg but there was more impatience than sympathy in the gesture. Sort of the way Mother used to do when she determined we'd cried enough. A firm, decisive motion, sort of between a sympathetic pat and a spanking. More of a "let's cut the crap" slap. A "If you keep this up, I'm really going to give you something to cry about" whap.

One chair over from Georgia was Dayton Babcock, who, with his legs crossed and foot circling in an unconscious mimicry of her, rocked back and forth, studying her shoe and ankle and bosom as intently as she did herself. His hands were clasped in front of his knee, a position which, on the forward rock, if he craned his neck, gave him a better sight line down the front of Georgia's bustier and also threatened to split the rear seam of his too-tight navy blazer. Dayton was jiggling and bouncing and rubbing himself so obviously, I couldn't wait to see what he'd do next. Whip it out, probably. That was the only thing left. As usual, he looked as if he'd gotten his clothes from the Goodwill—rumpled khaki pants, argyle socks and dirty, scuffed leather Rockport walking shoes.

The "nicer" crowd had established its bulkhead at the far right end of the row: Cordelia, a grieving statue in dark glasses, and the Chamberlains. Dickie had on a dark suit and a white shirt, and whenever I looked at him I felt bad and could hear my mother scolding me before dancing school not to be rude to Dickie Chamberlain just because he was chubby and sweated a lot. "He comes from an absolutely solid, solid, solid family. His great-great-grandfather was one of the founders of the Chesapeake–Rhode Island Railroad, and one dance will not kill you," she'd say. But I've never been any good at pretending and I never would dance with him and he's never forgiven me. Joan wore a black dress, double strand of pearls and a small black hat trimmed with a smart net veil and diamond clasp, and looked as if she were at a state funeral at St. Thomas's in Manhattan.

Directly behind them sat Anthony "Call-me-Tony" Antonucci, also in dark glasses, and accompanied by a gentleman I did not recognize. They both had on navy suits, white-on-white silk shirts, silk ties looped not tied, polished loafers and those dinky transparent short socks that Italian and French men think are so irresistible.

Sam Campbell happened to look over and notice Dayton carrying on. He got up, and Sam was big, probably double Dayton's size, and walked over to him. "You trying to get a free peep of my wife?"

"Huh?" Dayton's big brown eyes looked up at him and tried to focus. "Huh?" he said again.

"You little pervert. You keep your eyes off my wife's tits." And then Sam Campbell side-armed Dayton like a big bear hitting a little dog. Hit him right in the mouth and sent him flying up and off his chair and across the floor, where he slid into the edge of the fireplace and cracked his head. No one made a move to help him. See if he was all right. Of course he was. You could throw Dayton off a fifty-story building and he'd get up and want to fight about it. Just like a monkey.

"HEY," Dayton yelled.

"Keep away from my wife, you little slimeball," Sam growled.

"HEY," Dayton yelled again, wiping blood from the corner of his mouth and nose. "That guy hit me. You see that?" he said to everybody.

"See what?" said Tony.

I sat down on the left end of the second row. Tony looked me up and down through his Ray·Bans and gave me a little salute. Daniel French came in and sat in the empty chair next to Cordelia.

"Move over one," she told him. "I'm saving this for Harry."

Dayton, who had gained his feet and shook himself out like a bag of dirty clothes, tried to sit down next to me. "Move down a couple," I told him.

"Why? You expecting Harry, too?"

"No. I just don't want you to sit anywhere near me. But I do want to talk to you later."

"Yeah?" Dayton said like a petulant little child. "Well, you can't because I'm going out of town."

I waited for him to say, "So there," or stick out his tongue, but he didn't.

Harry appeared and pretended not to see Cordelia motioning for him to come and sit by her. He sat directly in front of me instead. Undaunted, she got up and walked over and sat next to him.

"Are you all right?" she said.

"I've been better," Harry answered.

"Me, too." Cordelia tried to take one of his hands but he kept them carefully anchored on top of his leg.

The absence of music, with the exception of the chanting Indians, had no discernible detrimental effect on Bishop Bennett. He advanced majestically and ceremoniously, as though up the center aisle of St. Paul's Cathedral, to his place in front of the handful of mourners, and a dozen or so empty seats. He stood quietly, frowning at the paltry crowd from beneath his bushy white eyebrows, tapping his prayer book against the palm of his hand, while Carlo, Harry's valet, guided the ranch hands, who were all turned out in their Sunday best, toward the chairs, where they stomped and shuffled and crawled over us like recalcitrant schoolboys going to daily chapel.

Chief Inspector Lewis appeared next to Carlo. They looked like brothers with their slight, prim, dark looks and thinning hair. Jack's little lieutenant stood right behind him, ready to take notes.

"I feel like I'm at a Sons of Italy convention," Dayton shouted down to me in what he thought was a whisper. He was right, though. Between Tony Antonucci and his buddy, and Jack and his aide, and Carlo, the valet, Rita Haye von Singen's funeral was developing a distinctly Cosa Nostra ambience.

Tony Antonucci's friend started to get out of his seat.

"I'm kidding," Dayton said to him. "I was just kidding."

"Keep your mouth shut," Tony said to Dayton.

"Jeez. Everyone's so jumpy around here today."

Hank extended his hands and raised his eyes toward heaven. "Let us pray," he ordered in his irrefutable, thundering style that makes people feel as if God himself had trumpeted the words directly out of his mouth. The ancient service rolled out in his basso profundo, patrician voice, exquisitely trained over the years to ring out over Wyoming's prairie winds and obliterate any earthly sound but his.

He had barely begun when Cordelia reached over and unpried Harry's hands from each other and laced her fingers through his. "I need to talk to you," she whispered and slid her hand down his leg.

Well, she might as well have just pole-axed him right on the spot. Me, too. I couldn't believe it. I mean, it was incredible. I wished my mother had been there.

Harry was so aghast, it took a few heartbeats for him to recoup. "Perhaps later," he finally whispered. "For the moment, I am trying to listen to my wife's funeral service." Harry disengaged her hand and plopped it back into her own lap and turned his attention back to the enraptured bishop who, thankfully, had not noticed the infraction and plowed merrily along.

Cordelia did not seem in the least ruffled.

"Would anyone like to tell us any particularly special memory about Rita? A small tribute perhaps? Or say anything?" Hank asked and looked carefully at each face. We all fidgeted and sat there like dumb mutes. Mercifully, he didn't belabor the point. So, eight minutes after he began, he ended, wrapping up in record time with the part of the service every good country-club Episcopalian likes best: the cocktail invitation. "The baron has asked me to invite all of you to stay for refreshments," the bishop announced.

We stood, the wranglers filed past Harry and shook his hand, each saying, "I'm sure sorry, Baron," or, as their mothers had taught them, "My condolences, sir," before passing through the dining room to grab a handful of cookies and then out the door and back to whatever they were doing until spring came. Craps and ESPN, probably. Daniel joined me where I waited behind Harry and started to say something when we both noticed Cordelia, who had remained seated, reach up and tug gently on Harry's sleeve and look at him beseechingly. "Please," she said quietly. He sat back down and she took his hands in hers and began to speak. It quickly became clear that neither one of them knew Daniel and I were there.

"I know this isn't the best time to say this," she said solemnly. "But I can't wait anymore. I'm afraid I've waited too long already."

"For what, Cordelia?"

"I love you, Harry." She began to weep. Her long, thin fingers brushed away tears that ran down her cheeks from behind her dark glasses. "I've loved you from the moment we met in Cap Ferrat."

A look of compassion spread across Harry's face. "Cordelia," he said, "don't do this."

"I can't help it. It's true. I've waited all these years and I'm sorry,

I know I'm embarrassing you, but I can't seem to control myself. I haven't slept for days, since the accident, knowing that finally I could tell you. And I was going to tell you at my house the other day; I don't know what happened to me. I got on completely the wrong track. I'm so sorry."

"Oh, Cordelia." Harry's voice was sad.

"I know that you don't feel the same way. Rita told me that you're in love with Fancy. But maybe you just think you are. She isn't even here. If she really loved you, she'd be here by your side looking after you. And I know I made a terrible mess of things. But if you'd just give me a chance." She covered her mouth with her handkerchief and sobbed.

Oh, brother, I thought.

"Let's talk about this later," Harry said gently and stood up, pulling her to her feet.

"You're right. I'm so sorry. I'll excuse myself and go to the powder room. I know I've made an awful fool of myself. Please forgive me."

Harry waited quietly and watched her go and then took a deep breath, patted the pockets of his sport coat for his glasses, squared his shoulders and turned to see Daniel and me standing right there. A surprised, funny, apologetic look crossed his face, and after a second's hesitation he crossed into the dining room.

Daniel gave me a strong look over the tops of his reading glasses. "Oh, my," he said. "Isn't this getting good."

Chapter Twenty

Where are Rita's remains?" I asked Daniel as we trailed in Harry's slow wake. Dayton was standing at the far end of the long buffet eating a rolled-up pancake with his hands. I imagined he'd already shoved a few into his pockets for later.

"Cremated." Daniel popped a tiny, bite-sized cranberry muffin into his mouth. "What I want to know is, where is Fancy?" He took out a cigarette and lit it with a flourish. "She'd better get her perfectly toned little butt up here, or I'm going to move in on her territory. I think Harry is simply the most enchanting man I've ever laid eyes on. Bar none."

"Hello there, Lilly," Tony Antonucci said behind me.

"Hello, Tony," I said. "How's business?"

"Oh, well, you know. We do what we can." His associate stood slightly away from us and Tony made no effort at introductions.

"You're right, it is awfully bright in here," I said. "Excuse me a moment while I put on my dark glasses." I pulled them out of my purse. "There, that's better. Now tell me, Tony, are you up here keeping an eye on your investment? Collecting on Rita's life insurance? Making sure the surviving partner fulfills his obligations? Seen any good wrecks lately?"

"Lilly," he said, "I think you have the wrong impression of me. Rita was my friend. Dayton still is."

"I never thought she wasn't. I think everyone's your friend. Tell me, Tony, who do you think killed her?"

"I wish I knew. Hits like that look bad. Wasting a woman. I'd like to teach the son of a bitch a lesson or two."

"And I'll bet you and your buddy here know some pretty good lessons, too." I smiled. Tony smiled. The friend didn't smile. "Then you think it was a man?"

The question stopped him. In his world, women were weak things that did not commit violent acts. "Of course it was a man. A woman would never do such a thing."

"What is this?" Jack Lewis said. "A Ray·Ban convention?"

Jack and I exchanged quick greetings while I put my shades away and then excused myself to check out the buffet table. Over by the windows, Harry and Daniel were laughing about something and it occurred to me that despite Cordelia's strong protestations to the contrary, maybe Harry could go either way. I saw *Cabaret.*

Joan Chamberlain interrupted them. She took Harry's hand and insinuated herself in a way that put her back to Daniel, freezing him out of the conversation. She spoke quietly to Harry.

"Do you think Harry and Joan are lovers?" Cordelia said behind me.

"Do you?"

She shrugged. "Possible," she said in a way that meant she did. I could tell Cordelia was a little wary of Joan, reluctant to say too much. "Have you talked to Dayton Babcock yet?"

"No. Not yet. Why?"

Cordelia sipped her coffee. "I just think you should."

"What will he tell me when I do?"

"That Fancy spent the night here Friday night. That she just pretended to be drunk so she could race up here and meet Harry. Dayton is absolutely livid. Oh, hello, Georgia. How are you holding up?"

"Oh, brother." Georgia Campbell picked up a large strawberry. "I can't wait to get out of here." She took a little nibble, holding the berry between her thumb and index finger. The rest of her fingers with their ultra-long nails arched up and flexed and moved like a deep-sea coral fan. "Merry frappin' Christmas. You know what I mean?"

"Georgia," I said, wondering why I had never in my life been able to nibble anything, "I was hoping you and I could spend a few minutes alone together this afternoon. I'd like to ask you a few questions about Friday night."

"Sure." Her face brightened. "How about now? We could go into the card room. Get away from all these jerks."

"Fine." I followed her through the living room into a small cozy book-lined game room that had large windows, brass standing lamps and two baize-topped card tables. One of them held a large antique wooden jigsaw puzzle, about seventy-five percent done, depicting Neuschwanstein in autumn, sitting on a hillside that blazed with color in Bavaria's fairy-tale landscape. The chair seats and draperies were of red-and-yellow chintz on a black field. We sat down by the puzzle and she took a piece of Doublemint out of her purse—a little, tiny black patent leather suitcase with a long thin shoulder strap—unwrapped the gum and folded it into her mouth. "Want one?" she said.

"No thanks."

She tossed the balled-up wrapper back into her bag and snapped it shut. "I've done almost this whole thing myself, I'm so bored out of my frappin' mind."

"Why don't you go home?"

"Sam wouldn't leave until after the funeral." She picked up a kidney-shaped piece of the puzzle, turned it this way and that, and then examined the picture on the box. "Maybe we'll get to leave today or tomorrow. He doesn't tell me nothing."

"You and Sam are staying here at the house, aren't you?"

"Yeah."

"Did you hear anything during the night Friday night?"

"You mean besides Sam snoring?"

I laughed. "Yes. Besides Sam."

"No." She put that piece down and picked up another.

"Did you hear Harry come home?" I asked.

"He didn't come home, here to the ranch, anyway. He lives at his place in town." Georgia reached over and fitted the piece into place, tamping it in securely with her long nail. "He doesn't come out here much. It was just Sam and Rita and me staying out here." She opened the purse again and took out her lipstick and compact. "But I didn't hate her as much as everyone thinks I did, if that's what you want to know." Georgia studied herself closely in the little mirror and applied the lipstick carefully.

"What do you mean?" I asked, taking out my own lipstick.

"Well." Georgia fluffed her hair. I swear, her fingernails were so long, it was like having a conversation with Edward Scissorhands. "That's a pretty color," she said to me. "What is it?"

"Blaze," I told her.

"Pretty." She closed up her purse, rebuckling the tiny latches carefully. "I just thought that probably someone told you that after everything that happened between her and Sam, them being lovers and business partners and all for so many years, that I'd want her dead, but actually I didn't mind the interference. No, sirree, Bob. I didn't mind it at all."

"There you are, sugar." Sam Campbell stuck his big fleshy head with its oily balding pate in the door. "I was wonderin' where you got off to."

"Oh, hi, honey." Georgia smiled at him. This girl earned every nickel. "I was missing you."

"Hi, Sam," I said. "Maybe you'd join us for a minute."

Sam Campbell looked at his watch. "Probably just about a minute. I told the pilot to get the plane warmed up. Georgia and I are goin' home today." He pulled out one of the little game-table chairs and sat down. His bulk drooped way over on both sides. "I think I've answered every possible question your Chief Lewis could ever think of, but if you've got more, I'm more than happy to help. Georgia, sugar. Why don't you go on up and get our stuff packed up? Get that little Mexican maid to help you."

"Yippee!" Georgia smiled and jumped to her feet. "Nice to see you again, Lilly, and if you have any more questions, I'd be happy to help. Oh, Sam." She bent and kissed him on the cheek, making sure he had a good view down her bulging front. "I'm so happy we're goin' home."

My question, and Sam's answers, were predictable and inconclusive.

Chapter Twenty-one

Tony Antonucci, Daniel French, Cordelia Hamilton, the Chamberlains and Dayton Babcock had all left while I was in the card room with the Campbells. Only Jack Lewis was still hanging around. "How's it going?" he said.

"Not much so far," I answered. "Lots of motives. Few dead ends. How about you?"

"I still think we're going to discover it was your client. The Prince."

"Baron," I reminded him.

"Whatever. Or his girlfriend."

"Who? Fancy French?"

"Sure."

"She didn't do it." I picked up a handful of those wonderful little muffins. They were like delicious little marbles. "And I'm not even so sure she's his girlfriend, anyhow."

"We'll see. I got your message about Dr. Stewart's gun; we should have it by now. Come on, let's go," Jack said to his lieutenant. "See you later."

Harry was leaning against the dining-room doorjamb, sipping a glass of champagne. I poured myself a cup of coffee and then said to him, "Let's sit down and talk for a minute."

We sat at a table by the window. Outdoors, the light was high and shone blindingly off all the fresh snow. "Let's start over," I said. "Did Fancy go to your house, wherever the hell it is, on Friday night?"

"Certainly not."

"Do I have to tell you that the circumstantial evidence against you and Fancy is very strong? If you are trying to protect her, it's a mistake. It just makes things look worse. Dayton claims she came out here to be with you after he took her home."

Harry frowned and studied me with his frosty blue eyes. "All right," he said. "I will tell you. First of all, the only people who know I live in town are my staff, Rita, Sam and Georgia Campbell and one other. As far as everyone else is concerned, I live here at the ranch. So, for Dayton to say that Fancy came out here Friday night, or for Fancy to tell Dayton that, is ludicrous. Someone did come to my home on Friday night, but it was not Fancy. And it was not here."

"Who is she?"

"That I can't tell you."

"You have to, Harry."

"I will not. But I will tell you she positively did not kill Rita. She was not a guest at the party that night, and my staff will verify that she spent the evening waiting for me at my apartment, that's why I left early. Please trust me when I tell you this because it's true. It would be far too risky to involve her; there is simply too much at stake."

We looked into each other's eyes and although I didn't like his ultimatum, I did trust him. And I believed him. "What if it came down to your revealing her identity," I said, "or going on trial for the murder of your wife?"

"I would take my chances in the courtroom."

"You really love her, don't you?"

Harry nodded. "I would protect her with my life."

"Could Cordelia and Rita have had a fight? A lover's quarrel or something, and . . ." I didn't finish the sentence.

"You think Cordelia shot her?" Harry said. "In such cold blood?"
I nodded and popped another muffin in my mouth.

Harry shook his head. "They fought all the time. Silly things. How paintings looked. Which sculptor was better. She helped Rita select the art collection for the ranch."

"I wouldn't put that on my résumé," I said, looking around at the nightmares hung on the walls. "If that's the case, I'm surprised Rita didn't kill Cordelia."

Harry barked out his harsh laugh. "Ja," he agreed. "It's quite dreadful, isn't it? I've asked Dayton to arrange for their disposal as quickly as possible."

"I heard what Cordelia said to you after the funeral. That she loves you and always has, but that you're in love with Fancy."

"Yes, I know. Can you believe these women? It's really quite appalling. Practically overnight, Cordelia's convinced herself of two lies." Harry held up his fingers and counted them off. "Number one, that she's in love with me, but that I'm in love with Fancy because, number two, Fancy has convinced everyone, including herself, that I am. How long has my wife been dead? Four days?" He removed a silver cigarette case from his pocket, took out a cigarette and lit it. "Well, for the time being, it's just as easy to go on letting everyone believe whatever they want. Fancy never would believe the truth anyway." He lifted the champagne bottle out of the bucket, let the melted ice run off for a moment and refilled his glass. "Sure you won't join me?"

I shook my head. "Why wasn't Fancy at the funeral?"

"Women." He held up his hands, palms out. "I give up."

The longer we sat there talking, the more attractive Harry became to me, and the easier it became for me to understand why all these women were practically killing themselves, and maybe each other, to get to him. He was extremely masculine and maybe a little brutal, and a little dangerous, and also, irresistibly perplexed and confounded by the opposite sex. I ate another muffin to suppress the urges I was feeling about him. That old "Let's just do it right now" thing. Sometimes food works as an elixir, sometimes it makes you rapacious. I teased myself by saying this one could go either way, but as things stood in my life at the moment, it wasn't really true.

"So they don't know about your mystery woman?" I said. His cigarette smelled delicious, but no longer tempting.

"No one does."

"I saw you talking to Joan Chamberlain."

"Yes." The baron frowned. "I found it intriguing that they attended, didn't you? I don't even know them. She told me how sorry they were not to have known Rita better, and that they would call me for dinner in the next day or two." Harry smiled. "'And,' she said, 'don't give in to the first woman through your door, because practically every woman in town has designs on you.'"

"Good advice," I said, still wondering a little bit in the back of my mind that if things didn't work out with Richard, what number Harry would give me in the line. I had a lot of time.

Just then, the enormous front door opened, and in came Fancy. She crossed into the dining room at a quick clip and set two bottles of Roederer Cristal on the table. She was swathed in mink and scarves and suede gloves and dark glasses and looked like a movie star.

"Oh, my honey, I brought these to cheer us up," she said after she kissed Harry on the lips with her glossy, cherry-red smackers. "Tell me, how're you holding up? Probably glad it's over, I imagine. Sort of like saying good-bye to your dog, isn't it? Oh, hi, Lilly. I imagine you were just leaving."

Harry and I both stood up. "I'm sorry you missed the service," he said. "It was quite nice."

"I didn't think it would be quite right," Fancy said. "You know what I mean? With us being so close and all. People might get the wrong idea."

Harry gave me a "See what I mean?" look and helped me on with my jacket.

"Fancy," I said. "Dayton says you came out here and spent the night with Harry on Friday after the party."

"Where in the world would he get such an idea?"

Harry and I looked at each other and laughed. "I can't imagine," I said. "Was Lulu at home Friday when you got there?"

"Are you serious? If Lulu could keep her bathtub and makeup in her car, she would never need to come home at all. Well, don't let us keep you from finding that killer."

Harry walked me to my car.

"Who do you know that has a navy-blue Porsche 914?" I said through the open window of my Jeep into the brisk air.

"My friend."

"Good luck," I said, and left him and Fancy to work it out.

Southern girls, like Fancy, interest me because they are so very different from western ones. They are as diffuse and obscure as their climate, while we are as clear and straightforward as ours. They are willing to zig and zag, and take their time to reach their goals, while we favor the more direct approach. Fancy might have spent most of her adult life in the West, but she was a Belle through and through. She had been willing to spend months dating and sleeping with Dayton Babcock just to be around Harry von Singen. That, to me, is a perfect example of sacrificing short-term pleasure for long-term gain.

There was no doubt in my mind that Fancy could have murdered Rita in cold blood and never gotten a hair out of place.

Chapter Twenty-two

Tuesday afternoon

I left the von Singens' and bumped quickly down the dirt road onto the hardtop and out onto the deserted four-lane which wound spectacularly toward town. The mountainside rose up on my left across the highway and the canyon wall fell steeply off to my right, plummeting a thousand feet to the river.

It was a perfect Wyoming afternoon. The space of the sky, the biggest sky on earth, always gives me a boost no matter what I'm doing or what's on my mind. I love it. Our sky is so big and so clear and so empty, you can just gaze off into it for hours and not even see a bird. Or a cloud. Today, though, clouds rolled and billowed like sea foam along a distant ridge behind me.

I wasn't paying attention because I as busy conducting and singing all the parts of Handel's *Messiah*, going about eighty—otherwise, I would have seen the car coming. It was a black Ford sedan with blacked-out windows, and it had come up right next to me, on my left, at an enormous speed and crashed into my front left fender. I struggled to keep control of my wagon and then realized he was going to do it again. He was trying to run me off the road. Trying to make my car flip over the guardrail and down the cliff. The guy was trying to kill me. Son of a bitch.

Well, this wasn't the movies where a long, tense, slam-the-cars-back-and-forth struggle ensues, screeching around hairpin corners and teetering off the bends. This was Wyoming and it was real life, mine, and I wasn't quite ready to check out. I tapped my brakes enough to let the sedan get a little ahead, put down my window, opened the center console of my Jeep, took out my big 10-mm Glock, pointed it out the window, sighted the red laser-dot square-ly on his right rear tire and pulled the trigger. I slammed on my brakes as his car spun wildly out of control, doing two three-sixties in record time, crashed sideways into the rail, did a slow-motion roll over the top and dropped from sight into the canyon. Boom. The whole transaction took less than twenty seconds.

I pulled over, stopping not far from where he'd disappeared, and gulped for breath as though I'd just run a mile at high speed. The danger had completely ripped the wind from my lungs. I picked up the phone and punched in 911. There was just enough cellular power reaching the canyon to create the link.

"Roundup Emergency."

"This is Marshal Bennett," I said. "There's been a crash on the interstate eastbound, about two miles east of entrance 42. A car has rolled over the rail into the canyon."

"Are there injuries?"

"Yes," I said. "Probably serious."

At that moment, the *ba-boom* of the exploding car thundered up the canyon walls.

"Please notify Chief Lewis."

"We're rolling, Marshal," I heard the voice say, as I grabbed my binoculars and ran to the rim. Far below, the vehicle, which lay on its top, half in and half out of the river, was a mass of flame, melt-ing the ice and snow nearby. A fast scan of the line of descent and the area around it revealed that he had not been thrown from the vehicle. Even if he had, there would be no way to get down to him without a rope, and from the looks of the car, even if his seat belt had been fastened and he'd had an airbag, he could not have survived the impact. I prayed he had, anyway. I prayed for him.

Baby watched everything with her large brown eyes. She was completely quiet.

A Highway Patrol car, lights going, pulled in close behind mine. The patrolman jumped out and came over next to me, glancing quickly at my smashed fender.

"You all right, Marshal?" he said.

"Yes."

"Any sign of life?"

I shook my head.

The officer excused himself and backed his car up the road a ways, leaving the lights spinning, and removed an armful of flares from his trunk and laid them in a row along the highway, effectively closing the right lane. He then took my statement and got back in his car to wait and talk on his radio. I got back in mine and called Elias.

"What's up at your end?" I asked, once I'd brought him up to speed on the situation, given my observations from the funeral, and asked him to check out a couple of things.

"Not much. Are you coming back to your office?"

"Yes."

"I'll meet you there. Bring you a glass of something warm to drink."

"Thanks," I said. "I've got something to check out first. See you in a couple of hours."

More patrol cars, a mountain-rescue truck, an ambulance and Jack Lewis arrived shortly. Rescue workers rappelled to the accident site. The man was dead. And burned to a crisp.

I drove into town to Fancy's high-rise condo, and then from there, as fast as I could, out to the Lorillards' Ransom Creek Ranch, where Rita had been murdered. It took forty minutes. And that was with some traffic. Late on a Friday night, with dry roads and a little luck,

I could easily have done it in thirty, and would have arrived as people were starting to leave.

The Lorillards' butler had told us that Rita had been in the chair for at least a couple of hours, say since ten o'clock. But according to the medical examiner, who examined the corpse at approximately one-thirty, she had not been dead for more than two hours, perhaps slightly less. A corpse goes through significant, specific transitions during the first few hours after death, and the differences between a two-hour-old cadaver, and a three-and-a-half-hour-old one, are major—state of lividity being chief among them. It doesn't matter how fat, thin, young or old you are—gravity's gravity.

Therefore, Rita's time of death was placed at somewhere between eleven-thirty and eleven forty-five.

Fancy could easily have returned. No one would remember one more car in or out, and even if they did, in the pitch-black of the night, they'd never be able to remember the make. And if people remembered seeing Fancy in or out of the main house, that wouldn't be especially remarkable because she had been a guest at the party and no one paid any attention to when she came or went.

Same for Dayton. I knew I had to talk to him, but I really agreed with Harry's initial assessments of the likelihood of Dayton's ability to kill anyone: even if he'd been able to control himself long enough to do the deed, he'd never be able to keep it to himself for more than five minutes. He reminded me of an old joke a guy told me once: "It takes me an hour to make love," he said. "Oh, how very lovely," I answered. "Yes," he said. "Two minutes to do it. Fifty-eight minutes apologizing." That was Dayton, except that it only took him one minute to do it, and after he was done, he never apologized, he only wanted to be sure that it was as good for you as it had been for him, and after that, he couldn't wait to jump out of the sack and race out and blab all over town whom he was balling.

Believe me, I know what I'm talking about.

Dayton was my first lover. Can you believe it? The thought stuns me today.

My parents must have been in a desperate, hysterical panic for those few giddy weeks I spent brainlessly, overheatedly, in love with him. Here's how they finally got rid of him, although it took me years to figure it out.

My father always thought he was an idiot and called him "Einstein," which my brothers instantly mimicked, until my mother joined in, and then the whole family called him Einstein. Which, naturally, made me furious. Being just seventeen, I was extra-sensitive to virtually everything, especially appearances (a condition from which I've never really recovered totally), and one night after he'd gone home, I went up to my parents' room and said, "Don't you just love Dayton?"

"Well," my mother replied, "we think he's lovely, dear. But I have one question. Something we've been wondering."

"Sure. What?"

"Well." She thought about her words for a moment. "We were wondering what it must feel like when he kisses you good night, and . . . well, you know."

"What? I know what?"

"When his hands only reach to the middle of your back."

"What are you talking about?"

"Surely you've noticed."

"Noticed what?" My face started to burn and my jaw started to set.

"Well, his arms are a little short."

"What in the world are you talking about?" I screamed. "There's nothing wrong with Dayton's arms. They're perfectly fine."

"Of course they are. Forget I brought it up. We think he's lovely."

I stormed out of the room, slamming their door behind me and called Dayton on the phone to tell him how much I loved him, just in case he'd somehow gotten wind of the exchange. Just to reassure him, and me, that I would love him always, forever and ever, even if he didn't have arms at all. But the seed had been planted. Unfortunately, both of my brothers had heard the confrontation, and began to call him Einstein Short-Arms. And it was true. Every time I looked at him, his arms grew shorter. One night at an agonizing dinner with my family, he talked about two new madras jackets he'd gotten that day from the Brooks Brothers representative.

"Why didn't you wear one of them?" I said.

"I had to leave them to get the sleeves shortened."

That was pretty much it for Dayton and me, because by then, I could have sworn his hands were growing directly out of his shoulders.

And today, all I can see is a short little man with hands like flippers at his neck. An impossible condition if you want to hold a gun and pull the trigger at the same time. If you get my drift.

Chapter Twenty-three

The clouds descended across town and the hill country as I drove home from my test run to the Lorillards'. It had begun to snow by the time I reached the Fort.

Linda had the doors open on the potbellied stove so the little fire inside was visible, crackling away, keeping the offices toasty warm, and she'd placed small red poinsettias on both of our desks and a dish of red, green and white saltwater taffies with Santa Claus faces on the coffee table in the reception area. Carols played from the little radio she kept next to her printer.

Through my office door, I saw a leg with a familiar-looking boot swinging slowly back and forth from the corner of my desk.

"Dwight?" I pointed and mouthed the name silently to Linda, who nodded.

"Whew," she said under her breath. "He looks like a Greek god."

I didn't tell her that a statue has more brains than Dwight, because it wouldn't have made any difference. He'd made another conquest just by showing up.

Dwight didn't jump to his feet to greet me when I walked in. He just sat there on the desk, rolling a bit of paper in his fingers, appraising me with his sandy blue eyes. His tongue touched the corner of his upper lip. "Merry Christmas, Marshal," he said and slid slowly to his feet.

"Merry Christmas, Dwight," I said casually, trying not to picture the two of us rolling around on top of the desk. I hung my jacket on the coatrack and placed my briefcase on the floor and sat down. "What are you doing here? Did you come on the prisoner escort?" I was expecting one of our VIP federal prisoners today for an extended visit in my cozy little jail.

Linda had followed with a stack of file folders, and as I sat down, she spread out a handful of pink message slips, like a fan of playing cards, in front of me.

"Yeah. There's this sign-up sheet to accompany the deputies, part of our training. I'm the only one who signed up for Bennett's Fort. Everyone else always wants to go to L.A. and stuff, but I wanted to see how you were doing. We'll be here until after the first of the year." He hooked his thumbs in his belt loops and began to drum his fingers on either side of his fly. I swear to God, every time I look at Dwight it takes all my energy to keep my eyes on his. "I know you're working on this big murder case and thought you might need some help."

"Not yet," I told him, "but I appreciate the offer. How're things going for you?"

"Boy"—Dwight shook his newly shorn head—"these guys kick your butt all day every day. But you know what? I like it. I'm in better shape than I've ever been in and I like the idea of actually doing something. My old man thinks it's stupid, but, well, you know." He shrugged. "Gives 'em something new to talk about around the Grosse Point Country Club besides their capital-gains problems."

"That's your father's problem," I said, recalling that his father was a tycoon who had mocked his son for not wanting to follow in his father's footsteps, starting with business school. "You're going to make an outstanding deputy."

Dwight brightened. "You think so? I'd sure like to be assigned to you, Marshal Lilly."

I laughed. "Honey," I said, "you'd die of boredom." I didn't say that I was afraid that if Dwight were assigned to me, boredom was the last thing we'd die of. Exhaustion, maybe. "Absolutely nothing goes on in this district, and Justice intends to keep it that way. My position as a marshal is mostly invisible—all the action here is Bennett Security stuff." I picked up the stack of messages. "I'd better be getting back to work, but thanks for stopping by."

"Thought I'd go down to the saloon and see if Buck's changed his mind about letting me date his daughter."

"You never know." I smiled at him. "It's Christmastime, and miracles do happen."

"Yeah." He touched his lips with his index finger for a moment, as though in thought. "I'd sure like to find you under my tree. Now that would be my idea of a miracle."

"Bye-bye, Dwight," I said.

"Bye, ma'am." He put on his hat and on his way out the door tipped the brim, first at Linda's breasts and then her mouth and then her eyes.

"Wow." She let her breath out when he was gone. "I've never met anyone like that before. That guy is a complete sex bomb."

"They're few and far between," I told her. "Thank God. Now, what's going on? Bring me up to speed."

"The marchése says the missing Titian can wait until you're available." She smiled, handing me a fax with an elaborate family crest at the top. "He's sure the painting hasn't left the family, that it's hidden in his cousin's palazzo in Florence and will not move anytime soon."

"It sounds so wonderful," I said, "I don't even want to think about it."

"Jack Lewis just called and left a message that Dr. Stewart's gun was missing. Not where he said it was. They're following up on it. He said you could call him back, but there was nothing more to add."

I shook my head. "John Stewart didn't kill Rita. He wouldn't jeopardize everything he's achieved because a customer disappointed him. If we all killed everyone who embarrassed or disappointed us, there would be no people left on the earth."

"Starting with my ex and our neighbor's daughter," Linda let go in a completely uncharacteristic huff.

I smiled up at her. "That's one I'll look forward to hearing about."

We both turned to look as the door blew open and Elias thundered in in a flurry of snowflakes. His arms were full with two large wicker baskets, and before long, he had set up a four-course picnic on my worktable, including three margarita glasses, their frosted green crystal stems in the shape of saguaro cacti, and a silver cocktail shaker. He put burritos in the microwave in Linda's office, shook some tortilla chips into a basket and put Marialita's homemade salsa into a small earthenware bowl. Then he poured each one of us a drink. I think I might have seen a shy little spark fly as he handed Linda hers.

"Perfect end to a perfect day." He sipped his drink and licked the salt off his lips. "Perfect."

"Where did Fancy go after she left the work-out studio?" I said. Elias was right, the margarita was perfect. "Because she didn't get to the von Singens' until about twelve-thirty."

"Her shrink. She is a pathetic mess."

"Or else she wants to look like one," I said. "Who would want Rita von Singen, and me, dead? We have no connection that I can think of, and both jobs were so professional, or almost professional—the second one pretty much backfired, but even so." Elias placed a steaming burrito, smothered in green chili, in front of me. "Fancy has cultivated this helpless persona, but I know she's like steel inside—that's what southern women are known for—and she's hell-bent-for-leather to have Harry von Singen. Maybe she thinks I'm after him, and set up the accident this afternoon to get me out of the way. What did her doorman say?"

"His log shows that she arrived back home at eleven-oh-one and didn't go out again. Lulu came in at four-seventeen in the morning."

"Is there any way she could have left without his knowing?"

"Sure. The building's system is sophisticated, but you can trick it if you want to."

"She did," I said. "I know it. I think she was pretending to be drunk."

Elias just ate his lunch and listened to me talk; didn't say anything. Finally I ran out of gas and the three of us sat quietly—eating and thinking. I kept reviewing Fancy's excessive, erratic behavior over the last few days. Happy, sad. Drunk, sober. Weak, strong. Elias flipped through my phone messages. "Three of these are from Richard," he said.

"Don't change the subject," I told him. "I'm going to get a warrant to search her place."

"I think it's nice." He ignored me. "I've never seen you so happy. And, if you don't mind my saying so, it's nice to see you go out with someone who treats you well. And who you treat well back. And who has a brain in his head instead of just a big snake in his pants."

"Elias!" I yelled and started laughing. "That is so bad."

"It's true and you know it." He straightened some papers on the edge of my desk. "I think you guys ought to get married."

"Now you're sounding like Mother. That's not going to happen. We're both too old to get married." But inside, and this sounds so corny but it's true, my heart actually skipped a beat and I agreed with Elias completely.

"Uh-huh," he said.

Baby jumped onto my lap and curled up for her afternoon nap. I stroked her head and gave her a kiss.

After lunch, I called the judge and arranged for a warrant to search Fancy's home and cars for a gun or any other evidence that could incriminate her, or anyone else, in Rita von Singen's murder. Then I tried to get ahold of Richard, but he was in rehearsal and would call me back, so I told Linda good night and drove home to the ranch.

He called the minute I walked in the door. "I have an idea," he said.

"What?"

"Let's pass on the Cramers' cocktail party tonight. It's just going to be the same old blockheads we see all the time. Let's stay home and cook some steaks."

"You always say the right thing," I told him. "If you can get here soon, we could go out and get the tree."

"I'm on my way."

The light was almost gone as we left for the upper meadow where I'd had my eye on a certain small spruce tree since August. Not that small, maybe seven or eight feet, and perfectly shaped. The snow-mobile bumped us over the rough, frozen road that had been torn up by the treads of the snowcat that dragged hay sleds to livestock in the outer pastures. We climbed a hill, passed through an aspen glen, kept climbing and then wound down into a wide open valley and finally pulled to a stop by my tree. The fresh snow on its boughs made it even more perfect than I remembered.

"Are you *sure* this is the one you want?" Richard hefted the chainsaw out of the sled.

"Absolutely."

"This tree is about fourteen feet tall."

He got it for me anyway. And had to saw a few feet off the bottom before it would fit into the house. But finally, there it sat in the corner of the living room, gloriously plump and fresh. Ready to party.

There were a lot of things I wanted to tell Richard about that tree, about all the things it represented to me. Such as being the first tree I'd ever had in my own house at the ranch, something I'd dreamed of all my life. I'd always had a Christmas tree in Santa Bianca, but having a Christmas tree in California is a little strange. But this was my tree, in my house, in the snow, at the ranch. Or about being the first time I'd gone to get a tree with a lover when things didn't turn into a big emotional mess, usually because one of us had expectations that were too high, usually me. Or else it all was going well and then

I'd get a call from the station and have to go and he'd say, "To hell with this." Or that it signaled the start of party season, and that I didn't think people should have to do any work from the middle of December until after New Year's.

I didn't say anything, though. All I could do was smile. Richard put his arm around my shoulders and we looked at the perfect tree.

"In my experience," Richard said, "getting a Christmas tree has always been one of the most overrated, gut-wrenching tasks of the year. Ever since I got divorced when the boys were little, I've dreaded it. But I think this went pretty well."

"Ditto," I said. All choked up. Estrogen has turned my life into a melodrama.

We sipped champagne and decorated our tree, even though everyone says you should wait a couple of days to let one settle. Richard was in especially good, happy high spirits because the dress rehearsal had gone smoothly. Nikki Pantallo had sung and acted circles around Eloise Scott. And I was cheerful too, because aside from having escaped some wild man trying to run me off the road, I felt the clues to Rita's murder beginning to fall into place in my mind. And also because Richard and I had shared such a traumatic thing as getting a Christmas tree so easily and comfortably.

Later, in bed, we watched a very roughly made video of a rehearsal of the Met's production of *Rusalka*, the opera about the water sprite who murders the prince. Richard had been right; once it was staged, it looked beautiful, but I still thought the music was lame. Of course, I was far from an expert because we turned it off before the end of the first act, while Rusalka still had hope.

I snuggled down under the soft, warm, goose-down puff, and with Richard and Baby both sleeping quietly beside me, the outside vast and silent, the black sky pricked with stars, and only glowing embers left in the fireplace, I re-examined the facts and my strategy. By the time I went to sleep, I had things pretty well arranged in my mind and felt ready to move on to the next stage in Rita von Singen's murder investigation: getting specific about how Fancy did it and taking her into custody. I dreamed about what I would wear to help the marchése wrest Titian's *Adoration of the Madonna and Child* back from his no-good Florentine cousin at a white-tie New Year's Eve party at the family palazzo. I knew it was a dream because I was sleuthing around in a slinky Armani.

Chapter Twenty-four

Wednesday—Ball Day

The Roundup Debutante Ball Committee

has the honor to invite

Miss Lilly McLaughlin Bennett

to be a Patron of the Debutante Ball

for the benefit of the

Roundup Symphony Orchestra Association

Wednesday, December the Eighteenth

Eight o'clock in the evening

The Rotunda

The Roundup Grand Hotel

Roundup, Wyoming

*I*f you want to see people, starting with those in Kansas City and heading on east, slap their sides and fall on the floor in hysterics, just tell them about the Debutante Ball in Roundup,Wyoming. They can't take it, and who can blame them? We don't play by their rules. How can we? You can really only be that kind of blue-blood, Main Line, old-family exclusive when you have a whole bunch of old families to choose from. We just don't have that many people out here. So, when it comes to selecting the young ladies who will be invited to curtsey at the bottom of the grand staircase in the rotunda of the Roundup Grand, to a representative handful of Roundup's social lions, exclusivity becomes a relative thing. Basically, it's just a great Christmas party and the debutantes add a nice touch and make it a major fund-raiser for the Roundup Symphony Orchestra.

Or, as my mother puts it so succinctly, in private, behind closed doors, at the committee meetings: "Just make sure you get their curtsey fees in the bank, in advance, or the orchestra won't make payroll next week." The curtsey is hefty, too. Ten thousand dollars. When all is said and done, the whole show, the whole Christmastime debut season can cost each family about fifty thousand. But mothers insist fathers pay it and remind them how lucky they are that they don't live in Dallas, where their tab makes ours look like going out for a cup of coffee. A big part of any debutante mother's rationale, to the girl's shell-shocked father, is that the daughter can use her debutante gown as her wedding dress. Sure. I know of about two times that's happened.

And parents want their daughters to make their debuts for a number of reasons. Sometimes, the family sees the invitation as a social coup. Sometimes, it's the daughter herself who wants to do it because all her friends are. Sometimes, the parents insist the daughter does it because she's a dog and the parents want to get her out there and attract a wealthy young man and get the girl married off as quickly as possible. Sometimes, the whole family sees it as just what it is: an outstanding opportunity to party, and, a handy stand-by social yardstick when you're older. It all gets down to money.

In my instance, I was such a wild girl, I think my father was anxious to have me marry just as soon as possible and get the responsibility off his hands, so even though one debut is generally considered sufficient, I was presented at the Roundup Symphony Ball, the Houston Grand Opera Ball, the Denver Symphony Ball, the San Francisco Cotillion, the New York Mistletoe Ball, the Versailles Orangerie and the Viennese International.

I cannot tell you how much fun it was. It was fabulous. I was on the Pill. I was thin. I looked good. The men were spectacular. What can I say? I decided I was never going to get married.

After twenty-four months of nonstop, intercontinental, first class on Air France, debutante parties, my father finally said, as I was passing through Roundup to pick up a fresh supply of bank checks, "What do you plan to do now?"

"I don't know," I told him. "I guess I thought I'd just keep doing what I'm doing."

"I don't think so," he said. I believe that was the first time in my life my father ever said No to me. "I think you're either going to marry Lawrence Williams, or you're going to get a job."

What a bummer. I called Lawrence Williams, an F. Scott Fitzgerald, Arrow-shirt-looking kind of guy from Westport, Connecticut, a sophisticated Yalie charmer who had been after me to marry him for a few months, and asked if I could come visit. We all knew what that meant.

"Mother and I would love to see you," Lawrence said. He lived in a lovely old terraced and parterred Sanford White estate with his widowed mother and looked after their investments and holdings from a quiet, paneled, leather-bound office next door to the Union Club in the city. He picked me up at Kennedy in his glossy black XK-E convertible. He gave me champagne and drove me up the Merritt Parkway to see his mother, and the next day we had lunch with his godfather—who had been his guardian since his father died when he was twelve—and his aunts and uncles, and the next day we drove into Manhattan to Tiffany's and picked out the biggest, most perfect diamond they had, and the next day his mother gave a perfectly lovely garden party for us, and, at three o'clock the next morning, Lawrence and I bumped into each other sneaking down the back stairs with our luggage.

"Where are you going?" I whispered.

"Buenos Aires," Lawrence answered. "I'm going to work at one of our companies there for a couple of years. I'm sorry, Lilly, I just can't do it. Here." He handed me a heavy ecru envelope with the family crest embossed on the flap and my name scrawled elegantly on the front in practically perfect copperplate handwriting. "I was going to leave this for you." Then he noticed my bags. "Where are you going?"

"Wyoming." I handed him my heavy ecru envelope engraved in red with the Circle B brand.

We both grinned and started to laugh and laughed so hard, we had to sit down on the steps.

"Will you give me a ride to the airport?" I finally said.

"It'll be my pleasure."

I don't know how long it was before people figured out we hadn't eloped. I don't even know when, or if, Lawrence came back from South America, because we never talked again. Not because we didn't like each other. We liked each other a lot, but not enough. And I realized I had to do something with my life besides being a wife and mother. I wanted to do something that was hard to do—mentally and physically—and had a lot of men around. That's when I went to Santa Bianca, California, and joined the police force. Which was significantly more rigorous and demanding than being a debutante and quite, quite different. I took a lot of flak, but I also did a good job and finally qualified as a full-fledged, professional, brave and dependable member of the team, and no one made fun of my debutante background again, because in law enforcement you earn your stripes, period. No amount of money can buy them.

I love our little Debutante Ball in Roundup. I like the anticipation, the preparation and the party itself. It all brings back such happy memories for me.

Chapter Twenty-five

Wednesday morning

I had planned to spend almost all day Wednesday getting ready. But first I worked out—second time this week—then pulled on some gray flannel slacks and a soft navy wool turtleneck, pearls and a bright red blazer, and drove through the sunny morning to Fancy's high-rise. The head of the building's security company was there to meet me while I waited for Elias to arrive with the warrant.

It was simple for us to figure out how a resident who wanted to, and who made an effort to study how, could escape detection by the unsophisticated video setup that kept an eye on the garage door. The building's single-guard system was designed to defend the main entrance, which in Roundup is considered sufficient, because, frankly, we don't get many terrorists.

"Our elevators have been on the fritz for a couple of weeks," the security chief said. He wore a navy blazer with the company emblem on the breast pocket. "It's been driving everybody crazy. Sticking between floors, getting stuck at floors, alarms going off. Some kind of computer glitch."

"Or man-made."

"Sure," he said.

"So a person could set off the alarm at any floor and then, while the guard was waiting for the other elevator to take him up to correct the problem, the person could go down the stairs and leave the building through the garage."

"Sure," he said again matter-of-factly.

"Do you keep a log of every time the elevators get stuck?"

"Should."

I followed him to the reception area, where the guard on duty, a Slav whose thighs and neck were as big as Christmas turkeys, sat behind a high desk facing a bank of monitors, and buzzed residents and their guests in and out. He knew almost everyone by name. Christmas packages buried the tables behind him and a large stack of Federal Express and UPS cartons, waiting to be delivered upstairs, was piled against his desk.

The boss leaned over the counter and grabbed the log and flipped back a few pages. "Here it is. Elevator stuck. Tenth floor. Eleven-oh-two Friday night."

"Let's say she left, undetected, at that time. Do you have a record of her coming back in?"

He ruffled the sheets back and forth. "Nothing," he said. "Oh, here. Ten forty-five A.M. That would be after her workout. Gets home about the same time every day. But there's no record of her leaving." He spoke to the guard. "Floyd, this is your initial, isn't it? Were you on duty Saturday morning?"

"Yes, sir."

"There's no early-A.M. departure time for Mrs. French—only her return."

The guard stood and leaned over the counter and looked into the log. "No, sir," he said. "She always leaves between eight-twenty and eight-thirty. See, here is Mrs. Cosgriff walking her Scottie at eight twenty-one, and Mr. Rawls going out at eight twenty-five, and so forth. No, sir. She didn't leave at her regular time on Saturday. I don't know when she left. But, yes, sir, here she is coming back at ten forty-five. Isn't that odd?"

"I think we just found the elevator glitch," I said to both of them. "I'm sure I don't need to tell you to keep this to yourself."

"No, ma'am."

I hadn't been in Fancy's apartment before, because the last time she'd invited me for cocktails, she and Lulu and Daniel had all still been living in her parents' big country-club home. Since then, their parents had died, and she and Daniel had come into their full inheritances. He'd stayed in the house on Spring Street and Fancy had bought an entire floor of Roundup's most exclusive building, filling it with several generations of family treasures, brought to our dry climate from Beaufort.

I rang the doorbell.

"Doesn't this make you a little uncomfortable?" Elias said as we waited.

"No. Why?"

"Searching an old friend's home. Makes me feel a little funny."

"She might be a murderer." I looked Elias in the eye. "It would make me feel funnier if I had suspicions and didn't do anything about them for propriety's sake."

"Yeah. You're right," growled the old Green Beret. "Let's bust her ass."

I laughed and shook my head.

The maid let us in—the señora and señorita were both out and expected back momentito. I explained to her, in Spanish, why we were there: to search for something, anything, that could help us in our investigation of Baroness von Singen's murder, and Elias showed her the warrant.

"Sí," she said about ten times, her eyes moving suspiciously back and forth between the two of us.

"Do you live here?" I asked her.

"Sí."

"Were you here last Friday night?"

"No, I'm living here only in the week. Not the weekends. I have my family on the weekends."

We followed her down the long entry gallery, where floor-to-ceiling mirrors on the left wall reflected a series of three gilt-framed eighteenth-century English landscapes. A Persian runner ran the length of the hallway to a tall American Colonial desk.

"I'll do Fancy's and Lulu's rooms," I told Elias as I snapped my latex gloves into place. "You start in the study."

"Right," he said.

We began the search. It was easy for me to be dispassionate, objective. The magnificent rooms ceased to be an old friend's. Cedar closets, shoes, sweaters, evening gowns and fur closets, lingerie and jewelry chests, bed tables, bathroom drawers and desks, all became hiding places for guns or gloves or any tiny shreds of evidence that could link Fancy French with the murder.

I was in Fancy's dressing room when Lulu came in. Her face was fresh and glowing, nineteen-year-old skin, and her burnished-golden hair was pulled up on either side of her face with combs. She always seemed older than her years to me—more a contemporary than the child of a friend. But after growing up fatherless in the care, or rather lack of it, of an alcoholic mother, a tortured uncle and haphazard grandparents, she'd never really had too much of a shot at childhood. Even the times she'd come to visit me in Santa Bianca, I'd dragged her down to the station where she'd spend her day bringing hot coffee to everyone in the squad room; and in the evenings I made her sit through every opera, ballet, play and major art exhibition I could find. Not always pleasant, I know, but quite necessary all the same. Somebody had to do it, and Fancy certainly wasn't going to assume the responsibility for her daughter's cultural upbringing.

"Aunt Lilly," she said, "what in the world are you up to?"

I would be lying if I said that this encounter didn't make me uncomfortable. Lulu was the closest thing I've ever had to a daughter, but the fact was, she wasn't. She was Fancy's daughter, and I was searching her mother's house for evidence to implicate her in a homicide. "I think your mother was involved somehow in Rita von Singen's murder," I told her. "And I've had a warrant issued to search the apartment and her cars for evidence."

"You think my mother did it?"

"I don't know who did it, darling," I said. "But Harry von Singen has hired me to clear his name, and we have reason to believe that your mother or Dayton Babcock might have been involved."

"That wouldn't surprise me a bit," she said. "I wouldn't put anything past those two. She and Dayton were obsessed with the von Singens." Lulu didn't seem even slightly surprised or alarmed at the possibility that her mother might have killed someone. She may as well have been speaking about the wallpaper for all the passion in her voice, and I realized that after all the years of parental indifference, Fancy had successfully rendered herself a nonentity in her daughter's life. "Is there anything I can do to help before I leave? I've got to get cleaned up and over to the beauty shop."

"One thing: does your mother have a safe?"

"Yes, of course," Lulu said, leading me into the bedroom. "It's right here." She swung a small oil painting of lovers in springtime on the banks of the Seine away from the wall. "Do you want me to open it?"

"Yes, please."

"I don't think she keeps much in here except jewelry and her passport." Lulu spun the combination lock expertly. "I know there's no money because I'm always short, and this was always the first place I looked when I was little. That was before I figured out that she never has any cash either." The safe door swung open and Lulu peered into the dark chamber. "Nope," she said. "Looks pretty normal to me." She began to reach in.

"Let me do that," I said, and stepped forward and reached into the safe as Fancy's footsteps raced down the hall.

"What in the Sam Hill is going on here?" She burst through the door looking like Heather Locklear in her hot-pink work-out tights and thong leotard top and her hair pulled up in a barrette. "Lilly Bennett, what are you doing with my jewelry? And Lulu. What are you doing, opening my safe for anybody?"

I set a stack of navy velvet jewel cases down on the small French sideboard beneath the safe, and pulled the warrant out of my pocket. "She opened it because I asked her to, Fancy. We're conducting a search of your apartment."

"Why?"

"Unfortunately, all of the signs keep leading back and implicating you in the murder of Rita von Singen, and even though I hope you weren't involved, I have to follow up on them." I unfolded the warrant and held it out.

"What?" Fancy took the sheet of paper and read it quickly. She looked stunned. "How could you even think that after all we've been through? I've told you everything about myself, shared everything with you, and now you're accusing me of murder? Please tell me you're joking."

"This is no joke," I said. "I wish it were."

"What in the world are you talking about?" Her anger began to show. "Rita was my friend. Why in the world would I kill her?"

"I think you might have killed her to get Harry," I said.

Lulu laughed out loud and shook her head.

"What exactly does that mean?" Fancy whirled to face her daughter. "You think I can't get any man I want?"

"It doesn't mean anything, Mother." Lulu's expression sobered quickly.

"Well, let me tell you something, Miss World's Most Important Debutante," she snarled, "I work my ass off to stay in shape and I look a hell of a lot better than you do. And I can get any man I want. Any man. And I don't need to go around killing anybody to do it." Fancy turned to me. "You have a hell of a nerve thinking I would have anything to do with Rita's murder. I would never, ever, do such a thing."

"I truly hope you didn't," I said, disgusted, but not at all surprised, by the way she spoke to Lulu. "But you do have a very strong motive and there is a sequence of circumstances that can be strung together that all end up pointing in your direction."

"Like what?"

"I think it's possible that after Dayton brought you home Friday night, you returned to the Lorillards' and shot Rita."

"I was too drunk to tie my own shoes," Fancy said.

"Oh, that's terrific," Lulu said sarcastically. "I thought you were on the wagon."

"I'm drinking because you are driving me fucking *crazy*," Fancy shouted at her daughter. She had gone into her dressing room and was peeling off her work-out clothes.

"I think you pretended to be drunk," I called through the door to her as I opened and closed the jewel cases, one at a time, and replaced them in the safe. "You knew Rita had passed out in the living room and would stay that way until Daniel and Cordelia took her home. You knew exactly how much time you had."

"Check with the guard. He'll have a record of my comings and goings."

"I already did. The elevator was broken. It would be easy to leave the building with the guard distracted. And they have no record of your leaving the next morning to work out, just of when you returned at ten-thirty."

"Hogwash." Fancy snapped her toothbrush against the side of the sink. "Besides, where is the murder weapon? I don't own a gun."

"I'll find it," I told her.

"Look all you want. I'm going down for my massage. Harry von Singen loves me and is going to ask me to marry him. You'll see." She pulled on a long white terry-cloth robe, and tossed a pill, presumably a Prozac, into her mouth and washed it down with two big gulps of water. "You think you're so fucking smart, but I'll tell you something: I'm smarter than you are and if I had murdered Rita you'd never be able to figure it out. Besides, you're just jealous," she jeered, "because you've never been able to get a husband, so you just want to make sure no one else does either. I hear your father's offered Richard Jerome ten million dollars to marry you."

"I hope it works," I called down the hall, as she left the apartment for the garden-level spa. "See you tonight." Fuck her.

Chapter Twenty-six

*E*lias and I didn't find anything in Fancy's apartment or in either car. No weapons. Nothing.

As I drove to the beauty salon, where I joined the festive spirit by having a large cup of French roasted coffee and a number of glazed doughnut holes, I began to wonder if Fancy really did do it, or if I just wanted her to.

"Any breaks on the you-know-what?" Sparky Kendall said.

"No, and I don't want to talk about it," I said and sat down.

In addition to Sparky, two old friends—Mary McArthur and "Pitty-Pat" Palmer (Texas)—were there, and the four of us passed the time, as we did every week, visiting about the bond market, gardening, cooking, books and movies, and just generally nothing of any importance, which was fine with me because it gave me an opportunity to let the baroness's murder free-float along for a while as I soaked my hands in hot eucalyptus oil.

Four debutantes and their mothers were in various stages of getting fluffed for the big night. Two of the girls, clearly best friends, ecstatic at being home for Christmas from their first fall away from college, wandered around the shop and read everyone's horoscopes out of all the different women's magazines.

"Hmm," one of the girls said when they got to me, "you look like a *Cosmo* girl." She riffled through the thick magazine.

"Well," I said. "I certainly *used* to be one."

"Sign?"

"Leo," I said.

" 'Finally,' " she read, " 'he will release all those passions you've been keeping pent up since the last time.' " Or something like that. I know it had passion and pent up and release—all of *Cosmo's* horoscopes did.

"Thank God," I said. "A girl can take just so much pent-up passion before she goes wild." Look at Fancy.

I went home and had a Lean Cuisine for lunch, but I think it was probably too late to have any thinning effect—I should have been eating them for several weeks—and then took Ariel out for some afternoon exercise of barrel racing. Art timed us. Baby always tries to keep up for the first few rounds, but then she'll just sit down next to Art and bark as the horse and I dart our way through the three-point dash. It was hard work for both of us, racing like hell and then slamming on the brakes to pivot through a tight three-sixty without clipping the barrel or slipping and falling because the turn's too tight, and then doing it again, and then again, and then bolting, all-out, for the finish line. In my mind, barrel racing is sort of the ultimate in interval training. Ariel's and my competition days are far behind us, but the fun and excitement and challenge of racing against the clock never get boring. And so what if your personal best gets a little slower every year? It's just yours, and it's still fun.

Later, I called Harry and brought him up to speed on my day and my theory about Fancy's returning to the Children's Hospital party and murdering Rita.

"Do you seriously believe Fancy could do such a thing?" Harry said.

"Yes. I not only believe she could, I believe she probably did."

"She asked me to take her to the Ball tonight. What should I do? Go ahead and go?"

"Absolutely."

I could practically see Harry shaking his head. "I think I'd rather just call the whole thing off and stay home." He sounded discouraged. "I can't tolerate intoxicated women, and Fancy has become especially tiresome. And in addition to that, she has developed this fixation on me that makes me very uncomfortable because it's a complete fantasy. I don't want to give people the impression that I am seriously interested in her, and now, if it turns out that she murdered my wife . . ." He paused for the right words. "Well, it all becomes just entirely too improper."

"Obviously," I said, forcing myself to be calm but truly alarmed that he really might not go, "it's completely up to you what you do tonight. You're paying for my counsel and I'm giving it to you. I don't blame you for not wanting to go, but I have a gut feeling that something is going to happen at the Ball. That even if Fancy didn't do it, she'll lead us to whoever did. But your physical presence will be the catalyst."

"I'm thinking," he said.

"Look, Harry," I said. "How's this: do me a favor. Just take her to the Ball, not for her sake or yours or mine, but for my mother's."

"Your mother's?"

"Yes. You're seated next to her at dinner and if you don't show up, she'll kill me."

Harry laughed warmly. "In that case, I wouldn't think of staying home. Besides, how could I resist with all those beautiful debutantes—past and present—around?"

"There you go," I said.

We hung up and I smiled at myself in the mirrors around my tub as I turned on the hot water and poured on the gardenia bubbles. "Yes!" I balled my fist like a ten-year-old who's bagged a soccer goal. I was on track. Something was in motion, swirling and pulling as inexorably as the tide. I sank deep into the scented water and was contemplating how becoming fog on a mirror can be, when Baby started barking.

Richard was home.

"What did Jack Lewis say about the guy in the car?" he yelled from the kitchen. The muffled pop of a champagne cork floated up the stairs.

"Burned beyond recognition," I yelled back. "Car rental with a stolen license and credit card. No surprises. One other thing: Cordelia Hamilton's gun—the one we took out of her car—is brand-new. Never fired. She said she'd fired it once or twice. Not true."

"So what do you do?"

"I'm running a check on the ID registration. Find out when this one was bought."

"What time are we supposed to be at the hotel?"

"Six-thirty," I called. "The helicopter's leaving at six-fifteen."

"Perfect," he said, standing there next to the tub, all tall and good-looking in his gray pin-striped suit and cowboy boots. He handed me a glass of Dom Perignon and smiled. "That means I don't have to rush."

"Let me ask you a question," I said.

"Shoot."

"Has my father offered you ten million dollars to marry me?"

"Yes," Richard answered, "but I told him I wouldn't consider it for less than twenty."

"Good. Drive a hard bargain."

He handed me a towel. "Come in here," he called from the bedroom. "There's something I want to show you."

I had to start over on my hair, but it's short and naturally curly and pretty easy to redo, and I didn't mind at all.

Chapter Twenty-seven

By the time we left the house to drive the quarter mile to the helipad in the meadow where Christian's Sikorsky waited to take us to town, it was already pitch-black.

Mimi, Christian's tall, thin, elegant wife, who was all in black velvet, had arranged an exquisite, crisp cloud of black tulle over her white-blond hair, which was slicked back into a smooth chignon. With her full-length dark mink flying behind her like a cape, she looked like a Francesco Scavullo photo shoot for *Vogue* as she raced through the harsh glare of the heliport landing lights across the snowy tarmac from their car into the chopper.

Ellen Butterfield, Elias's sweetheart on and off for most of his life, followed Mimi. Her gown was heavily jeweled in sharp geometric patterns and jarring colors.

"Even in the dark that dress looks terrible," I said to Richard.

"You're right," he said.

I raced behind Ellen, wearing my bright new orangy-red gown with its tight lace top and huge satin skirt, and within seconds of sitting down in the comfortable cabin, Mimi had handed me a large yellow plastic mug of champagne and said how pretty I looked. I love Mimi. She's one of the nicest people I've ever known, and even though she knows how much better she looks than everyone else who's out there struggling to lose ten pounds and squeeze into a size eight, she always makes you feel that she wishes she could look as good as you do.

The men came right behind me, whooping and hollering, their starched white shirts almost fluorescent in the strong lights, their tailcoats flapping in the wind, their dress boots shiny, their cowboy hats held tight on their heads. Once they'd thundered raucously inside and the copilot had slid the door shut, we made a noisy, lumbering ascent, like a little tiny star rising slowly to the top of a Christmas tree, for that's what the countryside all around Roundup looked like on the fifteen-minute flight. Christmas lights blazed and twinkled from every ranch house and tree and fence. It was like flying through a wonderland in a royal coach that smelled of jasmine and tuberose, Old Spice and Mennen Skin Bracer.

Roundup rose to meet us from the prairie as we hurtled toward it at one hundred and seventy miles an hour. This experience of rushing toward mountains or buildings in a helicopter inevitably gives me vertigo and I gave myself the luxury of secretly taking Richard's hand so my brothers couldn't tell that I was afraid.

Suddenly we were close enough to see the city's decorations and as we passed up and down the streets to admire the lights, the illusion was one of becoming part of Christmastime, of being in it. Being it. Probably what it's like to take LSD.

"Wow!" Elias said. "This is so cool." I think he was the only one of us able to speak with any authority of that particular experience.

Roundup's annual Christmas display is a uniquely gaudy mess. Every office building, the civic center, all the trees in all the parks become monuments of sparkling lights in every color. Not only red and green, but blue and yellow, pink and lavender, orange and lime and turquoise, gold and silver. All the networks make fun of it every year on the national news. Naturally, we love it.

And while I'm on the subject, we call it a *Christmas* display, not a *Holiday* display, because if it weren't for Jesus, none of this would be going on. Know what I mean? So we just wish everybody a "Merry

Christmas," and not "Happy Holidays"—unless we know for sure the person we're talking to is Jewish or Muslim or something, although I don't know if we have any Muslims in Wyoming.

Gigantic trees made of strings of lights had been erected on some of the office-building roofs, and other buildings had immense wreaths on their sides, or lighted crèches or monumental angels soaring and swooping from the rooftops through the plazas. Red-and-green neon wreaths had been added around the necks of some of the cattle on the Roundup Gas and Electric Building's permanent display of neon cowhands who chased their neon herd. I nudged Richard's shoulder and pointed it out to him.

"Wonderful," he yelled over the whine of the engines.

"Take us around the park again," Christian called to the captain, who nodded, spoke into his radio and then peeled us off to the left and whipped around the parklike central plaza of City Hall and the County Courthouse and the Main Library and our art museum. I don't know about the architect for the Royal Palace in Lima, Peru, the only other building in the Western Hemisphere where you can see virtually every style of architecture since the beginning of time in a single structure, but unfortunately, in the case of our art museum, it was because our architect didn't know any better, and thought it looked great. Even more unfortunately, our city council agreed.

I know I shouldn't harp on this subject, but it really upsets me. Which mayor was it who appointed his blind-drunk buddies to the commission to make these design decisions? Jabba the Hut's brother? Conan?

"You should see what they've got in mind for our new library." Christian seemed to have read my mind.

"Bad?"

"Yikes," he said.

We flew low over long lines of automobiles that wound slowly through the civic complex. The parents and children and grandparents inside the cars gawked at the incredible display and sang along with Christmas carols that echoed over loudspeakers. A spotlighted Santa waved from a silver sleigh, while his elves wove among the cars passing out red-hot cinnamon and lime-green Jolly Rancher candies, and Baby Jesus lay in his manger surrounded by the menagerie of three camels, a burro, a cow and a lamb, which are brought over each afternoon from the Roundup Zoo to attend him.

Moments later, we settled on the roof of the Grand without crashing into a single building or spilling any champagne. I swear to God, I don't know how those pilots do it, except that they were both former Marine aviators. That's how.

The Grand is an elegant relic—a ten-story national historic landmark constructed in the early part of the century of locally quarried, smooth-cut blocks of pale limestone, trimmed with shiny black wrought-iron window boxes and an ornate glass-and-iron marquee. The hotel is built around a marble-floored atrium lobby, known as the Rotunda, where on a typical afternoon visitors gather for tea or whiskey and listen to the only harpsichordist in Wyoming bang away enthusiastically. But on the night of the Debutante Ball, all the furniture and carpets are swept away to make room for a large orchestra and dance floor. Every balcony railing, all the way to the tenth floor, is decorated with fresh greens and red velvet bows and tiny lights.

We took the elevator down from the roof to the third floor, and when the doors slid open, the noise and laughter and gaiety of the crowd and the fragrance of all the fresh green poured in and boosted our spirits even higher. All the balconies, up and down, and the lobby below bustled with people dressed in their finest evening clothes, wearing their best jewels, their hair and nails done to perfection, drinking expensive champagne and good whiskey. Dozens of uniformed and plainclothes police, and hotel security personnel, milled with the crowd and stood in groups of three and four at the hotel's entrances, and in pairs here and there around the Rotunda dance floor. A chamber orchestra played Mozart.

"Have you been to the Ball before?" I asked Richard as he guided us slowly through the crowd to the Ike and Mamie Eisenhower Suite. My parents, the Ball's lifetime honorary co-chairmen, hold forth at Ike and Mamie's every year, and throw a cocktail bash before the presentation for the committee members and the debutantes' parents.

"Of course," he said. "Twice."

I was floored. I don't know why. It was the same deal as the Children's Hospital party. I mean, why wouldn't he have gone to the Ball? "Who with?"

"Well, last year with Joan Chamberlain; of course she wasn't named Chamberlain at that time. She was Joan Dennis at that point, I think."

Well, shut my mouth.

Mother stood outside the suite's double doors, greeting her guests. I imagine Daddy was at the bar inside.

"Mama." I kissed her cheek. "You are looking wonderful." She was, too. Once her hair started to turn gray, she began wearing softer colors, giving the effect and impression that she was a gentle, kind, refined older lady. Soft and sweet. Of course, those of us who knew her, knew she was as sweet as a cinnamon bear who lived in a cave with two rattlesnakes as best friends.

"I always feel my best when I wear this shell-pink and my pearls and diamonds," she said loudly, a danger sign she'd decided not to wear her hearing aid. "I think it's an especially becoming combination."

'I agree completely," Richard said.

"Lorraine Elliott is wearing paste," Mother said.

Although Mrs. Elliott had her back to us, and was a little ways away, I knew she heard the remark. And even though I didn't exactly see the arrow go in, I did see her twinge a little.

"Mama," I said. "You don't have to shout, we can hear you." She didn't hear me.

"And wait until you see Mrs. Howell," Mother forged recklessly along. "I can't believe a woman her age would wear a backless dress, can you? I mean, just because she was Miss Wyoming in nineteen forty, good God. Somebody needs to get some clothespins and clamp all that skin back up onto her shoulders. Oh, well," she sighed, "what can one do?"

Richard and I just shook our heads and laughed. What can one do? Short of taping her mouth shut. Besides, I was still getting over the Joan Chamberlain/Richard deal.

"Lilly, darling, I'm so glad you're here with someone worthwhile for a change." She held both of our hands. "You know, Richard, she has come to this party with the most frightful men. One of them smoked cigars—the cheap, dreadful kind with a plastic holder already attached, the ones George Gobel's wife used to advertise on television in the tight evening gown and cheap white mink stole— and he wore sneakers, a white dinner jacket and a clip-on tie."

"Mother," I said. She pretended not to hear.

"Another was some champion bull rider who was so nervous at being at such a fancy social occasion he got completely smashed and threw up over the balcony. That was a very difficult one to explain away." She gave me a look. "Believe me. Did she tell you about the one with the short arms?"

"Mother," I said. "I think that ought to do it. And I think it was Tennessee Ernie Ford's wife who sold the cigars, not George Gobel's."

"Ernie Kovacs's," Richard said, but no one paid any attention to him.

"You're quite right, darling," she said. "I'll not say another word. We don't want to let this one get away, do we? Now, Richard, dear, tell me, how is *Ada* coming along?"

"It's coming," he answered.

"How about the ticket sales?"

"Sold out. Selling the tickets is easy compared to putting on the show. Those buffalo are so damned big, they just do whatever they want."

"Well, after all, that's what you're paid for. Just two days till you open." She just never gives anyone an inch. "Go in and get a drink. Your father's in there somewhere, but it's such a mob scene I had to come out for some air. I think you know everyone. Dickie and Joan Chamberlain are here. Honestly, she is such a snob."

"I thought you liked her," I said. "You said she was absolutely blue ribbon."

"Don't be fresh, Lilly."

We entered the big living room with its knotty-pine-paneled walls and rawhide lamp shades and dun-covered twill upholstery imprinted with fishing scenes.

Senator and Mrs. Baldridge were talking to my father, who was looking especially snappy and dignified in his white tie and tails. Senator Baldridge was one of my father's oldest and best friends. They'd grown up together, great-grandsons of western pioneers, and they were both lucky enough to remember their grandparents and great-grandparents, the men and women who'd been here first, who'd survived the massacres and claimed the land, founded the towns and guided the territory to statehood. If you touched them, you touched the start of the Cowboy American West. They had the look as well they should: they were the real thing. So am I.

"Hi, Daddy." I kissed him on the cheek.

"I was just telling your father a story," the senator said, "about the government's latest lamebrained scheme to make our life out here a little more comfortable."

"Don't let us stop you," Richard told him.

"Well, I was just saying that a couple of weeks ago, I was at a White House cocktail party for some ambassador or other, and the President was raising hell with our esteemed Secretary of the Interior about the fact that all of us westerners are all riled up, and rightfully so—of course that makes no difference with anyone back there—about his wanting to raise our grazing fees and put some more goddamned regulations on how we use the public land. And the President says, straight-faced, mind you, to the Secretary, 'Listen to me, Bruce, I've discovered there are over one hundred thousand cattle guards in Colorado alone. I want you to fire half of them.'

" 'Yes, sir,' the Secretary says.

"Few days later," the senator continued, "I hear that a congress-person—who shall go nameless—from Colorado has introduced a bill on the floor of the House demanding that Interior hold off firing the cattle guards for six months, until she can get them into a retraining program."

My father, who was working his way through a large dark glass of Jameson's, laughed until tears ran down his cheeks. He hated the Ball. Almost as much as he hated the government and the opera. But he went anyway. Did his duty. Only friends like Baldridge with stories like that made it endurable for him.

We moved a few feet through the glittering crowd.

"You know," Joan Chamberlain said to me, "I came to this party with Richard last year." Her pale-blond hair was parted in the middle and held in place by diamond clips that matched an enormous diamond necklace that sparkled spectacularly on her lightly tanned skin. I wondered if she'd worn the floaty white chiffon toga at one of her weddings.

"So I hear." I used to detest people like Joan, who moan and groan out every single ghastly, dreadful word. Now they just fascinate me. She had a cigarette holder.

"I don't need to tell you what a simply *divine* catch he is. Every woman on the Eastern Seaboard has been scheming for *years* how to get him. Did he tell you how I absolutely *humiliated* myself over him?"

"No."

"Well, he wouldn't, of course. But I'd just gotten divorced from Billy and I knew Richard was out here, so I absolutely *forced* myself on him, insisted he invite me to visit, and of course there's simply *nothing* there at all between us, no fire, not even any *smoke*." She punctuated the last with a large drag on her cigarette. "But at least the trip wasn't a complete waste because I met Dickie."

"How many times have you been married?" I said.

"Dickie's four. I've just had simply *dreadful* luck with men." She glanced across the room at Harry and Fancy, who wandered in just as Richard and Dickie returned from the bar with our drinks. "Oh, thanks, dearest," she said to her husband. "Honest to God, you are such a saint. Oh, Lord, here comes Cordelia Hamilton. She is nothing but *bad news*, Lilly, in case you didn't know. Dickie, let's scoot down and check on Dottie—trying to keep these girls sober long enough to get them down the stairs to curtsey is practically more than humanly possible. We'll see you at the presentation."

Richard had been grabbed by a couple of opera patrons I didn't know who wanted to hear all about his rehearsals and Friday's opening, so I headed in Harry and Fancy's direction. From a distance, she appeared radiant, almost shimmering, in a pale-blue satin dress that matched her eyes, but by the time I'd worked my way toward them, they'd disappeared. I know she saw me.

"I just stopped in to say a quick hello to your parents, before I go back down to that bedlam of giggling hormones," Cordelia interrupted my thoughts. There was just something about her I never could put my finger on. One moment she was delightful and charming, and the next, cool and reserved, but she was always calculating, suspicious and manipulative. She and Joan were cut from the same cloth—that defensive, in-your-face fabric that drapes rich married women who don't work when they get around women who do. Tonight, Cordelia looked unusually striking in a Japanese ceremonial robe, with a massive carved jade necklace and earrings. Her hair had been lacquered into a glossy helmet that hung in a perfectly straight line, Cleopatra-style, right at the edge of her eyes.

"I'm glad I ran into you before the evening gets away from us," I said. "Maybe we could just go in the other room for a minute and have a quiet word or two."

"I don't think it's necessary to leave." Cordelia smiled. "I haven't done anything wrong. What can I do to help?"

"I wanted to ask you about the gun we took from your car."

"Oh? What about it?"

"You told me you had fired it."

She nodded. "Yes," she said. "A couple of times." She sipped her champagne.

"Well, the weapon that we removed from your vehicle was brand-new. It's never been fired."

Nonplussed, Cordelia frowned and shook her head. "No," she said. "I've taken it to the range twice."

"Not this gun. Maybe some other Glock nineteen."

People around us grew still.

Her face colored and she laughed a little. "I—I don't know what to say."

I studied the nature of her discomfort, and on the surface it seemed to be more the result of embarrassment and being perplexed than nervousness. There was no tremor, no dampness, no change in her pupils.

"You don't have to say anything," I told her. "I'm certainly not accusing you of anything. I just wanted you to know what we've found. Who, besides you, has been in your car or had access to it since last Friday?"

"Probably dozens of people." Cordelia shrugged and shook her head, aware of the quiet circle of listeners. "Maybe we should talk about this later."

"That's basically it," I said, and laid my hand on her arm in a comrade-like gesture. "I'm sorry if I embarrassed you. I just knew you'd want to know."

"Well." She laughed it off gracefully. "I'm sure everyone's glad to know." Nervous laughter mushroomed around us, followed by a headlong rush into conversation. "What's become of Daniel?" Cordelia searched around vaguely. "We've got to get going. Oh, Lord, there he is. How does he get into these things? He should know better. I'll see you later."

Daniel French had gotten trapped in an incoherent conversation with the Higleys, who were already drunk. Mr. Higley's toupee had started to slip, and Mrs. Higley, who wore flat shoes like a lot of alcoholics, the theory apparently being it is harder to trip and fall down in flats, was pitched heavily to the right on her cane, which she had wedged into the corner where the wall met the floor. Cordelia grabbed Daniel's arm and dragged him away.

I went to the bar, got another drink and then joined Elias and a few other big-shot ranchers who, along with the Governor and First Lady, were listening to one of the ranchers—a great big nice guy I'd known for years named Walter Gunderson—report to the Governor on a meeting he'd attended a couple of night before in Sheridan. The subject was predator control, meaning coyotes, and the federal government's latest half-assed solution, meaning some new harebrained waste of the taxpayers' money dreamed up by some lamebrained twenty-five-year-old who'd never crossed the Potomac, much less the Mississippi.

"Hey, sugar, come on in here." Walter put his arm around my shoulders and gave me a squeeze. "So we're all gathered in this big banquet room in the Holiday Inn in Sheridan," he continued his report. He had on a formal western suit, not a tuxedo, and his stomach, without a cummerbund to rein it in, hung over his low-slung pants like a baby in a sling. "And these two pantywaists from back east are complaining about everyone's smoking, which of course just made us all smoke all the harder. Few guys I know don't even smoke, were. So one of these girls takes his suit coat off and rolls up the sleeves and loosens his tie like he's one of us, and so does his buddy. They're just so danged earnest, these government fellows. Just earnest and just board-dumb. And he announces, from a microphone at the head table, that he and the government have come up with what they consider to be a workable, acceptable-to-all, solution to the coyote problem.

" 'What we're gonna do,' he says, 'is start a coyote trapping program, and we aren't gonna kill them because, as you all know, that's ecologically irresponsible and gets the environmentalists upset, but what we're gonna do is remove the testosterone from their system, remove their aggression. Make them not want to kill anymore.'

"'How're you gonna do that?' someone asked him.

"'We're gonna castrate them.'

"Well," said Walter, "as you can imagine, it got pretty danged quiet in that banquet room and then Sam Henry finally stood up and took off his hat and says to this earnest young greenhorn from Washington, 'Son,' he says, 'you don't understand. They ain't fuckin' our sheep. They're killin' 'em.'"

Chapter Twenty-eight

Let's go see what else is going on," I said to Richard.

We grabbed fresh drinks and said hello, hello, hello all the way down to the second floor, where the debutantes and their parents had taken over the mezzanine suites early that afternoon, to relax and get dressed. The suite doors now stood open and the fathers, in their white ties and tails, milled around out on the balcony laughing loudly and gulping strong cocktails and initiating or concluding business deals with their buddies and checking one another out in their formal evening clothes, making nervous jokes and gibes.

Inside, the mothers fussed over the twenty-five young ladies—all college freshmen, most of them plump, a few anorexic and sylph-like—who giggled and acted silly and sneaked drinks and cigarettes, and self-consciously admired themselves in their white ball gowns. Some of the gowns were elaborate and some were simple, and every year, there was always one that was absolutely breathtaking, worn by a particularly beautiful girl whom no one really knew because she'd always been away at boarding school or wasn't really from Roundup at all. She would spend the evening unapproachably alone with everyone admiring her, but, except for one or two people, they would be shy and unwilling to make contact. So ultimately, through no fault of her own, everyone would end up whispering that she was a stuck-up snob. Inevitably, this girl would get a job somewhere else and never come home again. In a few years, her picture might appear in *Town & Country* at a party in Palm Beach or somewhere, married to a big executive, but more often than not, she would probably just disappear. Never really amount to much, besides being thin and pretty and rich. This year it was Joan Chamberlain's daughter, Dorothy Jefferson. And she was positively stunning—no wonder everyone avoided her.

I made a point of introducing myself to her, telling her how beautiful she looked and how glad I was to meet her and how much I'd heard about her, knowing it probably didn't mean anything to Dorothy, but would mean a lot to Joan. In many ways, I was sort of new in Roundup, too, and therefore, like Blanche DuBois, we had to depend a little on the "kindness of strangers," and believe me, a little goes a long way.

Richard and I joined the Kendalls. A jeweled, black tulle snood covered Sparky's streaked hair and she was wearing trousers. I wondered if my mother had seen her.

"Don't you love this party?" Sparky said.

I nodded.

"It brings back so many memories. It always makes me think of my mother."

"Get a load of that one," Tom said to Richard.

"Which one?"

"The fat one in that scary, ruffly, lacy job that has the big muttonchop sleeves. Her arms look like ham hocks," Tom said. "Reminds me of Sparky."

"What are you talking about?" Richard said. "Sparky's tiny."

Sparky and I started laughing.

"Lilly's and my mother had taken us to New York in August to get our dresses, just before we left for college," Sparky told him. "And we were both so cute and thin. And we got the most beautiful gowns. But unfortunately, during my first fall term at Stanford, first time away from home, I gained about forty pounds eating doughnuts in the Student Union cafeteria. And when I lumbered into the house for Christmas vacation, my mother went absolutely crazy. She spent the five days before the Ball in complete hysterics—I think she must have taken at least a thousand Miltowns—while the seamstress ripped the whole dress apart and stitched a flounce over the bodice and sewed in these gigantic panels. It was awful. My fairy-tale dress looked like some kind of Mexican wedding cake." She looked at the young woman who had started the conversation. "I know that poor girl just feels like killing herself."

"Tell me what Lilly was like," Richard said.

Fortunately, Sparky could not answer because we were interrupted by a man's raised voice coming from one of the suites. "Goddamn you," he shouted angrily. "You are such a bitch. You take that back."

"Never, never, never," a woman shrieked.

Next came the sounds of a slap, a scream and a thud, which were immediately followed by a very red-faced Daniel French racing out of the door, pushing his way through the groups of fathers. The fast-moving blur of Harry von Singen and Fancy flew by next. She had her hand over her cheek and was crying and Harry had one arm around her shoulder and the other around her front, shielding her from view as they rushed down the hall away from the startled crowd. His eye caught mine and I knew if he could have killed me at that moment, he would have done so, with great joy. He indicated with a jerk of his head that I should get into the suite, just as a loud wail emerged from the open door.

"I can't stand this anymore," Lulu wept, with her hands covering her face. She stood in the center of the room, where all her friends circled her like virgins circling Aphrodite, but no one got close.

I went to her. "Come on," I said and put my arm around her and led her into the bathroom, where I shooed out a couple of girls and closed and locked the door.

Lulu completely dissolved in my arms. "Oh please, Aunt Lilly. You've got to make her stop. Why can't she act like a grown-up? Just for tonight? She called Uncle Daniel the most terrible names.

Sometimes I think they're going to kill each other."

"I'm so sorry," I said. "So sorry."

In a few minutes, she began to pull herself together, and shortly after that, with the help of a lot of cold water, several deep breaths and completely fresh makeup, she was back to normal.

"Who's your best friend?" I asked her. "Leonie?"

Lulu nodded and lit a cigarette with trembling fingers.

"You wait here," I said. "I'll get her. They're about to start getting everyone squared away. Do you want me to stay with you, or get your Uncle Daniel?"

"See if you can get Harry, please. Mother and Uncle Daniel are drunk."

Chapter Twenty-nine

At seven forty-five, the Roundup Symphony Orchestra jumped with both feet into the "Theme from Star Wars." The music thundered through the atrium, sending chills up everyone's spine. Everyone, that is, except those aesthetes who bitched that the Ball had turned the orchestra into nothing but a band, and Dorothy Mae Jenkins, the Ball Committee member charged with organizing the debutantes and their fathers into proper order for the eight-o'clock presentation.

Dorothy Mae Jenkins had always been in charge of the lineup, even when I was a debutante, and she wore the same stiff, navy-blue taffeta dress and white kid gloves every year. Her navy-blue, bugle-beaded handbag dangled from the crook in her arm and she carried a clipboard and a whistle, and she didn't take any crap from anybody.

At seven fifty-five, the orchestra segued from "Star Wars" into "The Syncopated Clock"—don't ask me how—and the excitement mounted higher as guests juggled politely for good viewing space.

Richard had staked out a perfect vantage point by the second-floor railing, halfway between the top of the stairs and the receiving line, in the midst of a crowd of old friends, most of whom I hadn't seen since I moved back.

Harry joined us, clearly relieved to be free of Fancy for a while. "I'm considering withholding the other half of your fee," he grumbled semi-good-naturedly.

"I don't blame you," I told him.

Down below, on the lobby floor, the debutantes' mothers, who hold nothing back in the gown- and jewelry department—I mean, if you don't wear it all tonight, exactly when would you wear it, then?—were being assembled on a riser behind where the receiving line would stand. When I was younger, I used to look at all those mothers and think they looked like a bunch of old bats and busybodies, but now I knew some of them, we'd grown up together, and I thought they looked pretty terrific.

I studied Fancy, who was chatty and ebullient with the other women, and wondered if maybe she and Harry had planned it all together. Or Joan, who stood at the opposite end of the riser, a pleasant expression on her face, but she was really outside the close group of most of the mothers, which I don't think bothered her in the slightest.

If you move to a new town and bring a lot of money, then, on the surface, it's easy to get invited to all the best parties and openings and join influential tables at benefits, but don't expect to make friends anytime soon. Especially if you waltz in and six months later your daughter is invited to make her debut. Some of these mothers slave on the committee for years to make certain their daughters are invited to curtsey, so even if they're polite and gracious—which in Roundup, believe me, sometimes we don't even make the effort to be—they're still resentful and suspicious and will probably talk about you behind your back for the rest of your life. They take it very seriously, because it anchors you at a specific social level in the community. Sometimes I think they get a little carried away. But then, on the other hand, maybe I don't take it all seriously enough, because I take it for granted.

At precisely eight o'clock, the music stopped. The conductor,

Maestro Williams, paused, drew himself up, raised his arms and baton, turned his head slowly from side to side, surveying the musicians and quieting the crowd, and then, almost as though without warning, even though everyone was expecting it, exploded the orchestra into a blasting, blazing, hair-raising, spine-tingling, deafening version of the "Theme from *The Magnificent Seven*." Whoa. The crowd hollered and clapped and whistled and cheered as the receiving line—my parents, the symphony chairman and her husband, and the Ball chairman and her husband—took their places on the opposite side of the lobby from the bottom of the wide circling staircase, and prepared to receive the young ladies of Roundup into Society.

During the ceremony, the guests lean over the balconies and crowd the edges of the main floor to watch each girl, who carries a large spray of white lilies tied with a white satin ribbon, take her father's arm and pause at the landing while her family background and her college are read. Called out, actually, by Westy Rhodes, the "Voice of the All-Western Rodeo Cowboys' Association."

Even though, at the Ball, Westy never actually says, "In chute number one, Midnight, the WRCA 1994 Champion Bucking Horse, out of Millie-Be-Good by Sawtooth, ridden by Tex Howard from Miles City, top money winner in his last ten outings," but says, "Miss Patricia Wilcox van Buren, a freshman at Scripps College, daughter of Mr. and Mrs. Newell Anthony van Buren the Third, and granddaughter of Mr. and Mrs. Wainwright Wilcox and Mrs. Newell Anthony van Buren, Jr., and the late Mr. van Buren, is presented by her father, Mr. van Buren. Her escorts are Gerald Thompson Nicholson, Jr., and her brother Newell Anthony van Buren the Fourth. Miss van Buren." The impression is the same. It still comes out sounding like, "AND IN CHUTE NUMBER ONE . . ."

After Westy calls out all about the girl and her family, she and her father descend the final eight steps, where they are joined by her two escorts. The foursome then proceeds slowly across the floor to the receiving line, where the debutante dips into a deep curtsey and her father and escorts bow. And everybody smiles and nods.

Another thing we do in Roundup that would be considered extremely déclassé elsewhere and sends my mother into absolute orbit, is clap and yell and whistle as each girl curtseys. My mother smiles graciously at each debutante and her father and then immediately scowls up at all the swells in the balconies, hoping to frown them into silence and good manners, as my father pats her arm. Happens every single time. "People should know better," she always bitches. "This isn't a cattle auction, it's a very lovely evening." I agree it's a lovely evening, but face it, it's not exactly the Court of St. James's. I don't tell that to my mother, though.

Once the trumpet fanfare stopped reverberating, Westy tapped his finger on the microphone to make sure it was hooked up, and the presentations began.

Dayton Babcock shouldered his way through the three-deep crowd to stand next to me, pulling his date along with him. At a glance, she appeared to be a girl whose age and IQ were about the same: twenty-five. She had a friendly, blank smile, and wore a tight, sequined dress.

"Meet Jackie Hunter," he shouted over the noise and gestured over his shoulder with his chin. "She's a senior at Harvard Law."

"Sure, Dayton," I said.

"No, really, she is. She's fucking brilliant. Head of the *Law Review*."

"Uh-huh."

"Well, I'll tell you one thing, she's got a hell of a lot more on the ball than that bitch Fancy. Mark my words, this stuff will catch up with her one of these days. She'll pay big time."

"Uh-huh," I said, as the daughter of an old classmate of mine curtseyed. She looked just like her father.

"Look," he tried to whisper to me because Harry was standing on Richard's other side, "I know she and Harry are the ones who put the bullet between Rita's eyes. I've heard them talk about it hundreds of times on these trips we all took together. Plan out how they were going to do it."

"Dayton," I said. "why don't you just shut up for a few minutes? I'm trying to watch."

"Oh, look," he said and pointed, "here comes that loser daughter of hers and that fairy of an uncle. I wonder if they share their undies."

Richard reached around behind me and grabbed Dayton by the scruff of his neck, tightening his collar and cutting off his wind. "Beat it, Babcock," he said and hurled him back against the wall.

"HEY!" Dayton yelled to the row of backs that had opened like the Red Sea for his ejection and closed against him just as swiftly. "Did you see that? He hit me."

No one paid any attention.

Then the presentation was done and the orchestra held forth with "The Little Heifer Waltz," and the fathers and daughters began to twirl and move, just as they'd been practicing for three days non-stop. The girls' faces said it all. Blushing, happy, all grown up, holding their fathers all to themselves, even if just for a waltz. The crowd around us began to disperse.

Harry and Richard and I watched Lulu and Daniel move gracefully around the white marble floor, both beaming and excited, the contretemps forgotten and her mother nowhere in sight. I pointed out Joan Chamberlain's daughter dancing with Dickie: her third, and newest, stepfather. She was doing her best to be poised and polite, but it was easy to tell she couldn't wait to get away from him, that she would give anything to be somewhere else.

"That's kind of sad," I said to Richard. "I'm sorry for her."

"You know," Richard said, "when people get divorced, no matter how civilized they are, and no matter how much they say they're still friends, and everything's fine, it never really is. Things like debuts or weddings or birthdays, anywhere that everyone has to gather and comport themselves with control and dignity, resurrect all those old feelings, all those old reasons why the rift and the wounds are so deep and never truly heal. No matter how many feet of concrete you pour on the cuts, they're always open, and everybody's just as vulnerable as hell. All the time."

Chapter Thirty

You all know," announced Fancy, not yet tipsy enough to be called drunk, "our ball is much nicer than the one in Denver. Although they are similar in many ways."

"Oh? What makes you say that?" asked my mother, who snapped out her starched napkin and laid it carefully in her lap. She had always been very fond of Fancy, and was delighted when I told her several days earlier that I'd invited her and Harry to join our table. "Aristocracy always adds a little zip, doesn't it?" she'd said. "And Fancy's such a glamour girl. She is still on the wagon, isn't she?" But unfortunately, Mother now had a serious case of the jaws because Fancy had obviously fallen *off* the wagon, and the conversation was as unstable as nitro. Do I need to say that it was all my fault?

I don't know how zippy and glamorous we looked, but after the presentation the ten of us—my parents, Christian and Mimi, Elias and Ellen, Harry and Fancy, and Richard and I—gathered in the Grand's formal dining room adjacent to the lobby. Our table was set perfectly with crisp white linens and a Christmassy centerpiece of red poinsettias entwined with curled French golden ribbons and a dozen votive candles, which made us all look tanned and as though we'd recently had our faces lifted. Each place glistened with cut-crystal wine-, champagne- and water glasses and polished silver that shot sparkling prisms of candlelight off to dance in our shining eyes.

A ten-piece orchestra played big-band tunes from the corner bandstand beyond the small dance floor, while six or seven couples, most of them older—which used to mean in their forties, and now, to me, anyway, means in their nineties or hundreds—twirled around. The ladies' chiffon skirts sailed out behind them and light flashed off their jewelry and the saxophone and trumpet.

Waiters served the first course, a cocktail of small shrimp mixed with red sauce and crunchy celery mounded on a bed of fresh butter lettuce, and poured glasses of white burgundy.

"Well, for one thing," said Fancy, who was seated between my father and Christian, and who chose to forgo the food in favor of more champagne, "we charge more for our ball so we can have fewer people, but the symphony still gets a big gift, and our dinner can be nice, like this. Theirs is like a fraternity feed or something. Believe me, I've been. They have these long, dead-ended tables of twenty or thirty people all packed in; the tables are just smack-dab next to each other, so the waitresses just stand at the end with these gigantic, teetering trays, and pretty much sling filet mignons and whipped potatoes and haricots verts down the way."

"Now, Fancy," my mother said, "I'm sure you're making this up."

"No, it's true. I swear to God, you feel like you're in *Oliver Twist* or *David Copperfield*. And that's in the expensive dining rooms, where the committee members and the patrons sit. I declare, I can't even imagine what it must be like if you've just bought a plain ball and dinner ticket. I imagine it's something like Salisbury steak and wax beans. Of course, it's so noisy and you're just packed in there shoulder to shoulder, no one can talk at all. It's just fucking *awful*."

Mother and Harry simultaneously drew in their collective breaths and shot me death stares.

"Oh, Harry, darling." Fancy reached across Christian and my mother to pat his hand, "I know I do go on. I apologize, Mr. and Mrs. Bennett, for saying 'fuck.'"

When Fancy and I were thirteen, we went to see *Gone With the Wind* every day for two weeks. I think she'd been back a few times since then. Listening to her tonight, I felt as if we were out on the front porch of Twelve Oaks at the Wilkes's barbecue, before the war, and Harry von Singen was one of those poor sweet innocent brothers, whatever their names were, or Melanie's pathetic brother, Charles Hamilton, whom Scarlett hoodwinked. Even Richard picked up on it.

"'Ah sweah, Miss Fancy,'" he whispered to me, "you're just a fuckin' *mess.*"

I swear, she batted her eyes, but by then virtually everyone at the table was ignoring her.

"Baron," my mother said, "we're especially pleased you could be here tonight. Under the circumstances, we weren't sure you would."

"Thank you," Harry said.

"You look so very elegant this evening," she continued, admiring the crimson moiré sash that crossed his chest, and the heavy gold-and-enamel medal that hung from a wide, tri-colored ribbon around his neck. Three smaller medals on ribbons decorated his left breast pocket. "Just the way I always think a baron should look. You should dress this way all the time."

Harry laughed. "Thank you again."

"Isn't he absolutely *divine?*" said Fancy, who raised her left hand and patted her hair and we all noticed it at the same time.

"Is that an engagement ring?" my father said.

"Why, yes, it is," Fancy answered coyly, holding up her hand to display a new-potato-sized diamond. "Isn't it lovely?"

"Who's the lucky fellow?" Daddy pressed.

"Well, I really can't say." She gave Harry, who looked just as dumbstruck as the rest of us, a giggling, flirty glance. "We aren't quite ready to say anything yet."

"Good God," Mother said. "Certainly not the baron."

"What Kate means, Fancy, to you and whoever the lucky fellow is," Daddy rushed in with the shovel, "is best wishes and congratulations."

Just then, as if on cue, Dayton stepped out of the party's giddy swirl and appeared behind Fancy. He laid his hand on her shoulder, making her jump, and leaned toward her.

"What in the world do you want?" Fancy said. "You almost scared me to death."

"May I have this dance?" Dayton whispered, afraid to draw attention to himself around my father.

"Of course you may not," Fancy snapped. "I'm betrothed."

"To who?"

"Whom," my father said loudly. "Betrothed to '*whom.*'"

"None of your business," Fancy said.

"Let me just have one dance," Dayton whined.

"No, Dayton. Ask someone else."

"Like whom?" His gaze fell on me and he made his way around the table. "Lilly, may I have this dance?"

"I'm sorry, Dayton; Christian just asked me."

"You all are so goddamned mean to me." Dayton seemed close to tears. "What'd I do to deserve it? I'm going to go home and kill myself."

"I'll come load the gun," my father called to his disappearing back.

"I wish you would," my mother added.

Conversation switched from subject to subject, never getting back to Fancy's startling, phony engagement, although it lay in the middle of the table, stinking like a dead elephant, and we all talked and laughed, and from time to time I'd look at Fancy and wonder if she'd really killed Rita. And, if she had, what had become of the weapon. I mused along in my champagne haze about where I'd have put the gun if I were her. She would have been too high from the act, experiencing too much of a rush, wanting too much to savor it, to have the presence of mind to dispose of the weapon, heave it from the car window into the woods. Besides, at that particular point in time, the gun would be her accomplice, her lover, her friend, the only thing she could share the thrill with. I had to find it. Without the gun, there was no case. It led me back to Cordelia's new weapon. She'd seemed authentically surprised. Had Fancy stolen Cordelia's gun and replaced it, knowing if it were found Cordelia would be implicated?

And then I started wondering all over again if she and Harry were in it together. It didn't fit. But it didn't exactly not fit, either. Harry was a big catch for a wealthy woman. Fancy wanted a husband. Harry needed a big infusion of cash, soon, if he was going to keep the Poker Creek project on target. And as long as he was a suspect in Rita's murder, her assets, along with their joint assets, were frozen, and Fancy had more than enough ready cash. Dayton, even more than Harry, though, needed for the project to keep moving forward. I don't know how long I'd been sitting there, lost in thought, but when Harry's voice said, "Excuse me," I jumped about ten feet.

"I didn't mean to startle you, but would you care to dance?"

"I'd love it." I laughed with embarrassment, and once we were on the dance floor, I asked him what was going on with the engagement ring.

Harry shook his head. "This is the first I've heard of her marriage plans. Believe me, I didn't give it to her."

"I know," I said. "What's the latest on Poker Creek?"

"I'm going to close it. I'm not opposed to marrying rich women, but I have no intention of remaining in the real estate development business. It was Rita's deal."

"What about your investors?" I said.

"They're Dayton's problem." That remark and the attitude behind it made me uncomfortable, but I decided not to give Harry a big speech about accountability and integrity at that moment. I needed him to stay at the party.

Dinner was served: filet mignons, whipped potatoes and haricots verts. Same as Denver. Jordan Cabernet. Partygoers moved from room to room, flowing around the tables like scented, sparkling streams, pausing to say, "How nice to see you," and "Merry Christmas."

"Fancy," Mother blurted out—the wine had misted all of our

judgments to some degree—"you simply must tell us who you're engaged to."

"Well"—Fancy's eyes suddenly flooded—"I especially can't say anything right now because Lilly thinks I'm the one who murdered Rita." And she burst into tears.

"Lilly!" Mother scolded. "How could you?"

"Mother," I said coldly, not even bothering to try and hide my annoyance, "this is not your affair." I turned to my father. "Why don't you and Mother go dance for a minute or two?"

"Good idea." He was on his feet instantly and had Mother out of her chair and on the dance floor before she even knew what was going on.

"I don't want to go to prison," Fancy wept. "I'd kill myself first." She washed down a pill with her champagne. "I swear to God I didn't do it, Lilly. But I've been drinking so much lately, I just don't know anymore. I just can't say." She took a handkerchief out of her purse and blew her nose and was dabbing carefully around her eyes when Cordelia showed up to say hello.

"Fancy," she said after all the greetings, "Lulu is this year's most beautiful debutante—there is no question about it. She is exquisite. So much more sophisticated than the other girls. You must be so proud."

"Why, thank you. What a sweet thing to say, but I was just about to tell you the same thing about Mary Pat; I think she's simply love-ly." Fancy had her game face back in place, and seeing Cordelia seemed to perk her up a little. "Yes, I suppose I am proud of Lulu." She patted her lips with her napkin, making sure that Cordelia would see the diamond. "Are you going to the powder room?"

"Yes," Cordelia said. "Do you want to come with me?"

"Yes. I think I will. If you all will excuse us." Fancy stood up, as did the men at the table. "Did you see my ring?" she said as they left.

"Yes," Cordelia said. "Who gave it to you?"

"It's supposed to be a secret, but . . ." She whispered into Cordelia's ear and Cordelia turned quickly and gave Harry a hard look as they left.

The mood at our table elevated instantly with Fancy gone, even temporarily, as though a heavy shroud had been lifted. Richard danced with Mimi, and Daddy danced with Ellen, and I danced with Christian. Elias, Mother and Harry remained at the table, smoking cigarettes and laughing loudly. Finally, I got to dance with Richard just before dessert. There was still no sign of Fancy.

"Jeez," I said, "I didn't think I'd ever get to dance with you. I think you're taking this good-manners thing a little too far."

"You aren't having a little tantrum, are you?" He grinned.

"Good heavens, no." I laughed. "Well, maybe a little bit." After two smooth swirls I forgot to pout anymore and just sailed along.

Dessert was served: meringue cups with vanilla ice cream and hot praline sauce. We had just taken our first bite when several ear-piercing screams echoed throughout the lobby, punctuated by a loud thump. For a moment the entire building was completely silent, and then it was bedlam.

I flew to my feet so fast, my chair knocked over the man behind me, and I raced out of the dining room into the Rotunda. Fancy French lay in the very center of the marble floor, front-right-side down, dead. From a distance, she looked as if she were sleeping. Satin shoes peeked from beneath her strapless ice-blue satin ball gown, and her arms were crooked, one above her head and the other in front of her face. Up close, they were broken and splayed. Small bones were visible in her hands and right arm. Her skull had cracked open and blood ran from it through her blond hair into a small, growing pool. The left side of her face was surprisingly undamaged and seemed to gape in horror at her ring finger. The diamond glittered like ice.

I knelt beside her and looked up into the ten-story atrium. Dozens of faces returned my gaze from the balconies. Police and security guards ringed the Rotunda floor, and the hotel manager, with a series of finger snaps and hand signals, dispatched his staff to bring a number of tall, antique Chinese screens to surround the body. The privacy screens materialized so fast, I realized that jumpers into the Roundup Grand's lobby, while probably not exactly a common occurrence, were not an unknown one, either. I kept my hand on Fancy's shoulder until the paramedics arrived and made me move.

Richard stood guard over me the whole time, as I stood guard over Fancy. "Where's Lulu?" I said.

"Harry's taken her home."

Chapter Thirty-one

Thursday morning

The next morning, Richard and I got up at our usual time and went for a ride in the silent, bone-chilling dawn.

I was unsettled by Fancy's suicide, a little suspicious. Her life had rocketed out of control, and maybe, with booze and Prozac in her system to distort her reality, envisioning herself in prison was too much to bear. But I knew her pretty well, and would not have picked her as an individual with enough courage to jump. It's a bad way to go, and takes an exceptional amount of self-loathing. I tried to tell myself that I regretted we hadn't had an opportunity to bring her to trial, but there hadn't been much there to make a case against her anyway. I had been trying to intimidate her into making a mistake. But she hadn't.

The truth is, in my heart of hearts, I knew that Fancy's death wasn't the end of Rita von Singen's homicide investigation. It had only complicated it. I would have to tell my client that we were farther from the answer than ever.

Richard and I cantered slowly, side by side, up through the snowy hills, occasionally following fresh deer- and elk- and mountain-lion

tracks but finding nothing. Every now and then I'd say a little something, but I was working quietly on my theories, and besides, I
couldn't really get a word in edgewise because, after a while, when
we were more awake, Richard did not stop talking for one second
about his two sons, who were arriving tonight for Christmas break,
and the opera, which opened tomorrow night. His excitement was so
irrefutable, so inescapable, and frankly, so unavoidable—out there in
the middle of nowhere as we were—it forced murder and suicide
right out of my head.

He rode up next to me and reached over and put his arm around
me and pulled me practically out of my saddle and gave me a big
kiss. "I love you," he said.

"You do?" I laughed.

"Yes."

"I love you, too." It was true. He absolutely took my breath away.

Now this was how Christmas vacation was supposed to start.

Bright sunlight and the rich smells of fresh, hot coffee and frying
sausages filled the house by the time we got back, and Richard went
directly into the kitchen and put his arm around Celestina's shoulders. "Mi híjos esta noche," he said.

"Sí." Celestina gave him a big smile. "Yo sé."

It didn't matter that his "híjos" were Princeton men. They were
his little boys and they were coming to town for Christmas. That
was all that mattered.

The phone calls started just about the same instant that Celestina
put breakfast on the table: huevos rancheros, chorizo sausages, fresh
hot tortillas with butter and honey.

"I would like it if you would stop by my pied-à-terre for coffee
this morning," Harry said. "There are some issues I'd like to review."

"Great," I said. "I'll be there about ten." We hung up. "Did you
know that we have pieds-à-terre in Roundup now?" I said to
Richard. "Can you believe it?"

He nodded and laughed. "I saw someone's maid at a bus stop the other day wearing a Louis Vuitton fishing vest. Think it might have been counterfeit?" He took a big bite of egg and salsa. "Wow! These huevos are hot. Want to split a beer?"

"Sure. Why not? It's almost seven."

Daniel called and asked to speak to Lulu.

"Lulu?" I said.

"She left me a message that she had gone to your house. I'll bet she's still asleep, isn't she? Well, just have her give me a call when she wakes up. You probably gave her a sedative or something, didn't you? I'll tell you, I could use one. I am just in a state here this morning. The telephone has not stopped. I'm so glad Lulu's with you, I just don't think I could handle her today. I mean, my God, right there in front of all of us. That is not the way Fancy and I were raised to do. I'm so glad our mama didn't live to see it—she would have been absolutely mortified. As am I."

"I'll have Lulu call you," I said and hung up.

"Who was that?" Richard asked.

"Daniel looking for Lulu. She told him she was here."

"Where is she?"

"No idea," I said. "It sort of bothers me, though. I hope she's all right."

The phone rang again. I answered.

"DID YOU SEE THAT MESS?" Dayton yelled. I hung up.

"Dayton?" Richard guessed.

"Yup. Are you going to eat that sausage?"

"Yup."

The next call was for Richard. He listened carefully. "All right," he said into the receiver. "Do you think it's legitimate?" He listened some more. "I see. Okay. Call her back and tell her you've spoken with me, and that I'll come to see her as soon as I get to town, and that I have asked my physician to come see her right now, and that from the sounds of it, he'll probably want to hospitalize her for a few days. One more thing. Call my secretary and have her get a large bouquet over there ASAP with a card from Augusta saying not to worry, that everything will be fine and she'll hold down the fort as best she can till she's back on her feet. Keep me posted." He hung up.

"Diva problems?" I said.

"Amy. Eloise Scott. Gastrointestinal problems. Opening-night stuff. She'll be fine."

"Who's Augusta?"

"Her understudy. The flowers should have Eloise back on her feet in time for lunch."

Dayton called back and absolutely insisted that I drop by for a drink after lunch.

"I'll see," I said. "I have a busy day."

"That's okay," he said. "I can be quick when I want to."

"Really," I said, and hung up.

"Dayton?" Richard said.

"Yup. Wants me to come by for a drink. What a wasted life. It's pathetic."

Mother called to bitch about the whole thing and so did Cordelia, who invited me to meet her at Tutto Bene for lunch.

"I'd love to."

Richard kissed me good-bye. "Don't forget to meet me at the theater at six. The boys land at seven-thirty."

"I'll be there."

Christian honked his horn out front, and Richard raced out and jumped into the pickup and they roared off to the chopper and Richard flew off to town to spend the day with his other sweethearts, Ada, that sweet little cattle baron's daughter and her wild, crazy and jealous neighbor, Amy, who now had an upset tummy.

He said he loved me. Can you believe it?

I got cleaned up and went to the office. Elias was already there, having coffee with Linda. She had her hair pulled back with a big clamp. I could tell Elias was evaluating her, trying to decide whether, if he took off her big, thick glasses and yanked the barrette from her gray hair, and tossed her on the desk and kissed her, she would turn into a movie star. I think she was probably thinking that if she took her glasses off and kissed him, she wouldn't be able to see he was so fat. This seemed, to me, a match made in heaven.

"Go for it," I whispered to Elias as I passed him on my way into my office. They both followed me. He was blushing like crazy. "Has the registration report come in yet on Cordelia Hamilton's gun?" I said to Linda.

She shook her head.

"Would you call and see what the holdup is? Ask them to fax it right away."

"You bet." She handed me yesterday's mail and faxes. "We had two interesting queries: one from North Carolina, missing person; and one from Colorado, real estate fraud."

"Thanks." I took the stack of papers from her. Real estate rip-offs are common everywhere, but especially in the West, where we think we can dupe the out-of-towners, but it's almost always the other way around. We're just too damn naive out here. "What are you up to today?" I asked Elias.

He shook his head. "Nothing much. Kind of depressed about Fancy."

"Chief Lewis is on the phone," Linda called from the other room.

"Morning, Jack," I said.

"I'm at CSL, at the morgue. Come on by."

"I'm on my way." We hung up and I put my jacket and dark glasses back on. "Call me as soon as that registration report comes through," I said to Linda. "And, Elias, will you get a little more information on those two queries? Thanks. Bye."

Elias needed a couple of assignments. Winters are indescribably long for ranchers. They get bored and depressed. Even at Christmastime.

Christ and St. Luke's Hospital had been built around the turn of the century in the elegant style of huge, old red brick American hospitals with their big windows and porticoes and white trim. Somehow, over the years, the hospital's board of directors, a classy blend of Roundup business- and civic leaders, five nuns, and a couple of doctors, had bucked the city's whacked-out architectural misadventurism and managed to keep the institution looking like itself. They had added a number of buildings, but done something unthinkable: they were all in the same architectural style. Wow. What a concept. The result was a graceful, beautiful complex of classical structures that inspired confidence in those who entered them. That's what patients said, anyway. And they are the important part, even though the insurance companies want us to think that *they* are the important part.

Christ and St. Luke's is the main medical center—including major emergency, trauma- and indigent care—for a big piece of Wyoming; consequently, the morgue is always busy. This morning was no exception, especially since it was close to Christmas, when people drink more than they should and have more crack-ups than usual.

I pulled into the official-business parking spaces by the emergency entrance at the rear of the main building and went in.

"Marshal Bennett." I showed the receptionist my badge, but before she could answer, Jack stuck his head out of one of the swinging doors. "We're in here." He motioned with his arm.

Examining corpses is not my favorite thing in the world to do, especially when the corpse is that of someone who'd been a friend and who'd been very beautiful and whose skull and face were now completely smashed in on one side. It's usually never quite as bad as I think it's going to be, but it definitely stays with me longer than I'd like it to. Fancy was covered by a sheet, and by the looks of her form beneath it, she was lying on her stomach, damaged right side of her face down, undamaged side up, just the way she landed.

"What's up?" I said to Jack after greeting Dr. Leavy, the pathologist.

Dr. Leavy pulled the sheet back and I saw that she had shaved the back of Fancy's head, revealing a small gash and a contusion to her skull and brain, slightly above and behind her left ear.

We all studied it silently for a few moments, just long enough for a yawning black hole of self-reproach to open in my stomach. I'd been on the wrong track.

"Is that enough to cause death?" I asked Dr. Leavy.

"No question," she said. "I won't know for a while if it *is* what caused her death, but the blunt trauma would certainly have been sufficient. It's perfectly placed in one of the skull's most vulnerable points."

I leaned over and examined the gash more closely. It was about two inches long, and deep. "Sure looks like the edge of a gun butt," I said to Jack.

He nodded. "That's what I think."

"See this secondary bruising?" Dr. Leavy pointed. "That could be the result of the impact of the balance of the handle."

"Is there anything else?" I asked her.

"No." She pulled the sheet back over Fancy. "Not so far. Her liver was a mess."

"That's no surprise," I said. "I hope you never get a look at mine. Thanks." I followed Jack into the corridor, where we stopped at the coffee table.

"This debutante business is more serious than I've been giving it credit for," Jack cracked as he stirred some Coffeemate and two sugars into his cup. "You rich folks play hardball."

I laughed. I don't know why. My whole case had just evaporated. I had zilch.

"Where does this put us?" Jack said.

"I don't know about you," I said, "but at least from my client's point of view, I know this is one he had nothing to do with, because he was talking to my mother at the time."

"Do you think the two are related?"

"Absolutely," I said. "But we're back at square one because I was pretty sure that Fancy was the one who'd murdered Rita von Singen."

Jack nodded his head and didn't say anything for a minute. "You know, Lilly, I never thought I'd say this, but I'm glad you're on this case and I want you to stay on it. You know this world, I don't. Your insight and access mean a lot."

Well, praise the Lord. The nose of the camel was now under the tent.

"Thanks," I said calmly. "I appreciate the vote of confidence. A lot of Ball guests book rooms at the Grand for the night," I told him. "Let's see who they were."

"Evan's over there meeting with them right now."

Evan. That must be his dithery little aide whose name I never can remember.

"Tell me," I said. "Have you come up with anything at all on the man who tried to run me off the road?"

Jack shook his head. "The guy was completely toasted," he said, and then paused for dramatic effect. "And had false teeth."

"Great."

I told Jack I'd stay in touch, and moments later stood squinting in the sun next to my car and pulled my jacket closed. Baby had her head and front paws hanging out the window and looked at me expectantly, tail wagging. Ready to go, wherever it was. I couldn't help but smile.

"Well," I said to her, "between Fancy's suicide/murder and our burned-to-a-crisp assassin's dentures, our day is off to a very interesting start. And it's only ten o'clock."

Baby barked several times. Let's go.

Chapter Thirty-two

My plan was to go directly to Harry's from the morgue. Linda reached me in the car.

"Two things," she said. "There was a call from Santa Bianca, Chief Inspector Borden. Wanted to let you know that Bobby Melhado was paroled from San Quentin last Friday. And the registration report on the Glock nineteen found in Cordelia Hamilton's car indicates it was purchased on Saturday at North's Sporting Goods on Broadway, but not by Mrs. Hamilton."

"By whom?" I said. My skin was prickling.

"Joan Chamberlain."

I took a deep breath. "Okay, thanks. Do me a favor. Call Mrs. Hamilton and tell her I can't meet her for lunch. And then call Inspector Borden back and tell him Bobby Melhado is dead. That he died while trying to run me off the highway."

We hung up. One mystery solved. One deepened.

Bobby Melhado was a Portuguese-American thug, a tough-talking, macho, Mr.-Big-Shot, gang leader, whom I'd apprehended eight years ago. The charges against him, reduced on a plea bargain from murder one to manslaughter, had put him out of business only very temporarily—he should have been executed—and cost him and his gang millions in drug cash flow. He spent his whole time in prison bragging about how he, personally, would get even with me and made sure I heard about it through every possible channel. Well, he'd cooked to death at the bottom of a frozen, desolate ravine in Wyoming, and I hadn't. The best-laid plans, and all that.

"Better luck next time, Bobby," I said out loud. "I guess I won that damn argument."

I needed to think. Needed to make some notes. And since it was a beautiful day, blindingly bright, and warm in the sun, I knew just where to go: the country club. I pulled into the parking lot and drove to the far end by the tennis courts and parked beneath a couple of big elm trees, their gray branches stripped of leaves, and stark for winter. Baby took off over the snowy golf course, a thrill that was so strictly forbidden that it practically had shoot-to-kill status, but I thought what the hell, it's early and no one's going to be playing golf today, anyway. I walked along the golf-cart path and thought about Rita and Fancy. After a while, I sat down on a bench in the sun and took out my notebook and laid the whole thing out.

The murder of the two socialites in five days was possibly not coincidental, but only wildly so. They were connected. By what? Harry and Dayton, for starters. And money, of course. Lots of money. And lots of sex. Someone had lured, or taken, or invited, or forced Fancy upstairs. Was it because she'd announced some kind of ersatz engagement? To Harry? Had someone else given her the ring? Or was it one she'd already owned, her mother's, maybe? Had she been abducted at gun point? Did they take the elevator? Did she think she was going for an adventure with a friend?

I'd not given Joan Chamberlain serious consideration as a suspect, because she portrayed such a predictable personality. She was so wedded to propriety, that picturing her as a murderess was like trying to picture my mother as one. They were both, to be sure, killers, but their weapons were their tongues and their disdainful looks, their wrath and their withering scorn. But actually to take a life? Well, my dear, it simply wasn't done. So, it was very difficult for me to place Joan in that role, but now I did. She wouldn't need to kill any of these people to get Harry. She had a proven track record of her ability to attract rich husbands without having to resort to murder. Well, I didn't really know that, did I? Maybe they—or all their previous wives—were dead. Maybe this was her modus. New towns. New husbands. She was cool and aggressive, and definitely had her own agenda. Maybe she wasn't like herself at all, maybe she had that secret, fatal flaw that forced her to places most of the rest of us chose not to go.

It would be interesting to see what Jack Lewis turned up on who had booked rooms at the hotel. Maybe Fancy was going for a secret rendezvous with her fabricated fiancé. When I talked to Cordelia earlier that morning, she said Fancy had still been in the ladies' room when she'd left, and that Fancy seemed upset about something that she didn't want to talk about, and had insisted that she would be fine and that Cordelia should go. So she had, and now she felt terrible, felt she should have stayed and probably saved Fancy's life.

"Spare me your recriminations," I'd said to her. "Tell them to someone who will believe you."

Robbery wasn't the motive. That big diamond ring, as well as all the rest of Fancy's jewelry, was there. The murderer had gone out of his or her way to make it appear to be a suicide.

Yes, I concluded as I pulled my gloves back on and whistled for the dog, the motive was love of Harry, because virtually every single one of these people had more than enough money. None of them was going to kill for a few extra million.

Did Daniel love him that much? But the bigger question was: Did Harry love Daniel at all? Maybe Daniel was Harry's secret lover. At Rita's funeral, Harry'd denied any interest in men, and knowing the little I did of Harry von Singen, I would be surprised to find out that he was gay. But maybe that was just wishful thinking. The fact is, you just never know. Frankly, I think a lot of men are saying they're gay to cop out.

Plus—and a lot of women will know exactly what I'm talking

about—a fabulously handsome, rich, charming, gay man can be incredibly compelling to a red-blooded woman. "Rich, handsome and charming" being the operative words. The possibility that you may help him see the light—rescue him from his sorry, fallen state—is a little outré, very naughty, thrillingly erotic. *And* (I speak with great authority on this subject after exhaustive research) it *never* works and is not worth the effort. Much more fun to think about.

My mind raced with possibilities, like a hamster on a wheel, as I drove along. Harry, Daniel, Joan, Cordelia. And none of them made conclusive sense. And yet they all did. And then there was Dayton with his Poker Creek project. Money. Love. Jealousy. Power. Around and around.

> *Sleigh bells jingling,*
> *ring-ting-ting-a-ling, too.*

I drove downtown to the Federal Courthouse, where I picked up a couple of search warrants from Judge Fullerton: for the premises of Daniel French and Joan Chamberlain.

Between being in love with Richard and having a double homicide on my hands that Jack Lewis admitted he needed my help to solve, this was shaping up to be the best Christmas I'd had in years. Maybe ever.

Chapter Thirty-three

*H*arry's apartment was hardly what I would call a pied-à-terre. According to the doorman, a friendly young fellow in formal green livery, it was a mansion taking up the two top floors of an old lime-stone-trimmed Beaux Arts building close to downtown.

Now an apartment house with a doorman is no big deal, except in Roundup, Wyoming. I'll bet when I left for Santa Bianca twenty years ago, there wasn't a single one. Now, although we have a few, they are few enough that people still always refer to them as "Oh, is that one of those ones with a doorman?" Sometimes they call them "concierges," but in Roundup we pronounce it "kon-see-arge," with the accent on the "arge," as in "barge."

"Who shall I tell him wants to see him?" the fellow said.

"Lilly Bennett," I told him. "He's expecting me."

"Okay, Lilly." He shook my hand as though we were lifetime friends. "I'm Bill. You go on ahead up and I'll tell him to keep an eye out. HEY, TEDDY," he suddenly yelled down the long corridor toward the elevator. "GOT A CUSTOMER."

Roundup's small, hearty cadre of friendly, enthusiastic doormen probably wouldn't last long in New York City or San Francisco. As a matter of fact, they would simply get eaten alive. Our guys could walk the walk, but they couldn't exactly talk the talk. We're just too damn congenial out west, just too damn equal, and we have virtually no understanding of deference or service. Drives me nuts. But I will say in our favor that we will get involved, step up to the plate. You're in trouble? Ask a westerner for help. You'll get it. If we really think you need it. But of course, we're a lot tougher than most people, so trouble and needing help become relative things. But then, on the other hand, we aren't as tough as New Englanders. Those Yankees are Tough. I think it gets right back to the climate issue I was talking about earlier. They have all those rocks in New England. And those gunmetal-gray winters.

Bill held open the ornate glass-and-wrought-iron interior doors and directed me up a short staircase and down the wide corridor whose mirrored walls were crowned with deeply carved, gleaming white moldings. A red-and-navy Persian runner covered the marble floor, leading the way to an old-fashioned gold-and-wrought-iron elevator cage, inside of which Teddy—a tiny five-hundred-year-old man in a green uniform with gold-braid trim and shiny buttons and enormous feet in spit-polished black lace-up boots—sat on the little fold-down seat, staring out the door. He looked as if he were dead, but stood up when I entered. I thought for a second I was going to have to catch him. Teddy waited quietly for my instructions, his eyes fixed straight ahead.

"Baron von Singen's apartment, please," I said.

"Yes, ma'am." His voice was very cheerful and he delivered the words in such a way, with such a tone, that it was as though he were warning: "Okay, but you'd better hold on tight 'cause this is going to be a rough, fast ride." His teeth rattled as he slid the old door shut, slammed the reel handle over to his right and steadied himself. Off we shot—a baby could have crawled the five floors faster than we went—into what I'm sure he saw as a galactic docking station inside the baron's pad.

Now, I thought, as the elevator doors opened and I stepped into Harry's entry hall and trailed along behind a footman, *this* is what a baron's home should look like. Gleaming parquet floors, exquisite antiques, gorgeous rugs, high ceilings, walls hung with ancestors cheek by jowl with old masters, a Christmas tree decorated like a Bavarian wedding cake and a very handsome, elegant man in satin pajamas and a robe sitting at a breakfast table by the breakfast-room window, reading the headlines in the morning paper about the suicide of his mountebank fiancée, smoking a filterless cigarette and sipping coffee. The baron obviously had had company for breakfast, since the extra plates were in the process of being cleared by his valet, Carlo. I wondered if the guest would make an appearance.

"What a lovely way to begin my day—looking at such a beautiful woman," he said. "May I offer you some coffee?" His family coat of arms was embroidered on the breast pocket of his robe. Cool.

"I'd love some, thanks." I sat in a pretty Louis XIV chair which Carlo pulled out for me. "This is a spectacular apartment."

"This was Rita's and my secret understanding. No matter where we lived, she always knew that I needed my own home with my family's furnishings and staff. A place where I could go and relax into my native German and surroundings. My heritage held minimal interest for her and she knew how little her contemporary art and American Indian politics interested me. From the first day of our marriage, we made a bargain: if I was willing to look after her, escort her, never embarrass her or act disrespectfully to her, never leave her—she would see that I always had my own world to which I could escape. It was a perfect arrangement. Most people, yourself included, think I am a destitute fortune hunter, but it's not true. Oh, thank you, Carlo," he said.

The valet had placed a cup of coffee and two toasted, buttery slices of cranberry-nut bread in front of me. Harry's breakfast china was crenulated Flora Danica. If that's what he used for breakfast, I wondered what he used for lunch and tea and dinner. How high is high? You know what I mean?

"I am able to provide an extremely comfortable living for myself—this building is one of several dozen that I own all over the world—but I never had nearly enough to underwrite Rita's lifestyle, and I certainly don't have enough to save her and Dayton's country club. As you know, few people are aware of this apartment, Lilly. But I trust your discretion."

"And who else's?" I indicated the last of the other person's breakfast dishes as Carlo carried them away.

"Yes," Harry repeated. "Who else."

"Did Fancy know about it?"

"No."

"Cordelia?"

"No. No," Harry said, emphatically. "None of those ladies. Only one special one."

"The one who met you here the night Rita was murdered?"

"Yes."

"And is here now."

"Yes."

I saw movement reflected in the mirrored door and then she entered and stood like a statue in the doorway. It took me what seemed like an hour before I connected the taupe satin, lace-trimmed negligee with the face. It was Lulu French. She looked like a young goddess.

"Hello, Aunt Lilly," she said.

"Oh, my." That was all I could say.

Lulu crossed the sunny room and stood behind Harry and put her hand on his shoulder. Her long hair tumbled around her beautiful face and down her back. She was tall and slim, and as I studied the two of them, I was amazed at how perfect they looked together. Just as a baron and his young baroness ought to look. Regal. Calm. Composed. Made to be together.

My head filled with a million different things to say—few of them critical. I've always been attracted to older men myself. That is, until I got older and they became no longer older, but simply old, men. I don't think it has to do with Freudian notions, at least not in my case—I never have wanted to sleep with my father, or replace my mother. No. For me, it had to do with money and power, access and sophistication, elements that younger men don't have. Why go out with a poor man, when you can go out with a rich one? Why have a conversation about changing diapers, when you can talk about presenting a case to the Supreme Court? Remember that song, "If I were a carpenter and you were a lady, would you marry me anyway, would you have my baby?" Well, for me, the answer has always been, "Absolutely not." I suspected, watching Lulu, that it was the same for her. That Harry saw her, and treated her, as a woman, not a coed.

"Oh, my," I said again. "This could get very messy."

"I could not hide it from you any longer," Harry said. "Things with all of these crazy women have begun spinning out of control since Rita's death. They have been chasing me like hounds. I needed your help. That's why I asked you to come over."

"How did you and Lulu plan to handle this before Rita and Fancy both died so conveniently?"

"It was a matter of time for Rita." Harry lit another cigarette and crossed his legs like a monarch in a movie. "Her health was wrecked. You saw how heavy she was and how much she drank. She was miserable, always had been, and there was nothing that could make her happy. She had virtually everything she ever wanted except Sam Campbell, and she knew that as long as her father was alive, she could not do anything permanent or legal about it, that her father would disown her. When Sam married Georgia two years ago, Rita knew he had given up, and she gave up, too. She resigned herself to the fact that her father would live forever."

"How sad," I said.

"She was suffering from advanced cirrhosis," Harry continued. "The doctor told her that if she continued to drink, he could do nothing to save her."

I shook my head.

"It was her choice."

I knew Harry was telling the truth because I'd seen Rita's preliminary autopsy report. Dr. Leavy told me Rita's liver was as big as a big, yellow, slimy basketball. It explained the heavy makeup, designed to conceal her yellow skin.

"I've just come from the morgue, Lulu," I said. "I saw your mother."

She stepped around the table and sat down, and poured herself a cup of coffee. "Aunt Lilly," she said, "I suppose I loved my mother, but ever since I can remember, she's tried to destroy me. I don't know why, I never did anything to hurt her. But it has always been as though I were her enemy, her competitor. You're more of a mother to me than she ever was." She slowly stirred hot milk and sugar into the coffee and then carefully laid the spoon in the delicate saucer. "I wish I could be sorry she's gone, but I'm not. I know that you don't think that nineteen is very old, but when you grow up with a drunk, you experience more pain and humiliation in a single week than many people do in their whole lifetimes. I thought about her all night, wanting to feel something, any sorrow that she's dead, but the only thing I know is true is that Harry and I love each other, and that he has saved my life."

"Please understand," I said slowly. "I don't disapprove of you and Harry at all. In fact, I'm very pleased for you, but, there's something I need to tell you." I fidgeted a moment with my coffee cup. "Your mother didn't kill herself. She was murdered."

"What?" Harry's back straightened. "Murdered? Are you sure?" Lulu's expression registered disbelief.

"Yes. Very sure. Lulu, where were you when your mother died?"

"At the dinner table in the Cattlemen's Room with all my friends. Do you know who did it?"

"No. But I have a couple of ideas," I said, and directed my attention to Harry. "I think whoever killed Rita, and now Fancy, is trying to remove obstacles to you, Harry, so I want to stress that neither Lulu, nor you, should leave here. Especially Lulu, because if whoever this is finds out about her, well, she is the next obvious target."

They glanced at each other. "That is not a problem," he said. "She can stay here forever."

"Besides," I added, "she's already told her Uncle Daniel that she's staying with me."

"Oh, I forgot to tell you," Lulu said. "You didn't say I wasn't, did you?"

"Of course not." I fidgeted a little more and then decided the direct approach would be best. "Harry, I need to ask you an extremely personal question, and you might want to ask Lulu to leave the room."

He studied me closely. I think he knew what was coming and weighed just how open he wanted to be with his woman/child lover. "What is the nature of your question?" he asked.

"Regarding your relationships with other men."

"What sorts of relationships?" he said with humor. "Business? Golfing? Shooting? Fishing? Intimate?"

I pointed at him with my finger. "That's the one," I said.

"I've told you before. I have none. That has never been an interest of mine."

"Never?"

"That is one area in which, I can tell you unequivocally, I have never dabbled."

"A number of people have confided in me that you and Daniel French are lovers."

Lulu let out a laughing gasp. Harry reached over and patted her hand.

"A number of *jealous* people, you mean," he said. "Who has told you that? I'll tell you who: Cordelia, I'm sure, is one, because she's after me like a woman possessed. And Fancy? She accused every man who wasn't interested in her of being homosexual. Who else? Let me think. Dayton Babcock? Dayton would tell that to everyone just so he could try to hold on to Fancy and the investors in the ranch."

"What about Joan Chamberlain?"

"I've told you before, I don't even know her. She seems perfectly nice, but we've never even had a conversation. Why would she want these women dead?"

"Your guess is as good as mine," I said. "Do you think Daniel is in love with you?"

"Anything is possible. He has never said he was but . . ." Harry shrugged his shoulders with the acceptance of a person besieged with admiration. The acknowledgment that people couldn't help themselves. And the fact is, he was a little bit right.

A white-uniformed maid appeared in the door, and Lulu went over and spoke to her quietly and easily in German. I was impressed.

"Rita never cared about children." Harry noticed my watching her. "And I have always wanted a family. I think Lulu and I will have a beautiful family together."

"I think you're right," I said. "I'm truly happy for both of you." I gathered up my purse and glasses. "Again, don't let Lulu leave here until you hear from me. And Lulu, give your uncle a call. Just check in with him."

"How is he?"

"In a flap," I said.

"He's worried about how it all looks, about how embarrassed he is, isn't he?"

"Yes."

She smiled and shook her head and her eyes flooded with tears, but they didn't spill out.

Chapter Thirty-four

My next stop was Daniel French's house near the country club, and, even though I had a warrant in my pocket, I hoped he'd invite me in, not make me execute it.

But as I turned onto Spring Street I saw him, at the far end of the block, wedging himself into the passenger side of a small Jaguar convertible. They were gone by the time I got to the house. I knew his and Fancy's relationship had become acrimonious and volatile, but even so I was very surprised he was going out to lunch so cavalierly. I mean, if I died, I'd appreciate it if my brothers at least pretend they were a little sorry, for twenty-four hours anyway. He was behaving stupidly.

The traditional red brick residence, its trim gleaming in the sun, sat back from the street. A brick walk led to the front door, which was in the exact center of the house, and on the right the driveway went beneath a porte cochere, past the kitchen, to a detached garage. Daniel's white Lexus sat in the drive outside the kitchen door. The neighborhood was weekday quiet.

I sat there for a minute and thought about that house and about Fancy and Daniel and all the fun we'd had when we were young, and we all had too much money for people our age, too much sophistication, too much champagne. The Frenches gave the most beautiful parties—garden parties, Christmas parties, Easter parties, Friday-night dinner parties and Sunday brunches. Constant parties. And so many times, people seemed to stay for days, just sitting around, basking in Mr. and Mrs. French's lovely Beaufort hospitality, having lots of drinks and screaming with laughter over nothing at all. And then we all grew up and went our ways and Fancy got drunker and drunker, and Daniel gay-er and gay-er, and the French family party turned ugly and deteriorated to where we were today, several years later, with Fancy dead. Murdered. And no one really very sorry she was gone.

Did thinking about the Frenches make me feel sad? Not especially. A little nostalgic, maybe, but I believe that we all have control of our own lives, and if they're going in a direction we don't like, it's up to us to change them. I honestly believe that anything can be accomplished with prayer, positive thought and action. I'm not kidding. But some people choose to hand over their control and then complain about what they get.

I asked my mother once what, at the age of seventy-five or whatever she was at the time, was the most important thing she'd learned so far. And she had said, "Never stop fighting." Well, as we all know, she's taken that credo to new heights, but the point is, Fancy and Daniel had handed themselves over to controlling forces, and now they were paying the piper. That's the way it works.

I rang the bell. It chimed a tune through the house, but no one came to answer. I rang again. And again. I went around to the kitchen door and knocked. No one came and there didn't appear to be any lights on in the house. I looked in the car windows. The doors were unlocked. I knew even before I found it that I would discover the weapon used for both murders in Daniel's car. My breath grew short and my heart started beating hard as I snapped on some latex gloves and opened the passenger door.

The brand-new Lexus stank of stale cigarette smoke, but beneath the stench, the familiar scents of cold oiled steel and fear-induced sweat and drying blood guided my hand home.

The Glock 19 was under the passenger seat. I stuck a pencil into its barrel and lifted it out carefully and dropped it into a zip-top plastic bag. The butt was smeared with what looked like blood. Easy enough to determine. A quick search of the rest of the car and trunk revealed nothing more.

Chestnuts roasting by an open fire,
Jack Frost nipping at your nose . . .

Tony Bennett crooned as I headed back down to the station, pretty sure I knew whose chestnuts we were talking about. Naturally, Jack Lewis wanted to move on it right away and I practically had to tie him to his chair to make him understand that we had to move cautiously. That we were dealing with someone organized and sophisticated. Someone who could afford a large team of expensive lawyers. We needed to have everything lined up perfectly before we did anything.

"Just stay cool," I told him. "Nobody's going anywhere. Keep the gun and anything you discover about it away from the press. We've tested so many weapons so far in association with the von Singen case, one more will simply be routine. Maybe we won't find anything. Maybe it's chocolate on the butt. And if I'm wrong, and you get canned, you can come to work for Bennett Security. Better pay, better benefits."

He looked at me hard. "You'd better be right, Bennett," he said.

"I am."

Chapter Thirty-five

Thursday afternoon

Well, I'd missed lunch and was running out of time before Mother's Mother-and-Daughter Tea Party, an annual day-after-the-Ball occasion, but I decided to go by and see what Dayton had been so anxious to add to the scenario, since the last any of us had heard from him the night before was that he was going to go home and commit suicide. I knew it had to do with money, and I was curious to see if he'd refined his approach.

Riding the elevator up to his penthouse—scene of my deflowering—didn't affect me nearly as much as I thought it would. Not at all, in fact. I had spent so many miserable, angst-filled hours there, when he was breaking my heart all those years ago, I really had expected that just setting foot in his building would give me the heebie-jeebies. All it did was make me more conscious of how little of the day was left.

The elevator chimed sedately and the door slid open in Dayton's foyer. His black maid, Bess, greeted me, her gray cotton uniform and perfectly pressed apron just as smart and pristine as I remembered.

"Lilly." She smiled. "It has been such a long time. I haven't seen you since you were just a child."

We embraced quickly.

"Come in and make yourself comfortable. Dayton is on the phone, but I'll let him know you're here as soon as he hangs up."

"Some things never change, do they?" Meaning that Dayton never let anyone feel that he or she was nearly as important to him as the phone call or meeting or conversation he always made certain to be having when that person arrived at his home or office. Bess knew what I meant.

"Never." She shook her head. "Even when they should. I'll tell you, he never had another one as good as you. Not marrying you was the biggest mistake he ever made."

"You're right," I joked. "But he has a lot of company. Dozens of men have made the same mistake."

As we spoke, I followed her down the wide hallway, which was floored with unpolished flagstone, and hung with what I consider indescribably tasteless art.

"This stuff is just as bad as it was then," I said, passing two of Mapplethorpe's boys French-kissing each other.

"Sometimes I just have to cover my eyes," said Bess. "This is not what I was raised to consider art."

"Me neither. Good God, will you look at that."

Dayton's living room was two stories high, with the western-facing wall all glass so you could see practically from one end of the range to the other. Across from the windows was a large fireplace, and above it hung Rita's screaming Indian warrior.

We both looked at the painting for a moment in silence. It had joined several other enormous works, which I found to be equally bad. There was not one single Christmas decoration anywhere.

"What's wrong with Dayton?" I said.

Bess shook her head. "Just cover your eyes, girl, and make yourself comfortable. Soon as he's off the phone, I'll get him," Bess concluded philosophically on her way through the swinging door into the kitchen.

"No rush," I called after her.

As I recalled, the circular staircase at the far end of the living room led to Dayton's bedroom. The double doors were only partially closed and I could hear him arguing with someone on the speakerphone. I went up the stairs and stood there, eavesdropping.

"You can't do this now, Harry. I'll find more backers. Hell, you need the money just as much as I do, but the last thing you should do is put Poker Creek on the market, or into Chapter Eleven."

"The bank called this morning, on the stroke of nine, and informed me they were going to start foreclosure proceedings today. I don't know what else I can do."

"Yeah, yeah," Dayton said without interest. "Well, I've got a couple of wild cards up my sleeve, so just get us forty-eight hours. Till Monday. You know the ropes, Harry. Just call those sons of bitches and tell them. You can stall them."

"I'll try one more time," Harry said with resignation. "But I don't think they'll buy it."

"Uh-huh. Uh-huh. Listen, I've got to go. Lilly Bennett's due here any minute and I need to finish getting ready."

"Why? You don't really think she'd consider an investment?" Harry asked.

"Possible. Possible. That's my plan. This romance she's got going with Richard Jerome is a joke. Look, I know the way around Lilly's track better than anyone in the world. She'd snatch me up in a second. She's carried a torch for me all her life."

"She doesn't seem to act like it," Harry observed cryptically.

"So what? I know where all her hot buttons are. Just give me forty-eight hours. We'll get things back on track. She can save our deal out of her grocery money."

"That was a long time ago you went out with her," Harry persisted. I could tell he was trying not to laugh.

Dayton snorted. "Chicks," he said. "They don't change."

I crept back down the stairs.

Seconds later, Dayton threw open the bedroom doors and strutted out onto the upstairs balcony. He was tugging the top button of a starched white shirt closed around his thick neck. A necktie was loosely tied. "Bess," he yelled loudly down over the balcony railing.

"Yes, Dayton." She came out of the kitchen.

"Where in the hell is Lilly?"

"Well, she's been sitting in the living room for about five minutes."

Dayton turned quickly and saw me on the sofa by the fire, flipping through *Country Life* magazine, another one of his affectations. "Hey, gorgeous," he called down cheerily. "I've got a bottle of your favorite bubbly."

"Oh, good," I said.

"Bess, would you bring the champagne bucket and glasses into the living room, please? Sorry, Lilly, I'm running a little late. I've got just one more quick call."

"No problem."

I drank a glass of champagne and then left. As I stood inside the elevator, as its doors began slowly to close, and watched Dayton crash heavily down the stairs, pulling on his jacket as he came, I thought how important this tête-à-tête must have been to him, because everything about him was shipshape except his shoes. He never could seem to get them shined.

"Goddamn it. Goddamn it," he shrieked and began to run toward the elevator. "So I keep you waiting for a few minutes. I said I was sorry. Goddamn it. Goddamn it. You can't leave. You are a goddamned bitch."

Time's up.

Chapter Thirty-six

*I*t took me about five minutes to get to my parents' big old Italian Gothic English country house on the edge of a park. The drive curves through ornate wrought-iron gates that Mother had hung with large wreaths. Miles of garland were looped along the fence. Expensive debutante mother-and-daughter cars filled the small parking area and most of the driveway.

Every year, the day after the Ball, all the girls and their mothers, and various and sundry friends and committee members, gather to debrief about the party. As far as I knew, there hadn't been a time, during my lifetime anyway, when there had been more to debrief about since 1963, when Mrs. Maarkisan's Nubian slaves had hacked Mr. Maarkisan to death with their scimitars as the couple returned home from the Ball, boozy and happy, to that demented Persian-style ranch of theirs.

Plus, I was sure this was the first time the Ball had been canceled in mid-stride, and hopefully the last. I'm sure the committee was a wreck, afraid a Neanderthal or two—someone like Dayton Babcock—would insist on a refund.

The afternoon was still clear and had turned cold, making the sky distant and pale, pale blue, almost white.

Mother gave me a look the second I walked into the living room.

I knew she would. Number one, I was late, and number two, I was wearing trousers. To a tea. They were good-looking, too. Bright red wool crepe with a red silk blouse, jacket, stockings and suede shoes. I looked up at the large portrait of my great-grandmother, and her little West Highland white terrier hiding in the folds of her dress, and touched my pearls, the same ones she had on in the painting. Even though she was hanging over the fireplace at the far end of the room, she saw me, and I think she winked at me in understanding. Great-grandfather hung above the fireplace at the near end of the room, and seemed perpetually occupied keeping his eye on Great-grandmother.

"Well," Mother said with a big fake smile, "don't you look nice." She looked impeccable, as usual, in old Chanel.

"Thanks." I kissed her cheek. "Grammy agrees."

"Uh-huh. Well, you come in and greet your guests. Everyone's in a lather about Fancy."

"The tree looks magnificent."

"Oh, you think so? Your father and I had so much champagne decorating it the other night, we broke half the ornaments." She started to laugh. "Did he tell you I fell off the ladder?"

"Good God."

"It was fine. He caught me."

He always did.

The large paneled dining room swirled with wonderful scents: expensive floral and spicy perfumes, Christmas potpourri, Earl Grey tea, Colombian coffee, caramelized sugar, cucumber and watercress, butter cookies and smoked-salmon canapés; and noise: the incredible hum and chatter and squeal of twenty-four elegantly dressed matrons and their daughters.

Two senior committee members sat at either end of the long mahogany table, with glowing silver services on large sterling trays before them. One lady poured the tea, the other coffee. A maid waited behind each, passing her a fragile tea- or coffee cup, with a matching, slightly oversized saucer to hold one or two of the delicious, ladylike treats. In the center of the table, arranged around a small Christmas-tree centerpiece, on dozens of shining silver platters, and in finely woven porcelain baskets lined with crisp, Christmas-trimmed linen, lay irresistible delicacies. Little sugary and savory treats. I hadn't had anything since the cranberry bread at Harry's, and the glass of champagne at Dayton's, and I was starving, so I popped about six little smoked salmon strips, rolled up with horse-radish and cream cheese and capers, into my mouth, one right after the other. Followed by two powdered-sugar-covered butter-and-pecan Swedish wedding cookies.

"Finding enough to eat?" a voice asked behind me. It was Sparky. She and Cordelia stood there giving me the eye. They both looked sharp and sophisticated. "Do you have any idea how many calories are in each one of those?"

"Yes," I said. "And I plan to have at least a hundred more."

"Daniel called me this morning right after you and I talked," Cordelia said, "and asked me if I thought it would be in bad taste for him to come to the tea, since Lulu's mother was dead, and he'd always been more her mother, anyway."

"You've got to be kidding," Sparky gasped.

"I'm not."

"What did you tell him?" I asked.

"I said, 'Oh no, of course it would be fine, Daniel. I mean Fancy's been dead for more than twelve hours. What could be the problem?'"

"He wasn't serious, was he?" said Sparky.

Cordelia stared at her. "You know," she said, "I'm not sure."

"You ladies don't seem too broken up over Fancy," I told them.

Sparky sipped her tea. "I'm not," she said indifferently, over the rim of her cup.

Cordelia nodded. "You know, Lilly," she said, "what you said to me this morning was right on target. Really snapped me out of mouthing a bunch of platitudes. One can do just so much, and then you can't be responsible anymore. Everyone has been carrying her along for years and when she stayed sober it was okay. I mean, we were all willing to go along with the 'He ain't heavy, he's my brother' philosophy. Be a crutch. But in the last few weeks, she was drinking more and more, and popping more and more pills, and getting needier and needier, and whinier and whinier. And she became a burden no one was willing to carry."

"Except maybe Harry," I said. Over Cordelia's shoulder, I saw Joan Chamberlain and her daughter, Dorothy, arrive. They stopped to talk with some ladies on the opposite side of the table.

Cordelia gave me a cool, analytical look. "Perhaps Harry. I talked to him this morning and he's devastated. He says it's over Fancy's suicide, but I don't think he cared two shakes for her. He's about to lose the Poker Creek project. I thought I'd go up and have dinner with him tonight. See if I can offer any solace." She put a tiny crab puff in her mouth. "Maybe take him a little suitcase of cash." She grinned.

"Really?" I said.

"I'd forgotten that you and Harry were old friends." Sparky took a minuscule bite of a cracker with nothing on it. "You all knew each other before you moved here, didn't you?"

"Yes, for years. We used to vacation with them in France," Cordelia answered. "And I'll tell you the truth: I would do anything for Harry. I've been knocked out about him since the day we met."

"Opportunity may be knocking at your door," Sparky said.

"That's just what I'm thinking." Cordelia gave her mysterious, sloe-eyed smile. "Now I'm the first on his doorstep with a casserole. Not second, the way I was yesterday."

Sparky and I both laughed.

Suddenly, a commotion erupted at the front door, raised voices, and then Daniel French burst into the dining room like a swashbuckler. He rushed over to the three of us.

"Oh," he said breathlessly. "I'm so glad to find you here, you won't believe it." Someone across the room caught his eye and he appeared to forget his news. He waved at the woman with his fingers, sort of a too-da-loo wave. "Oh, hi, Nancy. You look absolutely stunning. Lilly, this tea is gorgeous. Look at this table, I've never seen anything quite like it. Is this what your mother does every year? Oh, I can't believe what I've been missing."

By then, of course, all of us had stopped whatever conversation we were having. Some of the women spoke quickly behind upheld hands, some giggled, especially the daughters, and I thought about how much more sophisticated Lulu was than any of them, and that if any of this crowd had any idea what the day's real stories were— between Fancy and Lulu—there'd be no stopping them. The chitter-chatter would flash instantaneously to full-blown chaos.

"He's sort of like a fat Richard Simmons, isn't he," Sparky said under her breath.

"Daniel, darling," Mother said. "We're all so pleased you've joined us. What was your news?"

"Oh." Daniel clapped his hands together. "I almost forgot. Well"—he paused for effect—"I just got a call, and . . ." He paused again. "It's really too awful to tell, it makes me sick at my stomach, but . . . Fancy was MURDERED."

The announcement was received with stunned silence. Everyone's jaw dropped. Sparky gasped. Cordelia blanched. Mother raised her hand to her throat and grabbed hold of her three strands of pearls. And Joan dropped her cup and saucer, which shattered into a million pieces.

"Lulu called and told me," Daniel said. "They called her from the police department or something. But now it's all over the radio. And I'm just scared to death about who's going to be next."

"What makes you think someone's going to be next?" I said.

"Well, don't you? I mean, somebody wants something. I just hope I don't have whatever they want."

"I'm sure you don't need to worry about it," Cordelia told him.

"Certainly not," my mother jumped in. "You're too cute to kill."

Daniel smiled.

The room became a wall of sound—a true melt-down situation. A maid had cleared away Joan's smashed cup and saucer and brought her another, and she appeared to have regained her composure and was talking hurriedly to her daughter.

Daniel turned to me. "You're so nice to keep Lulu. I hope you don't mind."

"Mind?" I said.

"Well, you'll see. Keeping a nineteen-year-old at your house can be absolutely mind-numbing. She said you told her she could stay as long as she wanted, but truly, Lilly, if you want to send her home, I can find someone to stay with her. As you might imagine, my house is completely out of the question."

"I don't even want to think about what all goes on at your house, Daniel," I said.

"Well, it's not that bad," he snipped.

"Lulu can stay where she is for as long as she likes."

Sparky wandered back up just as I put a little watercress sandwich in my mouth. She frowned at me and then asked Daniel who he thought had killed his sister.

He shrugged his shoulders exaggeratedly. "I don't know, but it gives me the creeps. Poor Fancy."

"Where were you when it happened?" I said.

"Me?" His eyes widened and a sheen of perspiration appeared instantly on his face.

"Yes. Where were you?"

Daniel swallowed. "Dancing."

"With whom?"

"Oh, gosh. I'm not really sure. It must have been, let me see. I waltzed with Mrs. Willis. Did you know she was Miss California? And then did a fox-trot with Mrs. Davies and that wild rumba with you, Sparky; honestly, you are so fun." He squeezed Sparky's hand. "And then a frug with Mrs. Glenn."

"A frug?" I said. "In evening clothes?"

"You are so stuffy," Daniel said.

"Who else?"

"I just can't remember. But I know I was on the dance floor in the Cheyenne Room where we had dinner. Why don't you ask around, someone will remember if she was dancing with me then. Wait, let me think. Maybe I was in the men's room. I just can't remember."

"You can remember where you were, and what you were doing, when Jack Kennedy died, but you can't remember where you were, or what you were doing, when your only sister was thrown who knows how many stories and landed in the middle of the dance floor at the Debutante Ball? Come on, Daniel."

"I swear to God, I can't." He seemed close to tears.

"Well, work on it," I said. "You're the prime suspect."

I got to the theater just as *Ada*'s final dress rehearsal was winding up. The house was filled with members of the opera and the cast's and crew's families.

One of the most distinctive elements of Richard's directing style was the amount of creativity and energy he brought to choreographing the curtain calls.

"It's that last ten percent," he had explained to me earlier. "It's the same in any business: the profit is generated by the last ten percent you're willing to invest in your own product. If you don't spend the time and money to add on the glitz and gloss and the upgrades, and make that hundred-percent investment commitment, you'll still make some money but you'll never realize your maximum potential."

The buzz on the cocktail circuit about the *Ada* curtain call was that it was "classic Jerome," and I had never in my life seen anything like it.

The little conductor jumped about six feet off the floor as he hurtled the orchestra into the commanding reprise of the Act III "Cattle Roundup and Rodeo" scene. The massive red velvet curtain swung open to a stage empty of artists—only the bison stood staring out from their pens. Then, as mounted wranglers and their dogs herded out the rest of the stock, a large, billowy cluster of golden thunderheads descended from the fly loft and hung there in the painted sky, glowing in the warm bath of spotlights. The music grew more and more powerful, and suddenly, from the rear of the house, which is where I was sitting—and I swear to God, it almost scared me to death—in a big surprise of "whoop"s and "haaw"s, a stampede of buckboards, filled with the cast singing at the top of their lungs, thundered down the aisle. The last wagon, of course, was Amy's. It was traditional for the audience to boo Amy during the curtain call because she was such a no-good type, but this year she appeared to be ready for them. She stood, a big attitude on her face and her feet firmly planted in the bed of the rocking, racing buckboard, and picked out the booers in the audience and targeted them with her bullwhip, which cracked through the air like gunshots.

Finally, everyone was on the stage, except for Rex and Ada, who had died at the end of the opera, and the music got so loud I thought the walls would tumble down, and then there they were, stepping from behind the suspended cloud bank. They waved and waved, and once the company had exited in a headlong rush for the back of the house, they took their bows, and then, as the music roared to its final crescendo and the curtains closed, Ada and Rex disappeared back into the sky.

Holy cow. It was incredible. I was covered with goose bumps.

"Thank you," Richard called to everyone, once the house lights had gone up and Rex and Ada had been safely lowered to the stage. "That was perfect. We're ready. Get a good night's sleep."

I watched him lean forward, his arms on the rail of the orchestra pit, and have a quiet conversation with the conductor. Shortly, he turned and came quickly up the aisle to me. He looked red and rattled.

"What happened?" I asked.

"Just a little temperament," he answered tightly. "Nothing we can't overcome." He draped his scarf around his neck and shrugged into his overcoat. "Let's go."

"I honestly do not know how you stand all this cry-baby bullshit."

I followed him quickly out to the street, trying to keep up with his long legs.

"There's no creativity without temperament," he said and grinned at me. "We've been doing *Ada* for almost fifty years, and if you don't give her a big boot in the hindquarters every now and then, people'll stop coming. But such a big change, something like this new curtain call, makes the artists nervous. It's almost like adding a whole fifth act. Where did you park?"

We went for cocktails at the Elliotts' and then out to the airport to pick up Richard's sons. I was excited to see them, but apprehensive, too. They'd spent Thanksgiving with us, and it was terrific, but I worried that perhaps in the intervening three weeks they'd decided they didn't like me, and would try to sabotage Richard's and my whole deal. Kids do that, you know. And we were all going to be at the ranch together for ten days.

"Don't worry." Richard read my mind as we waited at the gate. "Everything will be fine."

And then they appeared. Richard, Jr., and Charles. Tall, handsome young men. I drove us home to the ranch, because Richard was too excited to drive. He was transformed with joy—all he wanted to do was talk to them. About them. And about us.

He never left me out of the conversation for a single second.

Chapter Thirty-seven

Friday morning

*B*ennett's Fort was mobbed with children lined up like a big snake that wrapped its way all over Main Street, waiting to see Santa—Cousin Buck, of course—who had enthroned himself in a red-velvet-upholstered, silver-painted sleigh, to which he had harnessed eight little yearling calves who had reindeer antlers attached to headbands sitting in their heads, and Christmas bells on their halters. Buck spent a lot of time every fall getting these creatures accustomed to the headbands and bells, and gentling them so the children could pet them and feed them grain and hay. If the youngsters saw that the antlers were fake, they never let on; they liked believing they were reindeer. Rudolph's nose looked real because Buck put a lot of rouge on it, and told the children it wasn't lighted because it wasn't dark out, and Rudolph didn't like to turn it on in the day, because it could wear out his batteries. "But boy, oh boy," he'd say, "on Christmas Eve, when we're on our way, look out. That nose is the brightest torch you ever saw. Some planes even think it's the Christmas Star." *Ohhh*, the children would say.

Their parents, secure that their little ones were safe, guarded as they were in the line by half a dozen of Buck's wranglers, who not only kept an eye on them but also made sure they had on enough sun screen, and who handed out mugs of hot chocolate and cinnamon cider, felt comfortable taking their time in Buck's Ye Olde Christmas Shoppes. The wranglers were under the supervision of Elias, dressed as an elf. It was a sight to see. My big old brother as a big old green elf—tights, pointy shoes with bells, red cheeks, red nose and pointy hat and all. He looked adorable.

"Mrs. Hamilton is on the phone," Linda said, when I walked into the office. "And Dwight called a few minutes ago and asked if you would stop by the jail."

Cordelia and I had a quick conversation, and then Joan called. These women did not like each other even a little bit, and each did her best to convince me that she thought the other was the murderess.

"Wow," I said to Linda when I'd hung up from Joan's call. "These girls are ruthless. Remind me never to get on their bad side."

"But you're about to, aren't you?" Linda said eagerly.

"Yes." I smiled. "And I can't wait."

The little jail was full of children looking at Wyatt Earp's desk and six-shooters and listening google-eyed to one of the wranglers, who, dressed up as a deputy marshal, told them stories of Christmastime bank robberies and shoot-outs in the Old West. Dwight and the actual deputy sat at facing desks behind a wooden rail partition. The two cells lay beyond them, but only one was occupied by an individual whose face looked familiar from a number of televised courtroom appearances. Dwight and the deputy jumped to their feet when I walked in.

"Good morning, Deputy. Morning, Dwight," I said.

"Good morning, Marshal," they both answered.

"Everything going all right?"

"Yes, ma'am," the deputy said. "Our prisoner asked to see you. Says he has some information you might find useful."

"Oh?" I was instantly suspicious. "Such as?"

"He wouldn't say, ma'am. But he said he didn't need his attorney here to tell it to you."

I met with the prisoner for about fifteen minutes. He was visiting our jail long enough to testify against an old colleague, before he entered the Witness Protection Program and hopefully disappeared from our screens forever. By the time I wished him luck and left, the emerging picture of Fancy and Rita's killer had grown even more sinister.

I used the phone at the jail to make a couple of calls, including to Mack Cleveland at St. Mary's Psychiatric Hospital, to see if I could drop in a little later. Then I told Dwight and the deputy a quick good-bye and went out to find Elias.

I was so proud of Dwight. He stood there straight and bright, never taking his eyes off the deputy marshal, locked-on every second in case an order should come his way. I didn't tell him how proud I was, of course, because I would never want to embarrass him. But I did want to give him a little hug—didn't, of course—wouldn't want to test his control. Or mine.

When Buck saw Baby and me heading back down the street and through the saloon's swinging doors, he signaled to Elias and told the kiddies that Santa had to go check on the elves in the workshop and see how the toys were coming along and he'd be right back. We met at Buck's booth. Three coffees and seven double shots of Wild Turkey materialized instantly.

"What," I said. "No Jameson's?"

"Not in the winter when I have to be outside."

Only one of the doubles was for me. Buck and Elias clinked each other's glasses and tossed the whiskey back before saying another word.

"I need you to do something for me," I said to Elias.

"Okay," he said. "What?"

"I want you to check out a couple of leads back east. It'll probably just be overnight." I briefed him on the phone calls I'd received that morning, not mentioning my meeting with the prisoner. "Your flight leaves at one. Your ticket's at the airport. Don't forget to change."

"Cool," said the big, smiling, drunk elf.

St. Mary's Psychiatric Hospital—an expensive, lush retreat conveniently located equidistant between the Roundup Country Club and the Wind River Cemetery—was an island of forced calm in the midst of Christmas. The only sign that it was the holiday season was a poinsettia on the receptionist's desk.

"We go out of our way to keep things low-key this time of the year, because Christmas drives some people literally out of their minds," Mack told me, as I walked down the hall next to him in his wheelchair. He pushed open the door of his office. "Come on in; do you want anything to drink? Something nonalcoholic perhaps?"

I laughed. "Have you ever had a meeting with Buck that did not involve a shot of something?"

"Never. I don't know how he keeps things straight."

"I'm not so sure he does. But, yes, thanks, as a matter of fact, I'd love a cup of strong black coffee."

I described the murders, the suspects, the evidentiary and behavioral trails, the phone calls from Joan and Cordelia, concluding with my deductions. "I know we're dealing with some kind of sociopathic behavior," I said. "I've met enough to recognize them, but this is a little different slant, and I'm not certain that's what this is. I need a refresher course on the kind of person who pulls the wings off flies or pins butterflies to boards, and some direction on how to proceed without tipping our hand."

"A sociopath," began Mack, as he slowly stood and moved himself into his desk chair, while a grimace contorted his handsome features. "You know, this rheumatoid arthritis can get lousy sometimes. Anyway, basically, a sociopath, or extreme antisocial individual, as we now call them publicly, is an individual who has expectations of people that the people themselves are unaware of. And then, when the innocent fails to live up to the expectations, the person must get even. This sort of individual sometimes carries grudges for years and years, waiting for just the right moment to inflict revenge."

"If you were to take the behaviors I've described," I said, "and push them to extremes, what would they be?"

"They're quite complicated. Oedipus and Electra are the classic cases. But if you want quick references, Ted Bundy is a modern-day example of the extreme: a man who wanted his mother, and even though his father abandoned them, and his mother remarried, Ted always saw himself as his mother's husband and saw her as a beautiful, vulnerable, young woman. But she would never accept him as a man, as a lover." Mack sipped his tea. "Of course, she was never aware that he expected her to. So to act out his fantasy, again and again, he kidnapped those beautiful young college girls, girls he saw as being as beautiful as his mother, and he would make advances to them, which they would reject, just the way his mother did, and then he would rape them and murder them, because he would never be able to rape and murder his mother, which was what he really wanted to do, because she continually rejected him. Although she never even knew it. It continued and continued, but still, he could not get his mother to love him as a man. She loved him only as her son."

His intercom rang. "Excuse me a moment." He picked it up and listened. "Calm down, Helen," he said patiently, and with such a kind note in his voice, it made me want to tell him all my problems, except I didn't actually have any except the one I was telling him about anyway. "Everything's fine. Of course we have room for you through the first. Do you want us to come pick you up? Don't cry anymore, the car's on its way." Mack hung up. "It's like running a hotel this time of the year. Sends our cash flow through the roof." Mack grinned happily. His secretary stuck her head in the door. "Send the car over to pick up Helen Simpson," he instructed her. "She's joining us for the holidays."

"And if it's a woman?" I asked, getting back to the matter at hand.

"Aggressively antisocial females, multiple murderers, are rare but becoming slightly more common. And by common, I mean still so unusual, you can practically count them on one hand. But the setup can be the same," Mack explained. "Just remember, Lilly, the keys are always: unknown expectations, followed by unwitting rejection."

"Thanks, Mack," I said. "I think that gives me some good direction."

"One more thing, Lilly, that I know you know well, but I'm going to remind you of it anyhow: don't forget, even for a split second, that these individuals are highly intelligent, usually brilliant. That's why they get away with this behavior for years, sometimes their entire lives. To catch one, you need to outsmart, rather than outmuscle him. Or her. As you know, they're the ones who enjoy the chase with the police, and often help. They play by a whole different set of rules, and have absolutely no sense of right or wrong, only of *being* wronged." He held out his hands, palms up. "That's about it, for the short version. I know you've worked on more than your share of cases with this type of personality. As a matter of fact, you probably have more experience with them than I do."

"Never an antisocial woman, Mack."

"They're a rare, deadly breed."

"Thanks for your help," I said. "I hope you and Joanne have a very Merry Christmas."

"You're very welcome. Give your family my best. Merry Christmas," Mack said.

Now all I could do was stay cool and wait. Wait for Elias. Wait for the results of ballistics and evidence tests on the gun. The serial number had already been confirmed. It was registered to Cordelia Hamilton. It was the gun she thought she'd had in her car.

I went home, worked out, and then fixed lunch for the boys— tomato bisque with croutons, and ham-and-cheese sandwiches, sauvignon blanc. Richard had already gone to the theater.

"Do you and Dad plan to get married?" Richard, Jr., asked me.

I was ready for the question, but I didn't know the answer. "I haven't got the slightest idea," I said. "We haven't even discussed it." And changed the subject. There was no way I was going to have that discussion with Richard's sons before I'd had it with Richard himself.

Talking to children about the undeclared possibility that you may or may not marry one of their parents is a strategy of which I disapprove. I'll bet these guys had had conversations with countless women on the subject, women who saw an inside track through them, and worked it to what turned out to be their disadvantage. It was a desperate, cheap tactic, and I've never been that desperate to get married, and never would be.

Chapter Thirty-eight

Late Friday afternoon

After lunch, I built a fire in the fireplace in my bedroom and stretched out on the chaise and ruminated all afternoon, and finally, just before I started dressing for the opera, I called my mother. "I need a big favor," I said, "and if I could think of any other way to pull this off, I would. But I can't."

"Oh? Of course, dear, what is it?" Her friendly, receptive voice glided gracefully on its frozen lake of suspicion.

"I'd like for you and Daddy to give a dinner party on Monday night."

"This coming Monday night?"

"Yes."

"It's two days before Christmas. Everyone's booked." She wasn't guffawing and saying, "Why, you must be mad." But she might as well have. I knew she'd hate the idea.

"I know," I answered. "That's why you need to give the party. No one will turn down your invitation. People spend their whole lives just praying to be invited for a glass of water at your house." I was really laying it on.

"Well, I don't know about that," Mother said in a tone letting me know she knew exactly what I meant, and agreed completely. "Are you sure it will help?"

"I promise. You might even get a meritorious badge awarded to you by the mayor. Helping to apprehend a criminal."

"I have more good-citizen badges than I know what to do with," she said, but I knew she liked the idea of one more, especially one where a little danger might be involved. I had to be careful not to let her know that there could be a great deal of danger. She might chicken out.

"Who all did you have in mind?"

"Before we get that far, you have to promise me, on your life, that you won't tell *anyone*, except Daddy, why you're doing this. Otherwise, it will fail, and instead of a badge, the mayor will be giving you a summons for obstruction of justice."

"Oh, my." I had her. "All right, I promise. Now, who shall we have?"

"Joan and Dickie Chamberlain."

"Fine." I could hear her writing them down.

"Cordelia Hamilton and Daniel French."

"Fine. They'll be at the opera tonight. But," she said, with a tone that was half skepticism, half seeing a challenge, indicating that the wheel mechanisms in her head had kicked up a notch, "the Chamberlains will be tough to get. They have a social schedule that would strike a hummingbird dumb. And I imagine they plan to spend Christmas with her parents back east. And I imagine Cordelia's planning to leave for her ranch in Jackson tomorrow morning. Well, let me see what I can do. Who else?"

"Baron von Singen and Lulu French, although they won't be at the opera tonight. I'll just give them a call."

"I thought Lulu was staying with you."

"Yes. Yes, she is. I'll just give her a call down the stairs," I joked lamely. I'd completely forgotten everyone thought Lulu was at my house, that no one knew about her and Harry except me.

"Well, with your father and me, and you and Richard, that's ten for dinner. I think that's enough. Don't you?"

"Not quite," I said.

"Oh?"

"Dayton Babcock?" I said with trepidation.

"Absolutely not. Your father will never agree to letting that little weasel into our house, much less into our dining room to sit at our table."

"Mother," I said. "This isn't really a Christmas party, we just need to get everyone there. You don't even have to serve the dinner if you don't want to."

"You mean one of these people murdered Rita von Singen and Fancy?"

"Yes," I said. "I believe so."

"Oh, my God. Wait until your father hears this. I'll tell you, Lilly, I'm sure it's Dayton Babcock. I think you should find another way to trap him, or just go ahead and arrest him straightaway. Or just go ahead and shoot him." She drew a deep breath and lowered the boom. "I'm sorry to wreck things, darling, but the more I think about it, I'm afraid I really am going to have to draw the line at Dayton. I just don't think we can have him in our house."

"It's not that simple, Mother. And there are a couple more things." It had gotten suddenly very hot by my fire, so I threw off my light blanket and began to pace, thinking, I'm never going to pull this off. I face bullets and danger and psychopathic wackos all the time, and my mother is going to kill me with a heart attack.

"Oh?" she said.

"Elias and Jack Lewis, the detective, will also be there."

"Speaking of your older brother, where is he anyway? Did he go out of town or something?"

"Yes," I said. "He took a quick trip for me."

"Dick Kelly called your father and said he thought he'd seen Elias at the airport this afternoon, but that this man he'd seen was wearing bright-red rouge, so he was sure it couldn't have been him."

"He must have forgotten to take off his elf makeup," I said. "He was a little drunk, I think."

Mother laughed. "That boy. He is something."

Now, isn't that just perfect? Here is my brother, drunk at the airport, wearing elf makeup, and my mother thinks it's darling. Do you know what she would say if it were me? She'd never speak to me again. I got grounded once for chewing gum during a field hockey game I was playing in.

"Don't you think your brother should bring a date?" she said, once she was done laughing at Elias's darlingness.

"No, Mother, I don't." Then I tried, unsuccessfully, to by-the-way the next strategy. "By the way," I said, "we'll be adding one woman to the serving staff."

"I beg your pardon?"

"It's okay. She's an undercover police officer, and Mañuel can show her what to do."

"Really, Lilly. We can't have policemen serving drinks to our guests. All they know about is beer."

I came within a heartbeat of telling her to forget the whole thing, but it was just too important. I bit my tongue. "She'll be fine," I said. "And she's a policewoman. Girls know how to serve drinks."

Ada was spectacular, and even though the opera itself wasn't that long—it had been scaled down by about fifty percent from its model *Aida*—it still took about three hours because the audience could not stay in its seats. Every aria, every whinny, every moo and bleat brought everyone to their feet with uncontrolled clapping and deafening cheers. And the new curtain call? Well, it even had some people in tears.

At the end of the second intermission, my mother had sidled up to me. "Mission accomplished," she whispered behind her hand, and disappeared back into the crowd.

Chapter Thirty-nine

Monday evening

Three days later, when Richard and I, bundled up and breathless from the cold, walked in my parents' front door, Mother and Daddy stood waiting to greet us.

"Thank you so much for doing this tonight," I told them. "Everything looks absolutely beautiful."

"Isn't it fun?" Mother said. Her eyes shone. "I think if you're going to give a party, then give a party, no matter the reason."

There was no question she had knocked herself out in the decorating department. The living room looked downright Dickensian.

The tiny white lights on the enormous Christmas tree reflected off the small diamond-shaped panes in the casement windows. Luxuriant, fragrant arrangements of freshly cut blue spruce and holly greens, trimmed with white poinsettia blossoms, crowned the mantelpieces at either end of the room, and lavish boughs of fresh juniper topped each painting. Silver cups and bowls, overflowing with buttery toasted pecans, ribbon candy and red- and green-striped candy canes, sat on every table and ledge, and the pungent, crisp, dizzying smell of sizzling fat, dripping from a rib roast on a fiery spit, drifted from the kitchen. Huge flames roared and raced across the stacks of big logs in the living-room fireplaces, and overhead two large banners, proclaiming "Joy to the World" and "Peace on Earth," had been added to the permanent standard collection which flew from the surrounding gallery. The Mormon Tabernacle Choir sang "O Come, O Come, Emmanuel."

Shortly, the other guests arrived.

"I think the cocktail hour is my favorite time of day," Mother said to Cordelia. "It's certainly the most civilized."

"Absolutely," Cordelia agreed. "My parents used to meet every evening at six-thirty in the living room and talk over their day."

"Mine, too. Wasn't it a wonderful picture? Mine called it the Hour of Charm—the time when you put all the day's trials and tribulations behind you, put the children in their playroom, and just relaxed with your husband and took stock."

Cordelia's helmety hair swung slowly as she nodded. She wore a plain hunter-green satin gown, and around her neck on a thick red satin ribbon hung an exquisite small, antique crystal perfume bottle, the kind it was fashionable to carry perfume in, in the 1880s, and cocaine, in the 1980s. It was etched with tiny pine trees decorated with tiny bright ornaments. Her earrings were dime-sized pigeon's-blood rubies—not one of my favorites, but with her coloring they looked okay. She always looked a little off to me, anyway.

"Very different from today," Mother was saying. "Children were not included. Now, of course, people drag their children along to absolutely everything, and think that everyone should find them as precious as they do. I think it's disgraceful. Tell me, dear, where do your parents live?"

"They're both gone. Mother died in a fire when I was about thirteen, and my father died five years later."

"How horrible," Mother said briskly, sympathy not being her strong suit. "But where are you from originally? Where were you born?"

"I grew up in Youngstown, Ohio, but after Mother died, Father and I moved to Pittsburgh. He owned a steel company."

"That's what I thought, that you were from Pittsburgh. Well, we're so glad you've picked Roundup. You bring a sophisticated flair we're greatly lacking, as I'm sure you've noticed." Mother's hand went automatically to her diamond necklace, which looked particularly commanding against the russet velvet of her long dinner gown. "We need all the help we can get." She took a second to scowl at Tina, the undercover detective, who was passing hors d'oeuvre. "Aren't these murders just horrible?"

"Awful," Cordelia agreed. "It's scary. Keeps you sort of looking over your shoulder all the time. Do you know what I mean?"

"Of course," Mother said emphatically. "Who do you think did it?"

Cordelia shook her head. "Well, to tell you the truth, I thought Fancy had murdered Rita, but that theory was obviously completely wrong. Now, I don't know. I guess I wouldn't make much of a detective." She took a little avocado-and-crabmeat cocktail tostada from Tina, who smiled at her blandly. "Who do you think did it?"

Mother shook her head. "I haven't the slightest idea," she said. "But I'm sure it wasn't you."

Cordelia struggled not to choke on the tostada, and once it was safely down, her face broke into a surprised smile, and she laughed easily. "Well, I'm certainly glad to hear that, Mrs. Bennett."

"Oh, excuse me, I must go greet Mr. Decker and the baron. I had no idea Paul Decker was joining us. Isn't he the most *interesting* lawyer?" Mother breezed past me on her way to the door. "Cordelia didn't do it," she muttered out of the side of her mouth.

"Who is that with Harry?" Cordelia said to Dayton, who had on one of those stupid Christmas bow ties that are electrified with blinking red and green lights. He was dying for someone to mention it. No one would. He chewed up a large shrimp with his mouth wide open and washed the mess down with a swig of champagne.

"Looks like Lulu French to me." Dayton looked down and spotted a large blob of red cocktail sauce on the starched white of his shirtfront. He tried to wipe it off with a cocktail napkin. You'd think he'd know better by now.

Cordelia frowned. "Why would she be with him? He's twice her age. And what has she done with herself? Are you sure that's Lulu?"

Dayton dug a piece of shrimp out from between his teeth and sucked it off his fingernail noisily. He was just a one-man pigpen. "She might be with him," he said, "because her mother was engaged to marry him, and he feels some obligation to look after her. Or, maybe they're out on a date. As far as I'm concerned, she's a dewy, delectably ripe little piece of ass, and I'm going to go say hello to her and see if I can get a handful of those tomatoes. Why should Harry have all the fun?"

Cordelia made a face. "Can you believe him?" she said to me. "I think he is the most disgusting person I've ever met. I'm a little surprised your parents would include him."

"Yup," I said. "Cordelia, do you know my brother Elias?"

"No, I don't believe I do. I saw you at the Ball but never did get to be introduced. I can't believe we've never met before. Roundup isn't that big."

Elias blushed. He was fifty years old and still could not meet a woman without turning red. "I stay mostly at the ranch," he said. "But I'm glad to meet you. I've heard an awful lot about you." He grinned at me.

"Doesn't Lulu look beautiful?" I said. She did, too. Her dress was a long slim column of navy silk chiffon, cut with short sleeves, like a T-shirt, and her hair was full and brushed back. It was glossy and wavy and she looked like a forties movie star caught in the wind. Her only jewelry was small pearl earrings, and a nicely large, but not garish, emerald-cut diamond ring. "She has absolutely no stomach."

"What do you want?" Cordelia said. "She's twenty years old."

"She reminds me of a fairy princess."

Dayton returned, rebuffed. "Runs in the family."

For a moment or two we all watched Harry and Lulu talking to my mother, who was oohing and aahing over Lulu's ring.

"Catch this," said Dayton through two caviar canapes which he spewed out along with his words. "She's got on an engagement ring. They're getting married."

"They're getting what?" said Cordelia.

"I think it's time for you to quit," Dayton added. "You've lost this one. You could work out all day, every day, for the rest of your life, and face it, the way she looks, you'll just never get a butt like that again. But"—he edged closer to her—"I still think you look pretty good. At least I'm willing to give you a little mercy fu———"

"Get away from me, you filthy little pig." Cordelia's eyes blazed. She threw her martini in Dayton's face.

"HEY," he yelled. "Did you see that? I could have been electrocuted. God, you are such a bitch." He blotted his face with his cocktail napkin, leaving a trail of red sauce.

"I just don't believe it," Cordelia fumed, ignoring Dayton along with the rest of us. "It'll never happen."

The Chamberlains arrived. Joan looked like an ice queen—straight, frozen, a perfect specimen, perfectly preserved in another, higher dimension. Her sharp cheekbones were brushed with coral blusher and her lips were highly glossed in the same silvery salmon-red as her dress. Her platinum-blond hair was strictly composed into two or three precise waves, held back on either side with diamond combs. Dickie stood next to her. Big, grinning and slick with oil.

I'm sorry, I know I shouldn't bring it up again, but I simply do not understand how some of these women who have married so obviously for money can stand it. How can they go to bed with these guys? What do they think about to avoid thinking about what they're doing? Do they think about the new fur coat, or the new house in the Hamptons, or the hôtel particulier in Paris, or a flat in London, or how they're going to redecorate the jet? Maybe they cost it out on a per-time basis. "If I do it x number of times, I get x num-

ber of dollars." Well, far be it for me to judge. It's the old-fashioned
way for a girl to get ahead, and evidently Joan, who came from a
wealthy family to begin with, had made a highly profitable career of
wedding these lost dogs no one else wanted. It was her job. My hat
was off to her. She had a stronger stomach than I. But then again, we
each had our intestinal strengths: I could spend hours in a murder
scene with people's insides splattered all over the wall, or walk
through an inner-city jail on a Sunday morning without throwing
up. Joan probably wouldn't do very well in that environment.

"My husband and I are so grateful you could join us this evening."
Mother took Joan's hand. "I cannot tell you how much we appreciate your rescheduling your trip east. I hope your father's not too
dreadfully disappointed."

"Oh, well," Joan sighed. "Mummy and Daddy will just have to
wait. Besides, when I told them it was for the Duke and Duchess,
they understood."

"I'm so pleased." Mother smiled graciously, and then added,
"Aren't these murders just the worst?"

"Positively ghastly," Joan said. "Dickie and I have been absolutely *horrified* by them. This sort of thing goes on in the City all the
time, but in Roundup? I thought I'd left all this behind me."

"Who do you think did it?" Mother asked, a twinkle in her eye.

"Heavens, I haven't the slightest," Joan said. "I mean, I scarcely
knew either of them. But I'm sure the police will nab whoever is the
guilty party. They always do."

"Well, you're right, of course. And I'm sure you didn't do it,
Dickie. Please come in and join the party."

The Chamberlains, with Dickie looking somewhat disconcerted,
moved happily off in my father's direction.

"Duke and Duchess?" I said to Mother.

"I didn't think the Chamberlains were going to come, so I had to
add a little sweetener. Sort of a bonus. I told them the Duke and
Duchess of Westminster had decided to come spend Christmas with
us."

"And they believed you?" I couldn't believe it.

"Don't be fresh, Lilly," Mother said with umbrage. "I don't think Dickie Chamberlain did it. Did he?"

"What about Joan?" I asked her, and as an answer received a look of such sheer ridicule, it could have stopped my heart, if I hadn't known the truth. "Do me a favor," I said. "Don't keep asking people who they think the murderer is, and telling them that you're sure they didn't do it. Okay?"

"I'm just trying to help." She giggled self-consciously.

"Well, don't," I said. "You aren't one of the Snoop Sisters."

"Weren't they darling?" Mother smiled nostalgically, and she and I wandered off to join my father and Richard and Cordelia. At that moment, my mother was the one who seemed darling to me.

Daniel swirled up, pink and glowing with Christmas cheer. "Everybody scoot together in a bunch," he said. "I want to take your picture. I'm the official photographer for the evening." A petit-point cummerbund, made for him a hundred pounds ago, depicting Santa and his sleigh and eight tiny reindeer, each with a little brass bell jingling at its neck, strained around his waist. "Ready?" He raised the small disposable camera. "Say 'Cheese.' Perfect. What's everyone talking about?"

"Your niece," said my father. "Congratulations."

"What in the world does that mean?"

"Lulu and Harry von Singen are engaged."

"Oh," Daniel sort of cooed. "Oh." His soft, plump hand with its nails that gleamed with translucent shell-pink polish flew to his soft, plump cheek. "Oh. Excuse me." He floated away in their direction. "I'd better take their picture right away."

"Love is in the air," said my mother gaily. "Isn't it, Richard?"

"Mother, behave yourself," I said.

Richard just laughed. So did my father.

"Elias," she said to my brother, "I'm so glad you're home. How was your trip?"

"Terrific," he said. "Once the stewardess helped me wipe the elf makeup off my face." He gave me a dirty look.

"Now tell me where you went."

Elias glanced imperceptibly at me, and I nodded. "Youngstown, Ohio."

"Isn't that a coincidence?" she said, turning to Cordelia, who was still seething and preoccupied with the news of Harry and Lulu. "Cordelia Hamilton grew up there."

"Really?" Elias said. "Nice town."

Mañuel appeared in the living room's archway entryway with Jack Lewis and his aide, Evan. Jack's tuxedo fit superbly, Evan's was clearly rented. You could practically see down his shirtback to his waist, the collar was so big.

"Now who is this, dear?" Mother said.

"Jack Lewis, the Roundup Chief Inspector, and his lieutenant. Evan, I think," I said. "Come on, I'll introduce you." I took her arm and led her quickly across the room like a naughty child. She was so taken with her new role as detective that she had become dangerously carefree about her champagne consumption. I didn't dare let her out of my sight for a second.

"What are detectives doing here?" I heard Cordelia ask Elias as we left.

"Something must be up," he said.

"Lilly," Mother whispered, "is someone *really* going to be arrested here? Tonight?"

"Yes," I whispered back. "That's the plan."

"I thought you were exaggerating," she said. "This is very exciting." Her eyes sparkled.

"I know. But, Mother, you've got to keep it under your hat for a little while longer. It'll all be over before we sit down to dinner."

"Are these gentlemen staying?"

"Yes. One of them is, Chief Lewis."

"Oh, good. I love to support our men in blue," she said. God forbid it should ever register with her that there were also women in blue. "Give them a glimpse at another world. I think it's good for their morale, don't you?"

"Uh-huh," I answered. "Fabulous. I think I'll have a big glass of soda water. Don't you want one, too?"

"Oh, heavens no. I'm fine. I'll just have a little more champagne."

Subtlety never works very well in our family.

Lulu caught my eye from where she and Harry were standing across the room. She smiled at me, excused herself to him, put her champagne down on the sideboard, and came to me. We embraced warmly.

"I'm so happy for you, Lulu darling," I said. "Is there anything I can do for you? Anything you need?"

"Only about a million things." She smiled.

"Such as? Tell me, I'll get them for you."

"Well, for one thing, I have absolutely no idea how to give a wedding. Will you help me? Sort of be my mother?"

"Will I?" My breath caught. My eyes filled with tears. "I can't think of anything I'd rather do. I would be delighted."

"Delighted to do what?" my mother had overheard the tail end.

"Lulu has asked me to arrange for her wedding. Isn't that wonderful?"

"Oh," said Mother. "This is marvelous. I've always wanted to give a wedding. Lilly is my only daughter, you know, and I always hoped it would be *her* wedding I'd give, but now it will be like giving my granddaughter's. Oh, this will be divine."

"Kate." My father appeared at her side. "She asked Lilly to help. Not you."

Lulu and I looked at each other and laughed.

Harry joined us. He placed his arm gently around Lulu's shoulders. "What are you all talking about?" he said.

"Your wedding," said my mother. "I think we'll have it at the ranch."

Lulu and Harry's engagement had completely captured the party; everyone surrounded them and Daniel snapped pictures like crazy. Lulu was so refined and composed, she would be a wonderful baroness. Harry, always handsome and elegant, looked even more so.

The room was noisy and warm and gay, and no one noticed that a dozen squad cars had pulled up outside and that there were officers all over the house, and positioned outside most of the first-floor windows.

My stomach was alive with butterflies, and my mind was focusing closer and closer on the target.

Chapter Forty

_I_ handed my glass to Tina, who looked about twenty and seemed to be handling her new assignment with dignified good humor. I could tell she was nervous, not about the party, but abut working with all the brass on a make-or-break bust. "Jameson's on the rocks, please," I said.

"Yes, ma'am." She returned in record time with what looked like about sixteen ounces of whiskey. I poured half of it into an African violet before moving to the center of the living room. "Excuse me," I called. "May I have your attention, please?"

The cocktail chatter was loud and it took another time for me calling out before everyone turned to listen.

The atmospheric pressure in the room changed perceptibly—at least for a few of us: Jack and Evan, Tina, Richard, Elias and me. I couldn't tell if anyone else had noticed that our adrenaline had begun to surge, our heartbeats quicken.

"I'd like to ask you all to take a seat for a few minutes," I said. "I have a few remarks to make."

"Do you think she and Richard are going to announce their engagement?" my mother said loudly to my father.

"No, Mother, Richard and I are not announcing our engagement. Mañuel or Tina will bring everybody a fresh drink, so please just make yourselves comfortable. The sooner we get this wrapped up, the sooner we'll get on to one of Mother's spectacular dinners."

Well, she liked that, and so did everyone else.

"Whatever you're announcing," Cordelia said, "it's going to be tough to top Harry and Lulu."

"I know." I grinned at her. "But I'm about to."

"I can't wait," Cordelia said. "Unless you're going to announce that Harry's changed his mind and is going to marry you, I'll kill myself. Or you."

"Nothing like that. Believe me."

I stood patiently in front of the Christmas tree, while Tina and Mañuel tended to the refills, hoping in the back of my mind that Richard found me irresistible, with my backdrop of small lights and glittering ornaments. He should, I thought. I mean, I had on a short black velvet dinner suit and every pearl I owned. He was leaning against the piano, legs crossed at the ankles, cradling an old-fashioned glass in his hands. Watching me. His craggy, weather-beaten face wrinkled into a slow grin. I smiled back.

Cordelia and Elias, who had been giggling and chatting since I'd introduced them earlier, sat down on the red silk damask settee to my right. She was flushed and schoolgirlish talking to him, and he appeared to be just as excited to meet her. She looked up at Mañuel and smiled and accepted another straight-up martini in a pretty stemmed glass. Elias already had a large tumbler of whiskey.

"Scoot over a little," Daniel said, and wiggled into the small space on Cordelia's other side.

Directly opposite me, Harry, who had worn what I suppose could be called minor cocktail medals: an enamel-and-gold medal on a tri-colored ribbon pinned to his breast pocket, as opposed to the major Ball medals he'd worn a few evenings earlier, took his place in one of the mustard satin, bumble-bee embroidered bergère chairs, while Lulu, too light to do any damage, balanced herself on one of the arms. She put her hand on Harry's shoulder and leaned down to say something. He smiled and laughed and patted her on the knee.

Naturally, Dayton had materialized instantly behind her, hovering, trying to peer down her high-necked dress.

Harry looked back at him, "Oh, Dayton," he said. "Here, let me find you a chair."

"No, this is fine," Dayton said.

"I insist." Harry retrieved a small side chair from along the wall and placed it on the opposite side of him from Lulu, and indicated with his hand for Dayton to sit. "Please."

"Sure, thanks," Dayton said, apparently knowing better than to make any lewd remarks to the baron about his intended. But he could not contain himself from motioning in Lulu's direction with his thumb, and saying out of the side of his mouth, "This is a good move, Harry."

"Thank you," Harry answered casually. "I know. I'm sorry about Poker Creek going into receivership, though."

Dayton was caught off guard. "What do you mean? What are you talking about?"

Mother had placed herself in the other bergère, and Daddy stood behind her and gave Dayton a hard look, which shut him up immediately.

The Chamberlains settled onto the matching settee facing Cordelia, who had moved slightly forward so her two chubby admirers could spread out behind her, all along the back of the small sofa. Joan never took her eyes off Cordelia, but if the scrutiny bothered Cordelia, it didn't show. She, Elias and Daniel had gotten a severe case of the giggles and they all looked like idiots, especially Cordelia, who was particularly hysterical.

Paul Decker was sitting on the piano bench talking to Richard.

"Must be kind of odd for you not to be the one up here addressing the gallery," I said to him.

He smiled and shrugged his shoulders. "Kind of nice for a change," he said.

Sure, I thought. Lawyers love to be quiet.

Everyone bubbled with Christmas cheer. Everyone except Jack

Lewis and Evan—who stood at parade rest in both the arched living room entrances—and all the rest of us who knew what was going on. A major arrest was about to come down. There could be no slipups.

Mañuel handed my father a drink, and retreated to the kitchen. I took a healthy belt and began.

"I'd like to thank my parents for inviting all of us here this evening," I said. "I know everyone's disappointed that the Duke and Duchess had to cancel at the last minute," I said to Joan and Dickie, "but at least it gives us an opportunity to get together and take care of some important business."

Everyone looked at me politely.

"I know you all have absolutely no idea what I'm talking about."

"Yeah," said Dayton. "Let's pick it up a little bit here. You're losing your audience. Right?" He looked around at everyone else. "Am I right?"

"Fine," I said. "I'll cut right to the chase. One of you murdered Rita von Singen and Fancy French, and will be leaving for jail tonight, instead of the dining room. How am I doing, Dayton?"

They all looked around the room quietly. No one seemed especially taken aback. Maybe all the genteel breeding had just bred demonstrative reactions right out of them. More likely, it was because they'd seen this identical scene on television a million times before.

"One of you has murdered countless times, not just Rita and Fancy, but others—we don't even know how many—over a period of what appears to be about twenty-five years, in order to achieve ends that are unattainable."

Virtually everyone looked at Dayton Babcock.

"Hey," Dayton yelled. "What're you looking at me for? I didn't do it."

"The truth is"—I smiled at him—"it's possible to provide a motive to murder both of these victims for almost every person here." Joan Chamberlain turned her blue-ice eyes on me, and the look gave me new respect for Cordelia's ability to ignore them. If eyes could march across a room and stab you to death, they would be Joan's. Made me shiver.

I looked away from her. "Dayton has very strong motives and had huge opportunities."

"Oh, right." Dayton's eyes reddened. "You've been out to get me ever since I dumped you on your pretty little ass, which incidentally isn't quite so little anymore. Probably not too pretty either." He laughed and elbowed Harry.

In less than a heartbeat, Richard had picked Dayton up out of his chair by the back of his jacket and held him off the ground like a rag doll, his clenched fist in front of Dayton's nose.

"Apologize, you little brat," Richard said. Dayton squirmed like a frightened kitten. "Or I'll give a bloody nose." Dayton wriggled and cringed. His bow tie flashed wildly.

"I'm going to count to three," Richard warned.

"Okay, okay," Dayton said. "God, nobody can take a joke around here. Everyone's so goddamned sensitive. Jesus. Okay. Lilly, I'm sorry."

"Thank you, Dayton. I accept." I smiled at Richard. "You can put him down now."

Richard carried the obnoxious little simian creep over and plopped him down in a chair next to Jack Lewis. "If he opens his mouth again, shoot him."

"You know," Jack said to Richard, "I haven't been to many parties as fancy as this one, certainly not at Mr. and Mrs. Bennett's, and somehow I thought you'd all act a little classier."

"Makes you sick, doesn't it?" Richard said.

"Honestly, darling," my mother said to my father, "isn't that Richard Jerome the most divine man? If Lilly doesn't marry him she's crazy."

"That's enough, Mother," I said. "Dayton has convinced dozens of small and large investors to put millions into the Poker Creek project, and when it began to go south and Rita's backers turned off their cash—and advised her to turn hers off as well—Dayton panicked. He needed a windfall so he could continue to pay dividends to his investors—anyone who has ever done business with Dayton knows that you receive occasional dividends, but no one ever recoups his original investment."

"That's a goddamned lie," Dayton said.

"No," my father said. "That's the truth."

"And," I plowed ahead, "the quickest way to get a big piece of cash into the operation was to murder Rita and collect the insurance."

"You know what you are?" he started, but Richard made a move toward him, and Jack Lewis reached into his jacket for his weapon. Dayton closed his mouth.

"Isn't this thrilling?" Daniel said to Cordelia and Elias.

"And," I said, "Fancy dropped Dayton like a hot tamale within minutes of Rita's death."

"What a bunch of bullshit," Dayton yelled. "Everyone knows I dumped her. She was a psycho. Just ask Lulu. Hell, ask Daniel. Look what she did to him—her own brother. She turned him into a queer."

"Save your breath, Dayton," I told him. "We all know you didn't do it. You don't have the guts."

"Oh right, you would say that. How the hell would you know?"

"On the surface it appeared as though Harry von Singen himself had strong motives for wanting to see his wife dead—their marriage seemed a mess and Rita's estate all flows to him—and two days after Rita was murdered, Harry was taken in for questioning."

"You know he's a Nazi," Dayton interjected.

"And although until a few days ago we couldn't prove that Harry hadn't killed her, he had a strong alibi with a number of witnesses: Lulu French first among them. When Harry left the Hospital Christmas Dance that night, at approximately eleven o'clock, he drove directly to his apartment in Roundup, an apartment few people knew about, and Lulu was waiting for him there."

Cordelia shook her head.

"And," I said, "Harry was the only one who knew that his wife was ill, that she had only a few months at the most left to live. Even her best friend, Cordelia, didn't know it."

"It's true," Harry said. "Rita knew about Lulu and me, just as I knew about her and Sam Campbell. We had no illusions of one another. No secrets."

"And," I added, "Harry and Mother were talking to each other when Fancy was smacked on the head and thrown from the balcony at the Ball."

"I was sort of hoping Dayton Babcock had done it," Mother said to Father. "I'd love to see him get the Chair, he's such an idiot."

"Now, let's talk about Daniel." I ignored her. "We could build a strong case that he's madly in love with Harry."

Daniel regarded me over the tops of his glasses. "I declare my niece the victor in this match," he said. "And close the subject."

"That's very gallant of you, Daniel," I said. "But the fact is that until about an hour ago, when you learned about Lulu and Harry, you've done everything in your power to attract him yourself."

"Lilly." My mother, who had been becoming more and more visibly distressed with the direction of my discourse, speaking of money and murder and homosexuality and all, could not control herself any longer. "This is getting to be a little bit much, I think, don't you? I don't really approve of having this sort of conversation go on in my home. I think we're all getting sort of uncomfortable."

"You're right, Mother. Maybe you ought to go upstairs until we're done. It's going to get worse."

Her eyes got big but she didn't move. My father looked at me and smiled. We both knew wild horses couldn't drag her away from this scene.

Chapter Forty-one

*A*s a matter of fact," I said, "most of the evidence points directly at Daniel, and he had lots of reasons to kill both Rita and Fancy."

Daniel had turned as pale as a sheet and looked like he was going to throw up. "I've never hurt anyone." He gasped for breath. "Never."

"You've always been a little extreme, Daniel, loved the dramatic flourish, and for a while I followed a path of reasoning that you thought that if you killed everyone who got close to Harry, eventually people would figure out that if they made friends with Harry, they'd die."

"Oh, God," Daniel wept. "That is just too sick. I didn't do it." Cordelia had her arm around him, and he had her other hand clutched in both of his.

"But, Daniel," I said, "most condemning of all"—I walked over to Elias, who patted both of his jacket pockets and then reached into the right one and removed a plastic bag, which he handed to me— "we discovered this under the seat of your car."

I held up the black-plastic-and-steel Glock that still had Fancy's hair and blood on its butt.

The room was silent. Even Daniel had frozen. I watched him catch his breath, his heart skip a beat, his mouth fall open. Realization briefly flooded his face and then he looked at me beseechingly, trying to hide his sudden knowledge. I gave him a small smile. Cordelia removed her arm from Daniel's shoulder, and her hand from his now-limp grasp. She folded both of her hands in her lap and looked at me without guile. Tina stepped forward and stood directly behind them.

"You're right, Daniel," I said, "you didn't murder all of Harry's alleged lovers so you could get him. Someone else did. We're dealing with something much more sinister than a motive of money; we're dealing with some very deep, above-average, intelligence, a complicated sociopathic behavior."

"Really," Cordelia said, "don't you think that's being a bit dramatic?"

"No, unfortunately, it's not. I couldn't figure out what the deal was with the guns. It was sort of a shell game. Cordelia had a weapon that she kept in her car, and she claimed she'd fired it a couple of times, but the weapon we retrieved from her vehicle was not only brand-new, it had been purchased by Joan Chamberlain on Saturday, the day after Rita von Singen was murdered."

"What in the world are you talking about?" said Joan.

"What's going on here?" Dickie frowned, first at me, and then at his wife.

"I'm telling you," Joan said to him, "I have simply no clue. I've never bought a gun in my life."

"Did Joan steal Cordelia's gun to perpetrate these murders, and replace it with an identical copy, thinking we'd never make the connection?" I wondered out loud and searched the faces. "Things are never as simple as they seem. But finally the tumblers began to fall into place two days after Fancy died, when I received two phone calls within minutes of each other. One from Joan and one from Cordelia." I sipped my drink.

"Joan and Cordelia have a very complicated relationship," I said. "I knew they knew each other, and didn't like each other very much, but I had no idea how deep all this went. Friday, after the Ball,

Cordelia called and told me that a few years ago, Joan had been married to a fellow named Bill Harrison, who'd been a major investment banker in Pittsburgh."

"Major, until he got caught with his hand in the cookie jar," Cordelia said.

"You be quiet," said Joan. "It was the eighties. Everyone was getting caught."

"Well, yes," I said, "he did get caught. What was it, Joan, twelve counts of securities fraud?"

She held her head high, looked me, and everyone else, in the eye, and nodded. "Yes. But he served his time. It's all behind us."

"To get back to what I was saying," I said, "Cordelia called and told me about Mr. Harrison's problems, and how Joan had 'unloaded' him—Cordelia's word, not mine—when he went to prison."

"It was his idea," Joan shot back. "I didn't want a divorce; he was the one who insisted, for my sake."

"Oh, right," Cordelia said. "Tell me another."

"Cordelia went on to tell me that you would do anything to continue to improve your social and financial position. Anything. She said she felt you would even resort to murder."

Joan was completely pale. White as a sheet. She began to tremble, as well she should. She'd seen the inside of a federal penitentiary. Not a pretty sight. "That's not true," she said. "I would never do such a thing."

"To continue my story," I said, "seconds after Cordelia and I hung up, Joan called, and told me a story that made the hair stand up on the back of my neck."

Joan raised her eyebrows and grinned over at Cordelia.

"She told me about her and Cordelia's close friendship over a number of years in Pittsburgh," I said, "and she told me about her husband's trial, which, apparently, was about two months long. Always on the front page. She described how Cordelia came to the courtroom every day and watched, but refused to speak to Joan. She even went so far as to run the opposite way down the courthouse hallway when Joan tried to approach her."

"I did no such thing," Cordelia said.

"You did," Joan said evenly. "You ran like a scared, giggling, stupid schoolgirl who'd gotten caught."

"I also learned," I kept talking, "that you visited Bill Harrison in prison a number of times and begged him to marry you . . ."

"Oh, dear Lord," Joan murmured.

"This is absolutely ridiculous," Cordelia raged.

". . . but then he died, still in jail, under mysterious circumstances, of something like untreatable food poisoning," I concluded, and paused for a moment. "Well, the behavior got me thinking. So I started by meeting with Mack Cleveland at St. Mary's and then checked with the Motor Vehicle Department, and found that Joan had had her driver's license replaced on Monday. A week ago today."

"That's right," Joan exclaimed. "I forgot my purse at the Hospital Christmas Party, and they never could find it." Her eyes grew round. "Are you saying someone stole it?"

I nodded. "Daniel," I said. "Will you please get up and go sit over there?"

"Why?"

"Just do it."

Cordelia stared at me grandly. Not believing. Tina stood warily behind her.

"Cordelia," I said, "you murdered Rita von Singen and Fancy French."

"That is the most preposterous thing I've ever heard in my life," she said. "I've never murdered anybody."

"I think we're going to find you've murdered your whole family: your mother, father, stepmother and husband. And possibly Bill Harrison."

"Are you crazy?" She laughed.

"No," I said. "You're the one who's crazy. The tip-off was your cold-blooded behavior at Bill Harrison's trial. It's why I had to consult with Mack Cleveland, to find out what kind of person thrives on cruelty, who gets a charge out of kicking people when they're down."

"And what did you discover?" She seemed to be enjoying the exchange. "Do tell. We're all on pins and needles."

"Well, you're going to have to fill in the blanks, but let me float out a few theories. I won't bore you all with all the psychiatric mumbo jumbo, but Dr. Cleveland said, 'The keys to this type of antisocial behavior are always: one, the antisocial individual has expectations of the victim, which are completely unknown to the victim; and two, these expectations are always followed by the victim's unwitting rejection of the antisocial individual.' The point is, the victim is doomed to failure, just as the individual is doomed to rejection, because these expectations, whatever they are, are unspoken, and unless the victim is a mind reader, he's going to screw up in the eyes of the individual. It gave us some direction, the break we were looking for. That's why Elias went to Youngstown and Pittsburgh, and why the bodies of your parents, Mr. and Mrs. Whittaker, your stepmother, and your late husband, Mr. Hamilton, will be exhumed this week."

Finally I'd gotten Cordelia's attention. My words jolted her like an electric cattle prod.

"I think we're going to find something in their remains," I said. "Some sort of poison. Something. What will we find, Cordelia? The same thing that's in Lulu's and Harry's champagne glasses? A little arsenic, perhaps?"

"I don't know what you're talking about."

"I watched you, as did the detective standing directly behind you, put a clear fluid into their glasses when they put them down on the table where they have remained. I believe we'll find the empty vial in your purse. As a matter of fact, Mañuel, I think it's safe for Miss French and the baron to have something to drink now. What would you like?"

"Thank goodness," Lulu said. "Champagne, please."

"Double Scotch on the rocks," said Harry.

The tension had broken momentarily and you could hear the whole room whistle out its breath.

"It's even possible," I said to Cordelia, "that Daniel unwittingly snapped a picture of you in the act."

"Strychnine," Cordelia said evenly.

"Why are you doing this? What have these people done to you?"

"It's really none of your business."

"That's not true, Cordelia. It is our business. But first, Chief Detective Lewis is going to place you under arrest and read you your rights. Paul Decker is here. You might want to consider retaining him now. I know I would."

"How thoughtful of you to provide counsel for your guests," Cordelia drawled sarcastically.

Jack Lewis stepped away from his position at the door, but Cordelia held up her hand to stop him. "Let me speak now before I lose my nerve. Mr. Decker, you are my attorney, and you can see that I am not under any duress; my words are my statement," she said.

Lieutenant Evan turned on his video camera.

Paul Decker, prepared to assume center stage, stood up. "I advise you not to say a word, Mrs. Hamilton," he boomed.

"Don't try to stop me," Cordelia said. "Just listen."

She turned her pale, robin's-egg-blue eyes on me, and they were as hard and glittering as stainless steel. Then she began to speak, very quietly.

"I think once I explain," she said, "you will all agree I had no choice. That to be able to live my life in happiness, these people needed to die. When I was a child, my father and mother fought constantly, and I finally realized that the only time Daddy was ever really happy was when he was with me. I knew he loved me more than he loved her. He never could admit it, of course, but by the time I was thirteen, it became obvious that she was destroying him. There was only one thing I could do."

"Murder her?" Daniel said incredulously. "You murdered your mother?"

Cordelia turned to look at Daniel, who huddled next to my mother as though she were the Statue of Liberty. "I had to," she said. "Don't you understand? Once she was gone, Daddy and I could be together. And oh, my, we were so, so happy. He bought American Steel, and we moved to the estate in Pittsburgh." Cordelia's voice grew stronger, as though she were telling us about her latest trip to London and all the sights she'd seen. "Things went wonderfully well for a few years, but when I was seventeen, he remarried." Cordelia shuddered. "Oh, my God, you cannot imagine how dreadful she was. Horrible. She trapped him, of course. All she wanted was his money. I told Daddy I couldn't stand for him to be married to her, and why couldn't he see that he didn't need anybody else? I remember his reaction perfectly: he laughed and told me that I would always be his little girl, and yes, he did love me more than anyone, but not like that. Not as a woman. He laughed. Can you believe it? He owed his whole life to me. All his happiness to me. I saw how wrong I'd been to love him so much. To put all my life into him. He tricked me." There was no emotion in her voice.

"You murdered your father, too?" Daniel said.

"And you all thought I was bad," Dayton piped up.

Cordelia seemed beyond us now. I don't think she heard either one of them.

"What happened after that?" I prodded.

"Oh"—she shrugged slightly—"I got married. But all he cared about was business and my money and having children. Once Mary Pat was born, he started running around with younger women. He was a bastard. And then, one summer, in the south of France, we ran into Rita and Harry. Remember how much fun we used to have?" She looked over at Harry. Her face glowed.

"I do," he answered. "We had a wonderful time."

"I love you so much, Harry. That's why I've done all this. For us. My husband. Rita. Fancy. All for us."

"I'm sorry, Cordelia," Harry said softly. "There is no 'us.' There never has been. There never will be."

The room was hushed. Not a breath. Not a sound.

"I know." Cordelia began to weep softly. "There's always someone else." Then, like lightning, before anyone could move to prevent her, she grabbed the miniature perfume bottle that hung on the ribbon around her neck, yanked out the stopper and drank the deadly contents.

Cordelia Whittaker Hamilton grew rigid with pain and her lips quickly turned dark blue. Then her eyes rolled back in her head, she thrashed through a couple of severe, quick convulsions, and thirty seconds later lay dead as a doornail on the red satin damask settee in my parents' living room, next to Elias, who still had his mouth hanging open.

"Good God," Mother said. "What has she done?"

Jack and Tina and I raced for her immediately, thinking that we would resuscitate her, but as the strong almond smell dispersed and reached our nostrils, we stopped. She would not be back. No one wants to perform mouth-to-mouth on a cyanide victim. The fumes are just too lethal.

"Get everyone out of here," Jack ordered, as Richard and the lieutenant threw open the windows.

He didn't need to ask twice.

Chapter Forty-two

*O*nce we got Cordelia's remains taken care of, the party turned out to be hysterically fun. There was certainly no shortage of conversation topics and goodwill.

Even Jack Lewis, at least two sheets to the wind from all the good wine and cognac, said on his way out the door, "I owe you one, Bennett."

"On the house," I said. "Merry Christmas."

Richard and I were the last to leave, and it was well after midnight: Christmas Eve Day. The temperature was ten below, and the stars sparkled and twinkled brightly in their black velvet sky. I snuggled deeply into my long fur and took my Richard's arm for the quick walk into the park to where Christian's S-76 waited. We were tipsy and happy, and I knew I'd never loved anyone so much in my life. We sat side by side in the chopper and fastened our seat belts and as we began our ascent, Richard leaned over and kissed me. A wonderful sweet, deep, rich kiss. A delicious kiss.

"I love you," he said.

"I love you, too."

He got up and spoke to the pilot. "Take us around downtown for one quick turn before going back to the ranch, please."

"Yes, sir," the captain said.

There it all was before us, all the wonderful Christmas lights on all our nutty buildings in our great little Wyoming town. We held hands and looked at the decorations like children.

Richard reached into his pocket and pulled out a small red leather box with gold trim. Even in the dark I could tell it was from Cartier. He held the box closed in his hand, and the blood was pounding in my ears so loudly, I couldn't tell if all the noise in the cabin was me, or the rotor blades.

He just sat there, looking out the window.

Well, finally, I couldn't stand it anymore. "What are you waiting for?" I yelled over the engine noise. "Christmas?"

Acknowledgments

I would like to thank Thomas Haney, Chief of Patrol of the Denver Police Department, and Denver psychiatrist William W. McCaw, Jr., for their generous professional guidance. My brothers, John and Drew Davis, and my former assistant, John-Paul Schaefer, get special thanks for their research assistance, as do Fr. John and all the Capuchin friars of the Mid-America Province for their Christmas carol expertise and prayers.

I am especially indebted to my editor, Sara Ann Freed, who maintained her outstanding sense of humor and composure as she guided me, calmly and patiently, through this process. And to my agent, Nick Ellison, who keeps me on the straight and narrow—a steady hand in an unknown sea. And to Harry Smith and Nelson DeMille whose enthusiastic support and encouragement have opened so many doors.

Finally, I thank our family and friends, especially my dearest darling husband, Peter, whose love, success and generosity make all good things in our life possible.

MARNE DAVIS KELLOGG
Denver, Colorado